The Eye of Purgatory

The Eye of Purgatory
&
Dr. Mops' Experiment
by
Jacques Spitz

translated by
Brian Stableford

A Black Coat Press Book

Acknowledgements: The publishers should like to thank Anne Lenclud, Laurent Genefort, Sylvie Miller and Juan Miguel Aguilera.

Visit our website at www.blackcoatpress.com

Introduction

L'Oeil du Purgatoire [The Eye of Purgatory] was initially released by the Editions de la Nouvelle France in 1945 and was Jacques Spitz' last published genre effort. The thematically similar, but earlier, *L'Expérience du Dr. Mops* [Dr. Mops' Experiment] was released by Gallimard in their prestigious literary NRF (Nouvelle Revue Française) in 1939. It was the ninth but last of Spitz's novels that they published and was perhaps a prophetic portent of what was to come.

Jacques Spitz was born in the town of Ghazaouet in 1896 in what was then French Algeria. His father was in the French military. He eventually went on to graduate brilliantly from the famous Ecole Polytechnique and subsequently lived in Paris, single, working as a freelance engineer, spending much of his time writing.

At the start of his literary career, Spitz was influenced by the Surrealist Movement and penned several mainstream novels in that vein, as well as a dark and cynical play about a comical, dystopian future, *Ceci est un drame* [This Is A Tragedy], published only in 1947.

In 1935, Spitz turned to science fiction with *L'Agonie du Globe* [The Agony of the Globe], which was translated in English in 1936 as *Sever The Earth* and in Swedish in 1937 as *När jorden rämnade*. In total, Spitz wrote eight major genre novels over the next ten years, becoming the worthy successor of Maurice Renard and J.-H. Rosny Aîné, and heralding luminaries of the 1950s and 1960s such as René Barjavel, Jacques Sternberg and Pierre Boulle.

In *L'Agonie du Globe*, Earth is bisected into two hemispheres, one of which eventually crashes into the Moon. The novel established the characteristics of Spitz' style: the use of realistic, scientific details, put to the service of a wild and surrealistic imagination and a pessimistic view of humanity, the result being a tragicomic satire on a "cosmic" scale. Unlike British and American authors, Spitz did not use science in a realistic context, to predict what might happen if…; his concerns were primarily about the society of men, and in that, he anticipated the so-called "New Wave" and writers like J. G. Ballard and Thomas Disch by at least 30 years. Yet, Spitz' novels are ever scientifically rigorous and logical in the unfolding of their plots, and never become grotesque or comical.

His next book, *Les Evadés de l'An 4000* [The Escapees from the Year 4000] (1936), is about a new ice age which drives men underground where they fall prey to a scientific dictature; eventually, some more enlightened characters escape and flee towards Venus.

It was followed two years later by *La Guerre des Mouches* [The War of the Flies], perhaps his masterpiece, and *L'Homme élastique* [The Elastic Man] (both 1938). The first featured the inevitable conquest of Earth by mutated flies animated by a gestalt intelligence. It is a particularly dark and pessimistic work, containing some fierce satirical observations about mankind, its foibles, and, ultimately, utter impotence before its implacable enemy. The realistic attention brought to the description of the details of everyday life brilliantly contrasts with the outlandishness of the story. The few survivors of Humanity end up in a zoo. *La Guerre des Mouches* is everything that someone like John W. Campbell would have hated with a passion.

By comparison, *L'Homme élastique*, with its means to compress and decompress atoms, enabling the creation of tiny super-soldiers and flaccid giants, is almost tame, but its handling of the theme of miniaturization is as ground-breaking today as it was when it was written.

L'Expérience du Dr. Mops (1939) and *L'Oeil du Purgatoire* (1945) both explored the theme of *farseeing* into the future. In the former, the hero discovers that he can't *see* beyond his own death; in the latter, Dr. Dagerloff's unhappy guinea pig, the painter Jan Poldonski, sees not the real future, but an increasingly aging present, where death and decay ultimately become overpowering sights. *L'Oeil du Purgatoire* is a dark, introspective novel, a reflection of the notion of time and aging, certainly unique in the annals of science fiction.

Spitz' final genre works included *La Parcelle Z* [Particle Z] (1942) and the somewhat more hopeful *Les Signaux du Soleil* [The Signals from the Sun] (1943), in which powerful Martian and Venusian Intelligences, unaware of our existence, discuss their plans to mine Earth's atmosphere for its basic components through sunspots. Their communications are discovered and deciphered by the hero. Fortunately for Earth, the aliens stop once they realize that our planet is inhabited by intelligent life. This is accomplished by encrypting *pi* into the ionization of the atmosphere.

Two more genre novels remained unpublished during Spitz' life: *La Guerre Mondiale No. 3* [World War III], which was finally published posthumously in 2005, and *Alpha du Centaure* [Alpha Centauri], which was either unpublished or pulped upon publication when its publisher was seized by the Germans (stories differ).

After 1945, Spitz, who had fought during two World Wars and had received the Legion of Honor for his bravery, abandoned science fiction and wrote only semi autobiographical and surreal pieces, but succeeded in selling only one more novel. He died in Paris in 1963. His Estate recently donated the personal journals which he kept between 1928 and 1962 to the Bibliothèque Nationale. They may still lead to new discoveries about this unfairly forgotten grandmaster of French science fiction.

Jean-Marc Lofficier

Translator's Note: The versions of the text that I have translated are those in the Robert Laffont edition of 1972, issued in the *Ailleurs et Demain/Classiques* imprint. I have not had the opportunity to compare them to the original versions issued in 1945 and 1939 respectively. Brian Stableford

Bibliography

La Croisière indécise [The Indecisive Cruise] (Gallimard, 1926) (*non genre*)

La Mise en plis [The Hairdo] (Editions du Logis, 1928) (*non genre*)

Le Vent du Monde [The Wind of the World] (Gallimard, 1928) (*non genre*)

Le Voyage muet [The Silent Voyage] (Gallimard, 1930) (*non genre*)

Les Dames de velours [The Velvet Ladies] (Gallimard, 1933) (*non genre*)

L'Agonie du Globe [The Agony of the Globe] (Gallimard, 1935) (translated into English by Margaret Mitchiner as *Sever The Earth*, John Lane, London, 1936)

Les Evadés de l'An 4000 [The Escapees from the Year 4000] (Gallimard, 1936)

La Guerre des Mouches [The War of the Flies] (Gall., 1938)

L'Homme élastique [The Elastic Man] (Gallimard, 1938)

L'Expérience du Dr. Mops [Dr. Mops' Experiment] (Gallimard, 1939)

La Parcelle Z [Particle Z] (Vigneau, 1942)

Les Signaux du Soleil [The Signals from the Sun] (Vigneau, 1943)

L'Oeil du Purgatoire [The Eye of Purgatory] (Editions de la Nouvelle France, 1945)

La Forêt des Sept Pies [The Forest of the Seven Magpies] (Maréchal, 1946) (*non genre*)

Ceci est un drame [This Is A Tragedy] (Editions de la Nouvelle France, 1947) (*theater*)

Posthumous:

Joyeuses Apocalypses [Merry Apocalypses] (Bragelonne, 2005) – omnibus volume including: *La Guerre des Mouches*, *L'Homme élastique*, *La Guerre Mondiale No. 3* [World War III] (unpublished novel) and six unpublished short stories.

DR. MOPS' EXPERIMENT

CHAPTER ONE

If the month of April had not been so rainy in Paris that year, nothing would have happened, or something else would have happened. But what good is it going on about the role played by incidental circumstances in life's great events? I no longer believe in causes and effects now—the laborious explanations that one forges after the fact in order to take account of a chain of events. All that is of no importance whatsoever, and it is only for the sake of vain mental satisfaction that one imagines a logical sequence in the course of events.

I had just returned to France to spend a year's leave there. One has to stay for three consecutive years in the Pacific islands—the Philippines, Timor, Bali—to understand what a return to France might mean. To rediscover trees, dairy produce, cool nights, mosquito-less slumbers, women whose eyes gleam and actually seem to signify something, old houses, ancient landscapes without scorpions, snakes or insects, and people whose language one understands effortlessly...

My first fortnight in Paris was delightful—for it was in Paris, naturally, that I began. After a fortnight of all kinds of folly, however, I woke up from the kind of intoxication into which that return had plunged me to become aware of the fact that it was raining perpetually, and that I felt chilly. My sojourn in the tropics had rendered me sensitive to cold. I could no longer set aside my fur-lined coat. Two weeks of rain had sufficed for me to be repossessed by nostalgia for the Sun that I had cursed for three years in the equatorial regions. The remedy did not require any great effort of the imagination. I was alone, free to go where I liked; I followed the traditional current that draws idlers southwards, and I woke up one morning in a couchette on a train moving along the Côte d'Azur. I got off in Monaco, because I had just finished my breakfast at that moment, and almost everyone had left the carriage. I could just as easily have stopped at Nice or Menton, but it happened to be Monaco.

The first day was execrable. Although the hotel was comfortable and the Sun high in the sky, I found around me nothing but people over 70: little invalid carriages; plaids; blankets over every knee; old mottled and twisted hands with swollen veins and outmoded rings; bottles of mineral water on every table; and, everywhere, the empty, discolored gazes of old people, awaiting death beneath checkered caps like those worn by American millionaires.

The following morning, to distance myself somewhat from that asylum of excessively rich old people, I took a stroll along a road that followed the coast through the pines and palm-trees overhanging the walls of villas. As I approached a little inlet, I perceived one of those tiny cars that one only finds in Europe, going along the road leading down to the sea. The road was little more than a pathway, and the badly-jolted vehicle had to be steered through the difficult sections with great care. It succeeded nevertheless in reaching the beach, and when the driver got out, I observed to my surprise that it was a woman—a young woman, to judge by her slenderness and the smoothness of her gestures. From the car's trunk, she extracted a bizarre instrument, which I recognized as one of those tricycles that move on the water, of which one sees a large number on the coast. Then, throwing off her robe, under which she was clad in a bathing costume, the young woman leapt nimbly into the saddle and began pedaling out to sea. One might have thought it an aquatic spider, a plaything like those sold by street-traders on the sidewalk.

When I arrived at the water's edge, she was already some distance away. After a moment's hesitation, I decided that my underpants could take the place of swimming trunks, and set forth in my turn into the transparent water.

I had no specific intention of joining the siren on the tricycle; I was merely giving way to a juvenile impulse to play in the water, as an example had been set for me on that sunny morning. I was a good enough swimmer not to have any fear of introducing myself in those conditions, and even of taking delight in a certain vanity—but the water in the cove, already warm, caressed my cheek so pleasantly that I was soon thinking about nothing but swimming. To be sure, the prospect of an adventure always occupies the mind of a man of my age when he has nothing to do and a year's liberty of which to dispose, but what adventure could match the simple pleasure of merely being in the infinite expanse of water, as clear as in the tropics?—and which, moreover, offered itself as far as the eye could see, without the barrage of steel nets that protect Oceanian beaches from sharks, I was free to go as far out to sea as I wished, my eye at the level of the horizon, cleaving the soft expanse with my arms…

If European seas have no sharks, though, they offer other inconveniences.

A motor boat arrived to pollute the essence of my marine surroundings with its horrible noise and odor. Returning to the surface, I found myself 50 meters from the young woman, who was still pedaling, high above the water, now steering for the shore.

The motor boat's wake struck the flank of the tricycle, whose floats were lifted up. I saw the apparatus sway. Its occupant tried to steady it, but was finally tipped into the sea. At first, I laughed—but a scream soon reached my ears, and I saw and arm waving as if appealing for help. I swam toward the overturned tricycle. One of the young woman's ankles was caught between the chain and the frame; stuck in an inconvenient position, she was unable to swim. I held her up with one hand, while bracing the other against the inverted machine, and she pulled free.

"Thank you," she said. "Just in time, I think."

A few strokes took us to the shore, pushing the apparatus ahead of us. I looked at her: the oval of her rubber cap outlined a very young face with exceedingly pure features. But women always look attractive thus, I said to myself, thinking of nuns and aviatrixes. Then I recalled the damp, firm figure that my arm had enfolded while I freed her.

"It's lucky you were there," she said, finally, in an entirely natural voice, which no longer retained the slight breathlessness of her cry for help. "I might not have been able to get out of it on my own."

She rubbed her ankle.

"Are you hurt?" I asked, with some hypocrisy, for I saw it as a pretext to touch her bare leg.

"A slight graze," she said, drawing away slightly. "It was the chain that trapped me."

My gaze moved back from the ankle to the face. With an abrupt gesture she liberated her rubber-clad hair: a surge of blonde curls, slightly damp around the nape of the neck, blossomed in the sunlight. As soon as she had shaken her head in order to permit her hair to resume its natural shape, I was able to estimate her age—about 20.

"I was trying it today for the first time," she explained, picking up the tricycle with both hands in order to reload it into the car, "and I haven't gotten used to it yet."

As I manifested some slight surprised at see her making preparations to leave so quickly, she said: "I've interrupted your swim. Forgive me." And she started the car.

I remained alone on the beach, rather disappointed to find the adventure cut short. Obviously, I had not expected her to throw her arms around my neck, telling me that I had saved her life, but she didn't have to leave so suddenly, without shaking my hand, or even uttering one of those polite formulas which at least permit the hope of a further meeting…

Lying in the Sun, I was meditating on the ingratitude of young women, while accusing myself of not having been able to take advantage of the situation, when two blasts of a horn made me lift me head. Having reached the cliff-top, the unknown woman had stopped her car and was sounding the horn to attract my attention. She waved her hand twice in a friendly gesture, then set off again.

That fashion of taking her leave, which revived my regrets, seemed to me a trifle perfidious. *She's a little tease*, I thought. I thought her lost forever. I didn't yet know that the Côte d'Azur is no more than a large village.

All afternoon, I dragged regrets and a morose state of mind though various dives in Nice. That evening, back in Monte Carlo, after having hesitated between roulette and the Russian ballet, I opted for the latter. Although the auditorium was mostly filled with the old people whose appearance I found depressing, the audience was elegant and my neighbor, in particular, set me dreaming. All that I could see of her was a fine, intelligent profile, but her perfume, which enveloped me rather insidiously, gradually effaced the memory of that morning's failed adventure. In the darkness, I let myself lapse into the game that consists of substituting for the nagging impression of a woman the presence of the one who might perhaps take her place. An already-dulled past regret was mingled with a not-yet-too-sharp future curiosity. My neighbor was veritably embalmed, and her slender hands, virginal of rings, were delicately taking hold of the reins of my reverie when I suddenly recognized, three rows in front of me, the golden hair that had glistened in the morning sunlight on the beach.

Instantly, I only had eyes for that blonde nape. From various slight movements, I understood that she was accompanying her neighbor, whose bald head reflected a fraction of the stage-lighting into the gloom. I was already assuming that he could not be a very serious rival.

This time, it was necessary not to let the opportunity escape.

During the interval, good luck helped to bring me face to face with the couple in the corridor leading to the boxes. I needed no further ruse; the unknown woman came up to me smiling, holding out her hand.

"Father, I can introduce you to my savior," she said, laughing, "but I don't know his name."

I gave my name; the bald gentleman murmured a name that I didn't catch.

"And this is my cousin Narda," she continued, indicating a slightly awkward young woman of about 17, who was standing to one side.

"Since you have saved her life," the father said to me, straight away, "I can entrust her safety to you. I must absent myself momentarily—don't wait for me."

He was speaking with a slight foreign accent, and his extraordinarily bushy eyebrows contrasted with his close-shaven head, which I had thought at first to be bald. He disappeared into the crowd. I went into a corner of the foyer with the young women. The morning's incident furnished a ready-made topic of conversation.

"A scratch that one can scarcely see through a stocking," she replied, still smiling.

My suit must have inspired more confidence than my swimming-costume, for amiability showed through the banality of the words. I learned that young Narda had arrived straight from her Swiss boarding school for the Easter vacation.

"...And she prefers going to the theater to going swimming with me," she added, teasingly.

To which Narda replied, in an almost child-like voice: "Yvane doesn't understand that the water of Swiss swimming-baths is much calmer."

I smiled, and turned back to Yvane, whose name I had finally learned. "If you wouldn't mind my company, I'd gladly accompany you on your next nautical experiment."

"We'd need a tandem," she replied, lightly, without giving any answer to my proposition.

The interval elapsed without my being able to obtain a firm engagement, which I could not solicit overtly. The bell rang and we had to go our separate ways. With a furrowed brow, disappointed once more, I was returning to my solitary seat when Yvane came toward me again, cutting through the crowd.

"I forgot to ask you to come to tea the day after tomorrow," she said, rapidly. "We live in the Château de la Colle, a few kilometers from Nice on the road to Vence. Ask for the house of Doctor Mops—my father-in-law—and you'll find it without any difficulty." Then, with a friendly nod of the head, she allowed herself to be borne away by the tide of spectators.

I had agreed without saying a word. The belated invitation reminded me of the adieu launched from the cliff-top. Was it typical of her turn of mind to return to unsettled situations? Or should I see these intentional postscripts as a demonstration that she was merely giving way to the obligations of politeness? I was thinking about that, recalling her words, when I was suddenly caught up by the term "father-in-law." I would not have thought that she was married, and, on leaning that she was, all the ideas that I had already formed in her regard were revealed as misleading. Nothing in her gestures or her costume—her simple long white dress and the absence of jewelry—indicated that she was in the power of a husband. As the curtain went up again, however, she turned her head slightly toward the auditorium and, meeting my gaze, made me a sign so manifestly ingenuous that I understood my error. "Father-in-law" has two meanings.[1] Her mother must have remarried Doctor Mops.

I was in possession of a baggage of impressions sufficient to give rise to pleasant dreams. After leaving the theater, instead of going to bed, I went to the hotel bar to get gradually merry. Full of assurance, I then found the means of buying a car from an Italian marquis of sorts, who had just been cleaned out at the roulette wheel, and who was drinking beside me. Anyway, a car would doubtless be useful. And in the juvenile delight procured for me by the slimmest possibility of intrigue offered that day by a precious hazard, I went to sleep on the threshold of drunkenness.

---

[1] Like the French *beau-père*, the English "father-in-law" can, indeed, mean "stepfather," although that meaning is almost obsolete.

CHAPTER TWO

My entry to the Château de la Colle was greeted by the barking of two Great Danes, fortunately enclosed in a kennel, which split my ears for nearly five minutes before the front door was opened by a Javanese servant. My surprise in confrontation with this Asiatic face, which I had scarcely expected, was redoubled by the sight of the colonial souvenirs—panoplies, trophies, wooden sculptures and masks—that cluttered the drawing-room into which I was shown. Even the window-panes were made of the alabaster-tinted translucent seashells that are used in Manila instead of glass. I found myself abruptly transported to the Dutch East Indies or the Philippines, when I had thought that I was in Provence.

I was still utterly displaced when the door opened on Yvane, whose blonde and blue apparition fortunately brought me back to myself in space and time. She understood the meaning of the grateful smile with which I welcomed her.

"What an idea to usher you into the midst of all this bric-à-brac!" she exclaimed. "My stepfather, who is Dutch, has spent many years in Batavia." She accompanied her explanation with an ironic gesture addressed to all the Oriental iron-mongery encumbering the walls. "Come on, we'll be better off elsewhere."

I followed her on to the terrace situated behind the main building, which overlooked a little valley. An olive-grove climbed the slope that was facing us, and vine were discernible behind the curtain of cypresses extended over the first ridge. It was an abridged version of the Provencal countryside.

"Here, I find you again," I said to Yvane.

Very simple in her dress of coarse blue fabric, she adopted a charming gaucherie, tinted with lassitude, in order to furnish the customary explanations.

"The property comprises some 20 hectares, but it hasn't been well-maintained. I ought to occupy myself with it, but I lack the resolve."

"Are you the mistress of the house, then?"

"Yes, since my mother's death two years ago. My stepfather leaves all the domestic details to me. As I have a horror of giving orders, that works out rather badly."

I assured her that even though I was an architect, I preferred untidy houses, with weeds growing in the pathways.

"Oh, you're an architect!" she said. Abandoning herself to the first association of ideas, she went on: "The gardeners have been pestering me to have the reservoir refilled, and I don't know how to do it…"

"Well, my visit won't have been useless," I said, laughing. "I'll give you a consultation."

We climbed the slope of the olive-grove, hollowed out at the summit of which was one of those large reservoirs open to the sky, such as one finds in Provence, and which, opening at ground level, are reminiscent of swimming pools. The reservoir was dry; the bottom was in need of concreting over.

"I'll contact a contractor and give you an estimate…but I scarcely expected to be talking business."

"Me neither," she replied, so sincerely that we both laughed.

"I'll change the subject, then, and pay you compliments," I went on.

"Why?" she asked, innocently, turning her large eyes toward me, which were the same color as her dress but which had the varnished gleam of Delft pottery.

"Because you speak French very well," I replied, caught off-guard by so much naivety.

"But I am French. My mother was French before she remarried a Dutchman. My name is Yvane Suyter—that's a Flemish name."

When we got back to the terrace, the tea was being served beneath a plane-tree, and various individuals were already busy about the table.

17

"Delighted to see you here, Monsieur Delambre," Dr. Mops said to me, with a briskness that I now knew to be Dutch.

In keeping with his status as a country landowner, he had coiffed his cranium in a Panama hat and was smoking a cigar. I was introduced to a relatively young man, Dirk Linard, who was his secretary. Narda was also there, engrossed in connecting the electric wire of the toaster to a power cable running along the balustrade of the terrace.

"You'll get your hands dirty," Yvane said to her.

"Well, I'll go wash them," she replied, with the imperturbable logic of a child.

As Yvane handed the doctor a cup of tea, he declared that he would prefer beer. "Here," he said, "it's not hot enough for warm drinks to be refreshing."

"That's a physician's theory," I said.

"No, a beer-drinker's," he replied, laughing. "Besides, that sort of medicine doesn't interest me. I'm a neurologist— but I won't bore you and all these young folk with the story of my research. It's quite enough that Dirk has to suffer my speeches."

Without saying a word, Dirk lost himself in the contemplation of a cricket that had strayed on to the table. Narda was now peeling the plane-tree, whose bark had been separated by the heat. All that was quite banal, but collectively, these various individuals gave a rather odd impression—which, nevertheless put me at ease. Instead of forming a more-or-less closed family circle, which always resists the intrusion of a new face, everyone here appeared to be following their own train of thought. Everyday companions did not seem to count for any more than a newcomer like me. I therefore had the impression of inserting myself painlessly into the middle of a cordial disunity.

Out of politeness, I made vague comments appropriate to the occasion. The doctor replied. By the manner in which he was holding his cigar between his teeth, I had already observed that he wore dentures. The care with which he smoothed his eyebrows, the only hairy parts of his face, indicated a certain affectation, which prevented me from taking him seriously, but when the servant brought a few letters on a tray, he put on his spectacles in a purposeful way that revealed a studious man, while his myopic gaze, circled with glass, acquired an undeniable intelligence.

"Well," he said, casually, "I'm going to go back to work with Dirk. On another occasion, Monsieur Delambre, I'll show you some unusual things that might perhaps interest you."

His departure seemed to lighten the atmosphere. Narda continued nonetheless to scatter pieces of bark under the table.

"Come on, stop it!" exclaimed Yvane.

"I hear you using the voice of a mother issuing a reprimand," I said to Yvane, while darting an amused glance at her young cousin. "What age difference is there between you?"

"Five years. Narda's 17, but she's been badly brought-up at boarding-school. She's an orphan, the daughter of one of my mother's brothers." Yvane offered this explanation in a low voice. "My stepfather accepted responsibility for her too."

There was a slight sadness in her tone that surprised me a little. I didn't press the point. We got up to take a turn around the property.

When we finally found ourselves back beside my car, she planted herself in front of me and said, brusquely: "I'm afraid you were bored."

I assured her of the contrary.

"Nevertheless," she said, not listening to me, "I'm putting myself in your place. I meet a young woman in the sea, go to her aid and pull her out of a perilous situation, then meet her again by chance at the theater—all that is bizarre enough, and sets my imagination working. I imagine a sporty fairy, some kind of star leading a luxurious existence, of a fantastic environment worthy of a woman fallen from the sky, and I find a poor girl living prosaically with her stepfather, almost alone in an old house. If I were you, I'd be disappointed."

19

"And the young woman, who also has a right to dream—what does she say when she only finds a great devil of an architect who promises to get her reservoir repaired?"

She laughed, tilting her head back, and the bursts of her laughter, which sounded young and fresh, lifted up her tanned throat. "Oh, I can see now that my reflection was indiscreet," she declared.

"The young woman remains more mysterious than she believes herself to be," I assured her.

Seeing her there in front of me, in fact, upright, simply-dressed, without make-up, with her eyes and hair bright, I found that she participated in the mystery of limpid entities and denuded artifices. She invited speculation, but in a truly magnificent fashion, as a pebble shining buy the roadside, a stem reaching up toward the sky, or a wild animal free in its movements encourages speculation about the enigma of existence.

"May I, as a good friend, come to collect you tomorrow in order to take you out in my turn—perhaps to Cannes?"

"With Narda?" she asked, after a moment's hesitation.

"Of course," I declared, starting the engine.

Having traveled a certain distance along the road, I stopped the car in order to light a cigarette.

The whole thing had been simple and rather odd at the same time. I looked at myself in the rear-view mirror. "Curious, curious," I murmured. I smiled. I no longer recognized myself.

When I presented myself the following day at the agreed time, I found Yvane in conversation with a gardener in the main pathway. "Narda can't come," she told me, immediately.

"I don't think that will alter our program. Your stepfather won't see anything improper in your going out with me, I hope?"

"Why should he?" she replied, in a surprised tone. Her tone and expression seemed decisive enough.

"I'd love to drive," she said, opening the door.

I yielded the steering-wheel to her, and she set off with a great deal of assurance. She weaved her way through the little crowded streets of Cannes rather skillfully. Authoritatively, she selected one of the best-known dance-halls in the town, and we parked on the quayside. When I praised her decisiveness, she replied, bizarrely: "I'm just struggling against my inferiority complex."

"One of your stepfather's terms?" I remarked.

"No—all the idiots are talking about their complexes just now. Haven't you noticed?"

I confessed my ignorance, and the recent date of my return to France. She listened distractedly, while dancing. She danced well. Secretly, I compared her with the women present; in the middle of all those faces made up with applications of cream and powder, her freshness and youth were imposing. The heat was stifling, though, and the orchestra really was making too much noise.

"Are you enjoying yourself?" I asked her.

She looked at me, searching in my eyes for the correct response, and replied: "No." We went back to the car and, abandoning the pleasures of the coast, set forth at hazard inland. A shared taste directed us toward deserted and honest places. By the side of the road a small inn appeared, whose terrace overlooked the region all the way to the sea. There were we able to drink lemonade in an arbor.

Her bare hand was lying on the corner of the table. Playfully, I covered it with mine, as if to compare their dimensions.

"My skin is darker than yours," she declared. "After two years here, I have the right to a certain advancement."

"If you'd met me in shorts on Bali, I'd have beaten you for suntan. I was no longer a white man in any but name."

She paused thoughtfully, and then declared: "Why do you think that I'm not curious about your past? Anyway, it's the same with everything. It's bizarre, at my age, but I don't experience any curiosity. The world doesn't tempt me. At times, I think that it's an illness."

21

I noticed that, without my being aware of it, the hand I had superimposed on hers had folded up to imprison it entirely. I didn't move a muscle, but I sensed that her gaze was lowered, like mine, upon our immobile fingers. She remained mute.

"I didn't do it deliberately," I said.

"I know that. It's like the tendrils of a vine. Have you seen vines in spring, creeping along a trellis? The tendrils only take a few hours to wind around the supportive wires; one might think that they were little conscious hands, and yet they don't know what they're doing, and more than your fingers knew…"

"Perhaps it's all the more revealing? The expression of a profound natural instinct…"

She looked me in the eye and said: "I know what you're thinking. You think that what I said doesn't mean anything, and that I'm deliberately misinterpreting a gesture that might have made a commitment you didn't intend."

"You read thoughts well," I admitted.

"Give me a cigarette," she said, then, abruptly enough for me to understand that she only wanted me to let go of her hand.

"Tell my stepfather," she continued, in a different tone, "that I can read thoughts. He'll be jealous—that's his great ambition."

"Is his research really serious, then?" I said, slightly disconcerted by the intrusion of the stepfather into the conversation.

"I think so," she replied, with some gravity. As I held out a match for her, she exclaimed: "I'm glad you don't have a lighter. I can't bear people who use lighters."

"Me neither—that odor of petrol, and the vulgarity of that movement of the thumb over the flint-wheel…"

Her expression brightened, and she added, precipitately: "Yes, yes—but I've discovered the real reason. Fire is a noble thing, and making fire is an operation so sacred that we must respectfully employ both hands to give birth to the flame.

22

When, with a lighter, you light the wick with excessive familiarity, it's a veritable blasphemy, a punishable triviality, like celebrating a mystery in a garage. The Sun, and fire are my personal gods…"

I listened to her with a half-smile on my lips. It was getting late. In front of us the Sun was hollowing out longer shadows in the rocky hillsides. The facades of small farmhouses scattered on the terraced fields were tinted in gold. In the pine-tree above our heads, crickets were singing. For a long moment, we watched the Sun setting on the plain in silence.

"The Virgilian hour," I murmured.

In a whisper, I heard her say: "*Majoresque cadunt…*"[2] As I looked at her in surprise, she explained, with a hint of irony directed at herself: "I have my baccalaureat."

The Fiat was waiting for us in front of the inn. I asked her if she still wanted to drive. She shook her head. Her mood seemed to have changed again; she remained silent. I could no longer sense anything of her but the hip that sometimes made contact with mine as we went around bends. Troubled, I could find nothing to say. It seemed that we were making a proof of our silences—the most redoubtable of all.

When I stopped the car in front of the gate of the property, the silence of the motor rendered ours even more perceptible and weighty. Noiselessly, for I can find no other word to render the significance of the movement that might, I sensed, release an internal storm within her, she turned toward me. Our faces found themselves so close that our lips touched lightly. She opened the door and, having leapt to the ground, opened the gate without looking back.

---

[2] *Majoresque cadunt altis e montibus umbrae* [The Shadows of high mountains grow large] is a popular quotation from Virgil's *Eclogues*.

23

CHAPTER THREE

The next day, if the weather had been less beautiful, less sunny, with less spring in the air, I would have found myself almost reasonable. A nice shower would have set me squarely on the right road, bringing me back to an awareness of the necessary greyness that is the background of any well-conducted life. But with all those colors—there were armfuls of flowers in every room in the hotel, and the casino flower-beds were nothing but living mosaics—my head still felt lacking in solidity.

No new rendezvous had been arranged, but the reservoir in need of repair furnished me with a pretext to manifest myself whenever I wished. Before the morning was out, I had already telephoned a contractor in Nice.

Then, as I was passing the casino, I happened upon Dr. Mops, who was climbing into his large Mercedes, driven by a Malay chauffeur.

"Gambling already?" I asked, in a familiar fashion.

"No, not yet. I'll probably try it in a few days' time."

"What?" I said. "Since you've been here, you haven't yet tried your luck?"

"I wasn't ready. I'm only here to measure the interval separating two plays at the same table."

Not caring whether or not I understood him, he replied with that slightly naive seriousness that had already struck me in his regard. I thought that he was preparing some kind of system.

"Be careful," I told him, "the mathematics are precise, and chance has laws that can't be subverted."

This time, he did not furnish an explanation, contenting himself with asking: "Can I give you a lift to La Colle?"

As the opportunity was there, I took my place in the big car.

The influence of spring was evidently not making itself felt in me alone, for the doctor's cordiality became even more expansive as we went along the road.

"Oh, Monsieur Delambre," he said to me, with the sharp accent that gave his words a child-like manner, "you're lucky to be young! When I think of my youth, though, of all the stupid things I did...would you think, to look at me, that there was a time when I thought I could photograph souls?"

I had scarcely expected that sort of youthful stupidity, and I burst out laughing.

"Yes, I occupied myself with psychic research; I photographed auras, vital bubbles. By night, I laid out sensitive plates to obtain the imprints of the states of my soul; I even slipped into my friends' homes. I wasted three years of my life in India studying the secrets of indigenous magic! And I won't mention spiritualist séances, daggers to cut through emanations, electrical recordings of prayers, of the *expir* and the *inspir*...

"My first wife was to blame. I married too young; I was in love. My wife was a theosophist; out of love, I devoted myself to the same follies as her. The worst of it was that we were both very wrapped up in the little circle that we formed, and my medical studies had given me an impressive vocabulary and an authority. How could one not be stupid at that point? That's youth...

"In our Northern lands, one does not mature as quickly as in your country, and one also remains young for longer. Then my wife died—she threw herself out of a window on a day of great inspiration; the *inspir* ought to have saved her. My eyes were opened. Afterwards, I read August Comte and Le Dantec,[3] to mention only your philosophers, and I burned that which I had adored, reverting to sane ideas. The brain secretes thought as the kidney secretes urine. *Der Mann is was*

---

[3] Félix Le Dantec (1869-1917) was a biologist and philosopher who wrote several books on evolution and one on atheism, taking a positivist approach derived from Comte.

er ist. Everything is inscribed in matter. There's still a lot of naivety in that, I grant you, but I resumed my studies, this time seriously. Science has completed my formation by submitting me to its discipline. I was one of Berger's pupils at Jena for six years.[4] I became passionate about his work on the electricity of the brain, before taking flight on my own wings."

I listened distractedly to this tale, which brought a smile to my lips with its extreme volubility. I had to say something.

"In my profession, we only have to deal with stones— it's less dangerous."

"A fine profession nevertheless," said the doctor. "A profession of artisans and artists…"

With these words he appeared to have exhausted the possibility of a discourse on architecture, for he continued without transition: "I'm glad that you've made the acquaintance of my girls. They don't see many people, and my company is scarcely agreeable. I make an effort from time to time to steer them this way or that, but everything that amuses most people bores me, and inversely…"

He followed this declaration with hearty satisfied laughter, which relieved him of all bitterness. As we were arriving, he suggested that I accompany him to his study on the first floor while we waited for lunch. I couldn't refuse, and I followed him into a sort of vast library, very comfortably furnished, with a wholly Dutch orderliness. Colored panes in the windows contributed to giving that interior the appearance and intimate atmosphere of a painting by a minor master.

A large photograph was standing on the desk. "My first wife," the doctor explained. Taking the photograph between his thumb and index finger, he made it pivot on its support. Another female face was framed on the other side. "The second," he said.

---

[4] Hans Berger (1873-1941), the director of the Jena Psychiatric University Clinic from 1919-1938, pioneered the use of encephalography in human beings, working on the correlation of brain activity with consciousness.

I did not linger over the comical aspect of that juxtaposition, moved though I was by finding Yvane's features echoed in the new face: there was the same nose, small and delicate, the same slight projection of the cheekbones, and the same obliquity of the features, which gave the face an expression reminiscent of a nervous hind.

"Whisky?" asked the doctor, abruptly. He added, perhaps by way of excuse: "An old colonial habit."

I accepted. He pulled a little wheeled bar toward him. Suddenly, he uttered a curse and rang for a servant. A barefooted Malay came in, and he spoke to him harshly in Dutch. Without saying a word, the servant went to move a large standard lamp that stood in one corner of the room five centimeters to one side.

"I can't bear the objects in my study not being in exactly the right place," the doctor told me. "The slightest modification of position upsets my thought-processes. For ten years, I've been working in unaltered surroundings. When I think that, one day, Yvane took it into her head to bring in a bouquet of flowers! It's the only time I lost my temper with her, the poor child!"

That little scene had made a slightly painful impression on me. My embarrassed gaze scanned the room. Half-hidden behind a movable staircase, something reminiscent of a grand plan of Paris was hanging in front of the books in a bookcase. The encounter with that familiar image gladdened my heart.

However, the doctor said: "It's an anatomical illustration, considerably enlarged, representing the internal face of the right hemisphere of the brain. It has hung there for ten years. I haven't been able to resolve myself to taking it down, and it remains in my lair like a sorcerer's owl."

Whisky in hand, he went to stand in front of the image, and laughed. "Nothing is as beautiful as a brain, truly. Every sinuosity, every groove of the pallium, has its meaning. And to think that I know all of that by heart! What a marvel of a labyrinth, in which one does not get lost! Now, Monsieur Delambre, if you like such things, here's a rather nice item…"

He lifted the lid of a varnished box, which revealed a solidified mass on a black marble pedestal, which I recognized this time as the lobes of a brain.

"A fine molding," I said, with a layman's slight nausea.

"A molding! It's an anatomical preparation, hardened in formaldehyde—a success that cost me rather dear, although I was able to make a good job of it. It's the brain of my second wife."

I could not repress an exclamation.

"I had asked that an autopsy be carried out on the cadaver," the doctor told me. "Wasn't it the least I could do to reserve a choice morsel, the favorite object of my studies? Preserve it in alcohol? Never! A slow petrifaction has made it into this work of art...

"In your architect's office, Monsieur Delambre, perhaps you have a view of the Parthenon, Rheims cathedral or the Empire State Building—what do I know? As an architect of the brain, why should I not give pride of place to a perfect encephalum?—the encephalum of a woman that I was pleased to imagine perfect for a long time. Others might have kept her heart, but we must abandon that organ to the symbolic significance that it has in the popular imagination. For us, who are much closer to the secrets of the flesh, a brain is much fuller of memories. You know, I often think that here"—he touched a region of the grey marble with the rim of his glass—"in the striated zone bordering the calcarine fissure, images of me reflected in my poor Gilberte's eyes formed many times over. The impulse that drove her arms, her beautiful bare arms, to fold around me, came from that frontal ascendant circumvolution, on the edge of the fissure of Rolando—and there in the region that extends from the mesocephalum to the rachidian bulb, where the 'central self' of that adorable being resided, along with the supreme regulator of all the physical functions, the entire personality of the departed doubtless remains, obscurely inscribed in the petrified fibers. What was she but a fragment of organized matter?—a cleverly-ordered atomic ballet; a bundle of cells ruled by this superior structure of which I conserve her very being, in a far more authentic fashion, much truer than within the vain memories in my own mind, or the superficial images that photographic prints evoke for us."

He had got carried away, perhaps slightly intoxicated by the alcohol, forgetful of my presence. The lunch-bell sounded opportunely, freeing me from the necessity of furnishing any reply. I felt rather ill-at-ease. When we met up with the young women in the hallway, their presence was a great relief to me. Yvane shook my hand in a comradely manner, perhaps with a slight hint of detachment. Dirk sat down at the table after having greeted us be clicking his heels. The doctor, at whose side he took his place, was the only one to offer him his hand.

During the meal, my uneasy impression dissipated gradually. The greater part of the conversation was abandoned to more-or-less overt attempts by Narda to obtain authorization from her uncle to remain at La Colle instead of returning to her Swiss boarding-school after the vacation. I appointed myself as her advocate. We finally obtained a "We'll see" from the doctor, which was almost a consent, and won me a covert smile from the young cousin. Entering into that little family comedy amused me, but I wasn't there to play the big brother. As we got up from the table, I asked Yvane to take me to the reservoir that I had to have repaired.

I had been looking forward to being alone together for a while. It was almost disappointing at first. She remained thoughtful, but gradually confided in me.

"Last night, I thought about the walk we took yesterday, and behind my thoughts, as if from a misty background, I saw the frightful 'What's the point?' that has pursued me all my life appear once again. The thought of your amity hasn't caused it to vanish…"

That sadness contrasted so strongly with her youth and the dazzling health of her body that I could easily have refused to believe it, but her tone was sincere. She was not acting out some comedy of coquetry, but seemed, on the contrary, to be surprised by what she was saying.

Far from being put off by her gloomy disposition, I experienced instead a desire to get closer to her, to help bring her out of herself, to force her to blossom freely and happily. It was akin to a devotional duty, a good deed to be done. I affected a great optimism, spoke with assurance, put on a display of vigor and will-power, in order to give her an exemplary tonic.

We were walking slowly, having forgotten the pretext for my visit. At the rear of the property, a little summer-house stood on the hill. I asked her to take me to look at it. The three rooms, on one floor, were surmounted by a *loggia*, which was reached by means of a ladder, and which looked out on to the mountains of the hinterland.

"Have you never had any desire to live here?" I asked.

"Well, no—you see, that's the sort of idea that doesn't occur to me spontaneously." She added, with a hint of bitterness: "The ideas that come to me spontaneously aren't good ones."

She sat down on the rim of the *loggia*, with her back to the column. Was it the shadow that the roof projected over her? Her eyes seemed to me to be brighter, bluer, and larger. A very vague smile floated sadly over her face. I had the bizarre feeling that I recognized it, and perceived that she was duplicating the expression her mother wore in the portrait that the doctor had kept. But the horrible memory of the anatomical specimen enclosed in the varnished casket was superimposed over her living image, and I had to make an effort to put it out of my mind.

She began speaking, in a deliberate and slightly strained voice, as if she were reciting a prepared text: "A gentleman goes for a stroll on the Côte d'Azur. Thousands of gentlemen go strolling on the coast. Why *this* gentleman? What difference is there between the day when, while taking a dip in the sea, one meets this gentleman, and all the other days when one takes a dip in the sea? The gentleman has certainly met a great many ladies who were also taking dips, in the sea or elsewhere. And is this gentleman asking himself: 'Why *this* lady?'" In a sharper tone, she added: "Yes, why should that meeting take on a serious significance, when nothing distinguished it, when it occurred, from all the other meetings in the world?"

"My word," I began, not knowing quite what I was going to say, "if it was a matter of chance, why complain about it? The clouds in the sky, the stars, life itself—everything is a matter of chance."

She sighed, raising her hand to her forehead. "Yes, yes—I'm very stupid when I let my poor head run on."

By way of protest, I had also moved my hand discreetly toward the head that she was slandering. Gently, like a trusting animal, she leaned forward to rest her forehead in the palm of my hand. It was the first time I had touched her face. Emotionally, I was allowing my fingers to model her temples and come into contact with the curve of her brow when the memory of the atrocious relic preserved by the doctor came to mind again. I felt that I had a duty to remove her from a depressing atmosphere and a deadening influence—the causes of the anxiety to which her thoughts gave testimony.

She raised her head again—the entire scene had lasted no longer than a few seconds—and said, in a changed and cheerful voice: "You have cool hands; you've cured me."

As we went back down the *loggia*'s ladder, an idea suddenly crossed my mind and, without further reflection, I exclaimed: "Would you rent this summer-house to me?"

She was momentarily nonplussed. "What an idea!"

"Quite seriously," I said, "I like the place. It reminds me of those bungalows in India that are open to the cool night air. You're not doing anything with it; for my part, I could live in it as easily as the hotel. If I have the impression of being in my own home, I would be more willing to stay on the coast for some time."

"But you'd be very badly lodged—the rooms are uninhabitable."

"It wouldn't take much to get them back into a proper state."

"Do you think so?" she cried, suddenly, with a childish spontaneity. "Oh it would be chic then!"

We began to study the place methodically. She brought to the domiciliary visit a zest and gaiety that she had not yet shown that day.

"Do you really think that it's possible?"

"Why not? If your stepfather will accept me as a tenant…"

"Oh, it will be perfectly all right with him."

I was sincere in my desire to rent the summer-house; the picturesque quality and the tranquility of the place, the olive-grove outside my door and the view of the mountains all attracted me. When I raised my head to interrogate the crumbling plaster of the ceilings, however, I nevertheless thought: *I'm in the process of putting a noose around my own neck.* But I thought it with some contentment, even delight. She seemed so pleased!

We went on to study the possibilities that I would have of reaching my home without passing through the property. There was a pathway along the estate's enclosing wall, which led directly to the main road. A door—long sealed up, admittedly—opened on to the path; all that was required was to find the key. Once the bundles of firewood that were encumbering it were cleared, the debris of a neighboring shed would furnish a garage for my car sufficient for the summer. Like children in the depths of a park, we were playing Robinson Crusoe. The intimacy between us was increased.

CHAPTER FOUR

None of what we had imagined proved impossible. Instead of putting the contractor's laborers to work on the reservoir, I sent them to the summer-house. I went to supervise the work every day. A week later, I was almost ready to take up residence.

If I had feared finding myself too close to the inhabitants of the château by renting the summer-house, that fear would immediately have proved vain. They exercised the greatest discretion in not disturbing my comings and goings. I had refused the items of furniture that the doctor had offered me, preferring to buy a few chairs or rustic accessories at random during my visits to the antique-dealers of the inland villages. Whenever I happened to meet Yvane, I asked her to accompany me on my excursions. Our searches amused her, I could tell. Once, she sighed: "And to think that these things would overwhelm me with boredom if it were a matter of my own house!"

There was a semi-admission in that, whose charm derived from her casual personality; it was an observation that she made innocently and unguardedly, whose real significance seemed to escape her.

I asked her to call me Pierre, since I called her by her first name. She did so immediately, without any reluctance. On occasion, she even addressed me as "tu" inadvertently, without anything ever having happened between us that justified a greater intimacy. That gave our relationship an air of pleasant comradeship, which would have been a trifle puerile if I had not found her grave and tormented on other occasions. Sometimes, her gaze became so vague that, plunging into her pupils, I had the impression that no matter how far I might go, sinking infinitely into the mists and blue-tinted heaths of her internal world, I would never succeed in catching up with her. But these sudden changes of mood prevented our meeting from becoming habitual, and the interest that I brought to them was ever on the alert. I could see her again and again without any monotony tarnishing her individuality.

One day, I was coming back from Biot with a consignment of earthenware pots that were destined for the decoration of my future dwelling, when I saw Dirk on the road, returning to La Colle on foot. In the course of the recent meals at which he had appeared, he had not opened his mouth. I wanted to be friendly and as I drew level with him I proposed that he get in. He did so without hesitation.

"Were you taking a little walk?" I asked.

He took some time before replying: "I was an assistant to a stockbroker in Amsterdam before entering the doctor's employ."

"Oh yes," I said. "I forgot to ask you. You haven't always studied medicine, then?"

"I'm primarily occupied with assisting in certain experiments, and spend a great deal of time in conversations in which I do nothing but listen."

"I was wondering what sort of collaboration you engaged in with the doctor."

"You'll have to give me a light, then," he declared.

I turned toward him to hand him a box of matches, but to my surprise, he had nothing in his mouth.

"A funny way of asking for a cigarette," I said. "Look, there are some in the pocket on your side of the car."

He took a cigarette for himself and lit it. "You're right," he said.

"About what? Never letting go of the steering-wheel? One can never be careful enough, and I have a whole lot of pottery there."

He seemed to be a million miles away, and his remarks were disjointed to the point that I suspected him of some secret intention. Where was he heading? Was it that my presence at La Colle near the young women had awakened a certain jealousy within him, which was responsible for his strange attitude toward me?

"She's very beautiful, and worthy to be loved," he declared, abruptly.

I started, and immediately brought the vehicle to a halt.

"Come on, my dear Dirk," I said, deliberately, "there's no need to play games. Who are you talking about? Are you talking about Mademoiselle Yvane?"

He drew on his cigarette awkwardly. His large round eyes were staring at me in astonishment.

"You've put it into third gear," he said.

The car had stopped. He was either mad or playing the imbecile. Irritated, I shrugged my shoulders and, without persisting further, engaged the clutch again—but, disturbed by what he had said, I did indeed go into third gear, and the motor stalled. I swore, pressing the starter again. The doctor's company must have unbalanced the poor fellow's mind. I abstained from speaking to him again during the few kilometers that we still had to cover, and I decided privately that, instead of dropping him at the château, I would leave him on the road, where the little path that led to the summer-house branched off.

He undoubtedly understood my intention, for even before I decelerated, he said to me very politely: "Thank you for having spared me a little of the road. I'd prefer to go back in discreetly now, without mentioning that I met you. I beg you not to mention it yourself. Goodbye, and thanks."

We were still 300 meters from the junction. He was a little premature in bidding me farewell. Having reached the path, I let him down. He bowed to me again, very amicably, but without saying a word.

Still under the influence of that bizarre scene, I arrived at the summer-house. Yvane was on the doorstep with a large armful of carnations.

"I hope I'm not being indiscreet," he said. "I came so that the vases wouldn't remain empty. Nothing is sadder, or even more ill-omened, than an empty vase."

Setting the flowers down on the window-sill, she came to help me unload the car.

"Don't you find Dirk truly bizarre?" I asked her.

"I don't know—I scarcely pay any attention to him," she replied.

"I'm wondering whether he hasn't conceived a grand passion for you," I continued, without meaning any harm.

She blushed violently. "What makes you think that? It's certainly not true, but the thought of it makes me ashamed. Yes, the most respectful homages, wherever they come from, seem to me to be a diminution of myself." She made a sort of angry gesture, and continued in a hurried voice: "I'd like it if no one ever noticed me, never gave me a thought, even of mere sympathy. That's why I live a solitary existence, not seeing people of my own age. It's an assault on my liberty for anyone to presume to dispose of me thus without my consent. It soils me—don't you think so?"

Visibly very emotional, she stood with her arms hanging loose, in complete disarray, as if struck in a sensitive spot.

I reproached myself for me abruptness, my misunderstanding of the extreme modesty of which she gave evidence. I was too awkward, too heavy-handed for that exaggerated sensitivity. She did not appear to hear my excuses, but she collected herself gradually.

"No," she said, "it's me who's ridiculous in letting myself go like that, but I can't control myself—forgive me. Just give me your hand for a moment, without saying anything."

I took her hand. We were leaning against the carnations lying on the window-sill. In front of us, the setting Sun was touching the horizon. The bleating of a goat rose up from a neighboring field, and all around us, the toads were already sounding their solitary note. In the calm air, the odor of flowers became more insistent.

We held hands like two well-behaved children. I respected her silence, which, as it became prolonged, gave a more serious significance to what I had thought to be only a caprice, which I did not understand. I looked at her: her eyes lost in infinity, her face turned toward the setting Sun seemed to be calling out to the languor of the evening, to the clouds stretching across the sky, to the fatigue of living. Little by little, in the rising shadows, I thought I saw her lose consciousness, becoming the soul of the night, distant and impalpable, barely alive. Becoming more emotional, I increased the pressure of my fingers. She shuddered, finally return to herself, and spoke. Her words, murmured in a soft, slightly sad voice, took on a strange sibylline resonance within the vast frame of silence that had preceded it.

"It's getting dark. I came to put flowers in the vases, but I won't have time to arrange them."

The dinner bell sounded on the far side of the little valley. She took a few paces. "I can't believe," she went on, "that you're going to live here."

"Yes—tomorrow evening, I assure you, I shall be here."

In my mind, these words only had the import of a polite reply, but on hearing them in the silence, after the long preceding scene, I was struck myself by the somewhat solemn character that they took on. It was like a promise, an engagement.

Yvane received it without saying a word, and seemed to bear it away beneath the silvery foliage of the olive-trees.

CHAPTER FIVE

Faithful to my promise, the next day, I made arrangements to leave the hotel. I had just paid the bill and emerged on to the casino plaza when I noticed the doctor's Mercedes among the parked cars.

He gambles, then, whatever he might say, I thought.

In fact the doctor, flanked by Dirk, appeared shortly afterwards. He offered, once again, to take me back to La Colle. Dirk sat beside the chauffeur, and I took my place inside. We had scarcely moved off when the doctor declared: "We had a good morning..." Taking a thick wad of banknotes from his pockets, he specified: "422,000 francs."

I uttered an exclamation. "Take care not to lose them," I added, at hazard.

"I can't lose—I'm betting on certainties."

"What! I'd really like to know..."

He shrank back into a corner in order to stare at me ironically. "You challenged me to find a system. It's a good thing that science is occasionally useful for something."

My curiosity was unsatisfied. Until then it had been rather difficult to take him seriously, but the wad of banknotes obliged me to revise my initial impression. I did not hesitate to press him to be more precise. He was reluctant to do so.

"It's a rather long story that requires appropriate explanations. Will you consent to accompany me to the laboratory?"

Desirous of clarifying the issue, I accepted the invitation. He doctor gave an order, and on entering La Colle, the car went around the main building to deposit us by a side door in the left wing. A little stairway climbed up to the first floor, opening directly into a sequence of whitewashed rooms exclusively furnished with scientific apparatus.

Very deliberately, the doctor began by putting on white smock with short sleeves. Then he donned the classic skullcap of the surgeon. "My dear Monsieur Delambre," he said to me, "you are not unaware that the activity of the brain is accompanied by electrical currents that are quite easy to detect?"

"My God," I said, without allowing myself to be intimidated by the solemnity of these preparations, "I have a strong suspicion that electricity must have something to do with what goes on therein…"

He smiled at this admission of ignorance, and rang a hand-bell. A Javanese in a white smock appeared, to whom he said a few words in Malay.

"We're going to begin with a classic experiment," he said.

The Javanese came back, holding a large rabbit by the ears.

"Watch this animal," said the doctor. "First I'll put it to sleep."

He injected the contents of a syringe beneath the rabbit's skin; it fell unconscious on the marble table-top.

With a few strokes of a razor, rapid and precise gestures, he shaved the top of the animal's cranium. Then he arranged his victim on a wooden block, immobilized its head, and, having connected an instrument like a dentist's drill to the electric current, he applied it to the exposed area.

"This marvelous little apparatus permits any skull to be made into a skimmer," he said. "Look, I'm making a few openings in this animal's cranium." Indicating a milky membrane reminiscent of the dome of a jellyfish in the middle of the hole he was cutting, he added: "And now you can see the *dura mater*."

That kind of operation always has an effect; I grimaced as I watched.

"The animal is obviously ready," the doctor declared. "You can see that it doesn't take as long as making a stew."

The Javanese, who was serving as an assistant, then transported the animal to an apparatus fastened to the ceiling, from which various wires hung. The doctor took one, which he introduced into the animal's ear; then he pointed out a sort of clock-face situated in front of us.

39

"The mirror of this galvanometer will inform us about the electrical currents running through the circuit."

A second wire was placed in direct contact with the brain of the rabbit, and the little mirror began to oscillate.

"Alpha waves in the occipital region," murmured the doctor, speaking to himself. Pricking the rabbit's paw, which caused it to shiver, he added: "Now we excite the animal. See how the motive impulse is accompanied by an electrical current indicated by a considerable deviation of the galvanometer."

In my incompetence, I thought it was going to a great deal of trouble to make a mirror quiver on the end of a ire, but I feigned great interest. "Have similar experiments been carried out on humans?" I asked.

"Of course!" he cried. "The cranial cavity isn't opened, of course; one simply puts the electrodes in contact with the scalp. What's more, I have a specialized premises for the study of encephalograms."

Abandoning the rabbit to the Javanese, to whom he gave a number of further orders that I did not understand, he preceded me into another large room in the middle of which was an armchair surmounted by a sort of crowd or helmet somewhat reminiscent of those which serve to perm feminine coiffeurs.

"I've acquired sufficient experience to be able to operate on myself," the doctor said. "The experimental apparatus here is a little more delicate, but is broadly the same as the one you saw just now. If we light this little flame, its image, reflected in the mirror of the oscillograph, will be projected on to this screen, and render the pulsations of the current visible."

Going over to the frosted-glass windows, he suddenly pulled down a black screen, which plunged the room into semi-darkness. Then, lifting off his white skull-cap with a rapid hand-movement, he sat down in the armchair and put his head inside the helmet.

"Don't move," he said to me. "I'll keep quiet for a few minutes to let the murmurs of my cerebral activity die down;

then I'll make the contact, and you'll see luminous oscillations on the screen corresponding to the rhythm of the Berger currents that are running through my encephalum."

Meekly, I fell silent. I was intrigued, as in a cinema, torn between a muted anxiety and the satisfaction of being initiated into the esoteric scientific mysteries. The doctor did as he had said, and after a few minutes, the luminous dot began to describe broad oscillations on the screen.

"You can see, now that I'm speaking to you," the doctor said, "the effort of attention that I have to make in order to slow down the rhythm of the oscillations that are muffled by other currents nascent in the zone of articulate language."

The displacement on the screen had indeed slowed down; it returned to its initial amplitude when the doctor had ceased speaking.

"The experiment is particularly striking when one performs it on oneself, for one witnesses it from outside and inside at the same time, if I might put it thus. Do you want to try it?"

"It doesn't do any harm?" I asked.

"None—it's just like being in a seat at the theater."

I took his place. He gently applied my head to the headrest, and I felt two little pieces of metal come into contact with my skin behind the ears.

"The blunted electrodes pass through your hair and won't prick you. Relax, and don't think about anything, as if you were going to go to sleep."

I obeyed. In the dark and silent room, the luminous dot gradually began its swaying. It was agitated by regular frissons, interrupted by calmer periods.

"Now begin a mental operation," the doctor whispered to me. "Recite the alphabet backwards."

I began internally: Z, Y, X… I was surprised to see the quivering of the dot on the screen die down. As I searched for the letter that ought to come after X, without finding it, the luminous dot became completely motionless, making my mental effort manifest. Before finding the letter, I had to recite the

41

entire alphabet forwards—A. B., C, etc.—and the oscillations resumed during that facile listing. Then I resumed with W, V...and hesitated again before recovering U and T—which provoked a further interruption of the pulsations.

The doctor was right; the experiment was quite striking. The variable efforts of attention were materialized on the screen by the quivering of the dot. It was as if one could see inside one's own head—something more impressive than seeing one's own heart beating. To make the little will-o-the-wisp that represented the spark of thought dance on the screen, it was sufficient to try to think, or not to think. No command more tenuous and more direct could ever have permitted the external development of a phenomenon. I was like the god of that dancing patch.

"We not only have the possibility of detecting the Berger waves that reflect the activity of thought," the doctor told me. "We can also reveal the specific currents due to affectivity."

I felt him moving some sort of metallic comb through my hair in order to push it to the right side of my forehead, where he seemed to be searching carefully for a suitable location. The luminous patch began to describe a little circle in the middle of the screen.

"Relax."

The luminous patch became almost motionless. Then, very softly, he breathed in my ear: "My dear Monsieur Delambre, what are your sentiments with regard to my stepdaughter Yvane?"

A surge of blood rose to my face, and I started in the armchair. On the screen, the little circle enlarged to the point of touching the edges, leading an extravagant dance.

"I don't see what that has to do with anything," I said, at hazard, my throat dry.

"Are you in love with my step-daughter?" the doctor persisted.

"You'll permit me to keep my sentiments to myself," I replied, with deliberate insolence.

"Alas, I fear that's impossible," said the doctor, whose eyes never left the screen on which the saraband of the luminous circle had lost all restraint.

"That's treachery!" I cried, furiously, removing all the instruments sounding my skull with a single thrust.

"Calm down, my dear Monsieur," said the doctor, removing the screens that were obscuring the windows. "My question is easily explicable. I don't seek to uncover secrets that do not belong to me without good reason. If you were only to be a temporary friend, I would owe you the consideration due to friendship, and nothing more, but if the interest you feel for my family responds to a more profound sentiment, it's perfectly normal for me to have confidence in you and furnish you with supplementary explanations regarding my work, under the seal of secrecy. Indeed, it would displease me now to be seen in your eyes as a person who earns his living gambling…"

My anger was not diminishing greatly.

"I don't know how I feel myself…" I began.

The doctor made a gesture, accompanied by a smile.

"I don't need anything more from you—what I've seen is sufficient. But everything that we've done to date is very little compared with what remains for me to tell you. You were curious to know my betting system, Monsieur Delambre, and your curiosity will be satisfied. Would you care to accompany me to my study? We'll be able to talk more comfortably there."

CHAPTER SIX

That session in the laboratory left me furious and some-what at a loss. The situation had been turned around. Dr. Mops, whom I had treated until then in a casual manner, had seized the initiative from me. I felt diminished, ready to submit to his ascendancy even though I forbade myself to do so. The thought that I might have been lured into some kind of trap also occurred to me. As soon as we had quit the experimental laboratories, he abandoned the rather solemn tone that he had adopted, quite seamlessly, to recover the polite and cordial appearance he normally manifested. That abrupt change of attitude only served to confirm that his customary joviality was an affectation, and that I had to be even more on my guard.

"A little Hollands gin?" he proposed, once we were in the study. "Schiedam is our Bordeaux, and carries the renown of the Netherlands throughout the world! My word, it's worth as much as Rembrandt!"

I swallowed the alcohol, and felt more secure on my foundations. The doctor lowered himself into an armchair, folded his arms, and began by caressing his hairy biceps a few times beneath the short sleeves of his white smock.

"I told you, Monsieur, that I don't want to have secrets from you. That will oblige me to remind you of certain histological data. They might not interest you, but they have their importance. A long time ago it was remarked that, unlike the ordinary cells that make up our organism, nerve-cells do not multiply. You are born with all your-nerve-cells and, their number being incapable of augmentation, they accompany you to your death. Thus from birth onwards, the material structure of the nervous system, which will support every psychophysiological edifice of your personality, is ready to play its role, to be loaded with all the knowledge that you will acquire. In other words, your brain is a blank slate that will be inscribed as you advance through life, and from which you cannot erase anything, since the particles that constitute it are always the same. That particularity of nerve-cells is rich in significance for the nature of human personality. There is no need to make any appeal to a supernatural soul to justify the conservation of the self in the midst of the general flow of things; the permanence of the cells is sufficient to explain it.

"I shall now pass on to the other extreme of philosophical speculation. I've already made you a profession of materialist faith. I believe that everything that happens in the universe, and everything that will happen there, depends on material factors, the evolution of which is regulated by immutable laws. Everything has been written since the first day of creation, and nothing can modify in any manner whatsoever the unfolding of the initial program."

After the scene in the laboratory, this philosophical conversation was somewhat anodyne—and, all things considered, I preferred it to experiments in which I served as the subject. I made a gesture of polite condescension, as if to reserve my opinion, and contented myself with drinking a mouthful of gin.

"What I've just told you is not essential to the consequences that follow whatever hypothesis one adopts, but it explains the orientation I have given to my research. I have been able to localize in the cerebral cortex the zones that preside over the organization of memory, and I have been able to detect, as in the experiments we have just made, the electrical currents associated with the activity of these zones.

"Just now, if you had not abruptly interrupted me, I would have shown you a curious but well-known experiment on the rabbit with the open skull, which consists of artificially imparting a rhythm to the electrical oscillations of the cortical currents. It is sufficient to submit the animal to periodic excitations, such as a lamp that goes on and off before its eyes, for the pulsations of the cerebral currents to reproduce the artificial rhythm of the lamp. Now, pay close attention to me…"

He got to his feet, extended a professorial finger to emphasize an important part of the speech, and continued: "Here is a subject. I localize the cerebral currents corresponding to the zones of memory. I impart an accelerated oscillatory rhythm, which has the effect of giving the nerve-cells of memory a more intense and more rapid activity than normal. I thus *age* the cells artificially, pushing them temporally, in terms of duration, to a point in their evolution that is ahead of the other cells. But these memory cells do not have two ways of aging. If, as I have told you, the film of the world's evolution is recorded at all times in the archives of the future, if what is going to happen is already contained within what had already happened, the cells age as they would normally age, but more rapidly—and, as a result, the hard-driven activity of my subject's memory precedes him in time, thus revealing to me the future that is already recorded, which nothing can modify. I finally obtain a subject who has a memory of the future…

"That subject, as you have deduced, is Dirk."

I sat there somewhat petrified, my head tilted back in the armchair so as not to quit the doctor's eyes, for I now mistrusted his every gesture. But the memory of Dirk's strange attitude during our last meeting came back to mind.

"Dirk," he continued, "who remains entirely normal with regard to his comportment, is presently living mentally one minute and 12 seconds ahead of the present. His life is unfolding in two parts: his body keeps company with ours, and he makes all the gestures he needs to make at the right moment, but his thoughts preceded it by 72 seconds, and from time to time, he says what he ought to have said 72 seconds later!" He accompanied these final words with a triumphant snigger.

"Did Dirk consent to this experiment?" I stammered.

"The question is irrelevant," the doctor said, dryly. "Now, you will easily comprehend the consequences. One only has to know how to take advantage of a 72-second advancement in the knowledge of the future. The average interval that separates two spins of a roulette-wheel is 70 seconds. Above the gaming table, after each spin, a figure lights up indicating the number that has just come up. I place myself, with Dick, so that I can see the signal. Twelve comes up and lights up. I ask him: 'Which number is lit up?' He replies: '28.' I know that 28 will come up on the following spin, and I bet the maximum. If he doesn't reply, it can only be because the interval between one spin and the next will differ from seventy seconds. This morning, I obtained four responses, which is four coincidences. Result: 400,000 and some francs. In a week, the principality has poured 12 million into my pocket.

My bewilderment was tempered by a prudent smile.

"That's your fortune made…" I said.

"Not yet," said the doctor. "My little ruse couldn't last forever, and this very morning I sensed that there were four inspectors of the gaming police spying on me. They can't prove anything against me, but they can ban me from the gaming rooms, under one pretext or another. I've collected 12 million in passing, but in reality, my ambitions are much greater."

I frowned, gripped once again by anxiety.

"Let's leave it there, if you will," said the doctor. "As for the rest, I don't want to go any further before being certain— selling the bear's skin before it's shot, as they say in France. I hope that you won't ask any more of me, and that we're still friends…"

My thoughts were utterly confused within my head. I got up, shook the hand that he extended to me mechanically, and went out.

I only came back to myself somewhat when I found myself in the open air again. I had taken too strong a dose of the doctor, unless it was the gin…

In any case, my first clear impression was an irresistible desire to go as far away as possible as quickly as possible. Everything that happened here seemed troubling, vaguely dangerous. I had committee a folly in wanting to install myself in the dependencies of the château. To set sail as soon as possible was the wisest course.

Little by little, however, the cool air under the trees in the grounds calmed my agitation. At the corner of a path, I happened upon Narda, in company with two Great Danes.

"Do you know that my uncle has given me permission to stay here?" she said. "I'm very glad not to be returning to Switzerland. If you hadn't been there at lunch the other day, I wouldn't have dared say anything."

It did me good to hear her frank girlish voice. It occurred to me to appeal to the judgment of her innocence regarding the matter that preoccupied me.

"Narda, what do you think of your uncle?"

"Him? He makes me laugh," she replied, laughing herself.

A happy age! I thought. *But who knows—perhaps she's right and one ought to laugh?* Her company brought me back to a saner view of things. I listened to her chatter. She told me, incidentally, with the precision that a child's words have, that Yvane was at the hairdressers in Cannes. Extraordinarily, I had not given any further thought to Yvane—but my mind was immediately invaded by her. Could I flee and abandon her?

From the summer-house, where I pursued my meditations, I could catch glimpses between the branches of the olive-trees of the left wing of the château—the one with the laboratories—a few hundred meters away. It was a sordid patch in the landscape, like a muted threat. Truly, I felt that prudence commanded me to tear myself away from this place. On the other hand, though, thinking of Yvane, I found that there was no immediate peril, that I could still wait to see how things went. In spite of everything, I remained undecided.

I cast an eye over the interior of my dwelling. The divan, comfortable beneath its bright cretonnes, seemed welcoming. In the entrance-hall, the flowers that Yvane had brought were slowly dying in the vases. The promise I had made the previous day returned to my memory. On due reflection, my malaise stemmed mainly from a vague dread of discovering secrets that I ought not to know, of finding myself an accomplice of deeds of which I would rather remain ignorant. And poor Dirk—what role was he playing in all this?

All things considered, I could not bear the idea of going to sleep so close to the doctor. He might have been able to influence my dreams, to devote himself while I slept to God knows what experiment upon me. Before nightfall, I leapt into my car and went to sleep in a hotel in Nice.

When one has a house, it's much funnier not to live in it, I said to myself, by way of an excuse.

CHAPTER SEVEN

When I woke up in my hotel room, the events of the previous day had settled down somewhat in my mind. My fears seemed exaggerated. I had a house waiting for me in the foothills; what was I still doing in a hotel, in that scorching town, when I hadn't seen Yvane for two days? Going through the market of the old town, I filled my car with flowers and, strengthened by that justification for my sojourn in Nice, I took the road to La Colle.

All was silence in the summer-house and its surroundings. The *loggia* was charming in the fresh morning sunlight. I began to unpack my belongings. Someone rapped on the window; it was Yvane, wanting to know how I had slept. I confessed to not having gone to bed there. She seemed distressed.

"What disappoints me more than anything else," she said, "is that yesterday evening I imagined you here, in your house, and I thought that I could see you here…and now I find out that it was false! I'm not used to my thoughts being mistaken. There was nothing in the house where I thought I could see you. How extraordinary that is!"

Although those sighs might seem rather puerile, it was impossible for me not to be moved by the inflections of her voice, in which the very essence of her being seemed to be distilled: a disarmed and disarming sincerity in confrontation with life.

To console her, as one consoles a child, I told her that I had found a little five-meter boat for sale in the old harbor at Nice, and that we might perhaps be able to buy it between us. My idea did a marvelous job of chasing away her disappointment. The "we" that she repeated had something clandestine and chaste in her mouth, which delighted me. She wanted to go and see the boat immediately. I yielded to her desire.

Confronted by the boat, it was necessary to try it out. I had to pardon myself for my inability to speak; I consented to everything. We refused the assistance of the sailor who offered to accompany us; the sea was calm, we could easily steer it by ourselves.

Yvane was charmingly unskillful, in spite of her docility in following my advice. The departure was rather laborious, but we got out to sea as best we could. Once the first period of activity was over, we finally found ourselves side by side, hands on the tiller. Then the thought occurred to us both that, for the first time, we were truly alone—for we exchanged a smile at the same time, which had that meaning.

She let herself loll backwards on to the false bridge, the nape of her neck in the gap, her eyes challenging the brightness of the sky, and her hair floating over our wake.

"It's as if I'd fished up a siren," I said.

Her little hand as resting on the tiller, brown and nervous; it no longer seemed to form part of her stretched-out body: a forgotten hand, sagely following the movements that I imposed on the rudder; a hand so alone, with a bone-structure so delicate, that it was heart-melting. I leaned over and I kissed it for a long time, in the valley hollowed out by the roots of two fingers.

"You're kissing me in September," said her voice, singing over the sea. As I didn't understand, she added: "You know how one counts the months on a closed fist: 31, 30 days…you're kissing me in September."

"Come closer," I said to her. "What are you doing so far away?"

She sat up again. "I was forgetting. That's what I was doing—forgetting."

"Forgetting what?"

"Everything. That's my dominant impression, for the moment: forgetfulness. And it's infinitely refreshing. As if I had left everything behind, to be elsewhere."

"Having left me behind with everything else?"

"No, not you—but me, I've left myself behind."

"Give it to me, then, and I'll look after it while you're not here."

With the gesture of an obedient little girl, she came to rest her hair on my shoulder. The sail carried us on silently, effortlessly. "A pretty self," I murmured, "brown and gold, perfumed with sea-salt, a self as light as a morning sky."

A sharp movement of her head, rolling on my shoulder, indicated a mute negation.

"A self that wearies me and makes me despair," she said. "I never know where it's going, what it will do—a self that drags me into dreams in which I lose myself... It looks me in the face: 'Is that me? Is it possible that there are so many differences between the self that you see from outside and the one that I see from inside?'"

"Then it's the one inside that it's necessary for me to look after."

"No, that's a wild, intractable animal," she replied. "I'd better give you the other."

"I want both of them," I said.

She shook her head pensively, but came back to huddle against me.

I too forgot everything. At that moment I was very far away from La Colle, the doctor, his frightful logic and his somber experiments. My usual indecision had given way to a certainty: the thought that, out of the entire life that I had been leading for thirty years, also without understanding very much, there was nothing to retain and carry forward but that very simple and marvelous thing, the living being pressed against me.

I steered into an inlet where the water was so calm and so transparent in the rays of sunlight that at twenty meters' depth one could make out the patches of sand and algae on the sea-bed. Leaning over the edge, Yvane said something that I would remember for a long time: "What strange and marvelous landscapes! Why are the drowned the only ones who have the right to stroll there?"

"What about divers?"

She protested against that prosaic notion. "There are landscapes in which it is necessary to go naked, caressed by the algae, one's hair at the mercy of the waves, one's eyes exposed to the sea. Ys, the city of Ys… those are my initials, you know. Y. S. I would love to walk the streets of my drowned city, the city of Ys…"

"I thought that I had fished up a siren!" Alluding to our first meeting, I continued: "From the first day, I should have known that…"

It was the first time that I found myself evoking a memory that we had in common. I asked her what she had thought of me that day.

She caressed the contour of my cheek with her hand. "Nothing. I couldn't know that you would be so indulgent to all my caprices, so welcoming to all my girlish ways. I've often been told that I'm no more than 12 years of age. I'd love that to be true—but I'd rather have an ageless mind. There's no one but you with whom I can say what I think."

The wind had changed and a slight swell was getting up. The boat's movements sometimes threw us into contact with one another, as if for a lesson in salutary rudeness, to remind us of our bodies made of muscle and bone. I hadn't the heart, however, nor the force of mind, for exacting gestures.

I was no longer a child, nor even a young man. Many times, it had been granted to me to enjoy the company of women who were said to be agreeable. In those past circumstances, the obligation to play a role, to be attentive to the impression I might be producing or to expected tasks, had always marred the pleasure of those encounters. In this instance, there was nothing like that. For the first time, I let myself go without thinking about it, without worrying about a game-plan—not because I let myself be led, but because everything proceeded of its own accord. "With you, I can say what I think," she had said. "And I too," I could have replied, "have only ever felt with you this impression of effortless wellbeing."

We did not return until the evening. And that evening, for the first time, I slept in the summer-house. The attraction of a virgin heart had borne away all the troubles and dangers that seemed to be roaming the pathways of the grounds. The event took on a symbolic value, and marked a step toward the acceptance of a situation that, sooner or later, would demand an official approach. It was, however, to take me nearly a week to decide to speak to the doctor.

CHAPTER EIGHT

I asked to see the doctor one morning. The painful impressions felt during my first visits assailed me once again as soon as I went into his study. Every object was occupying its immutable place, and if the stained glass panels in the windows were not projected their colors on to the carpet, it was because that morning's leaden sky was becoming stormy.

"It's some time since we've had the pleasure of meeting up," the doctor said, cheerfully. "One only needs to be neighbors not to see one another." I wanted to get to the point of my visit as rapidly as possible, but the doctor did not give me the opportunity. "Is your dwelling suitable for work? As for me, I haven't been wasting my time." He paused deliberately before announcing to me, with greater emphasis: "Dirk is 48 hours in advance..."

Everything that I had intended to say suddenly stuck in my throat, unable to compare with this extraordinary declaration. Having wanted to forget that entire frightful experience, I found myself brutally plunged back into it, and was gripped, my breath cut off as if by a jet of cold water.

"We weren't going to stop short after obtaining the first encouraging results," the doctor continued, apparently desirous of taking advantage of my surprise to proffer his confidences. "The treatment by artificial excitation seems to be acting more and more rapidly as we progress further. The difficulties encountered, would you believe, are of a much more trivial order—they relate to the measures that have to be taken to remain in contact with the subject. I anticipated the measures in question, but I did not imagine that they would have to be applied so delicately. In fact, not only can Dirk only talk if his surroundings are identical to those in which he will find himself 48 hours later, but it's also necessary that he situation of his interlocutors be that which will be reproduced the day after tomorrow. Only in these conditions is the connection made between the two components of his person, between his body and his mind, and, in consequence, the possibility of expression. Otherwise, he's out of phase, if I might put it thus, and says nothing.

"Do you understand now the importance I attach to the permanence of the décor around us? A simple bouquet of flowers on my table would suffice to paralyze Dirk. Moreover, as the questions that I ask him must be those that I will ask him the day after tomorrow, I'm constrained to keep a very strict timetable, scrupulously repeating myself every day—otherwise I could only rely on fortuitous connections.

"You seem incredulous, but I'll convince you. It will soon be 10 a.m., the time of my first daily interview with Dirk. In order that he will accept you as an interlocutor it's necessary first of all for you to promise to come and see me again the day after tomorrow, at the same time, dressed as closely as possible in the same manner. On that condition, he will tell you today what he ought to tell you in two days' time. Do you promise?"

Mechanically, I nodded my head.

"In any case, I'll find out immediately whether you'll keep your promise. If he recognizes you, it's because you'll come."

He got up, went to the door at the back of his study, and, with his eyes glued to his wristwatch, waited until it was exactly 10 a.m. to call out: "We're going to work, Dirk—will you come down?"

"Yes, Monsieur," said Dirk's voice.

"Those are our ritual phrases," the doctor explained, as I heard the noise of footsteps on an interior stairway.

Dirk appeared, calm and casual in manner, more at his ease than during our last encounter.

"Bonjour, Dirk," I said, in a slightly strangled voice.

"Why, Monsieur Delambre—I'm glad to see you."

The doctor addressed a glance of satisfaction to me, doubtless to thank me for the visit that I would pay him in two days' time. Going over to a window he opened it to the sky.

"What do you think of the weather, Dirk?"

"Bright sunlight," said Dirk. "A glorious day."

It had never been so black; the storm seemed to be about to break.

"Now you know what the weather will be like on the day after tomorrow," the doctor said to me. "Have no fear of thinking aloud—Dirk might hear you, but he won't make it manifest if it's not in the day after tomorrow's sequence."

"Do you really think it's fine?" I asked Dirk. "Don't you see any clouds?"

"You're joking," he replied. "The sky has never been so blue."

At that moment, there was a lightning flash; thunder reverberated, and I observed that Dirk had shivered.

"Did you hear that?" I asked him.

He didn't reply.

"Your question isn't one of those that will be asked in two days' time," the doctor explained. "The subject is disconnected—but my dear Monsieur Delambre, you must be aware that if I'm pushing this young man into the future, it's not merely to find out what the weather will be like, in order to get my umbrella ready in good time. As we have no more secrets from you, we shall continue the sequence of our daily labors in your presence."

He placed in Dirk's hands a long, rather narrow strip of paper, then went round to the other side of his desk and sat down, with a pencil in his hand. "You can begin, Dirk," he said. "Don't go too quickly."

"Central Mining 4215. Geduld 1700. Union Corporation 1,80. Areas 355. Anglo-American 511. Goldfields 698. Royal Dutch 6957. Rio 2486..."

I realized then that the paper strip from which was reading was one of those sheets that are unrolled by the apparatus recording share prices on the Bourse. The doctor noted down the figures.

Imperturbably, Dick continued: "Rosario 4250. Quilmès 5390..."

After a quarter of an hour, Dirk stopped reading.

57

"Do you understand?" the doctor asked me, then. "The figures on the roll are yesterday's share prices. This morning, as on every other morning, they were brought to me from the local branch of the Crédit-Lyonnais at Nice. I have them read by Dirk—who, in his former capacity as a stockbroker's clerk, never ceased to interest himself in financial matters. What he reads are not yesterday's prices, however, but tomorrow's. The consequence is easy to grasp. In a little while, I shall telephone my instructions. I can't say that I'm gambling, because I'm buying and selling on a basis of certainty. And my dear Monsieur Delambre, in the share market, we no longer find inspectors to forbid us entry into the gaming-halls!"

A diabolical flash of lightning made his gaze glitter behind his spectacles. He seemed to be waiting for some exclamation on my part. I refused him that pleasure.

The session was concluded. Dirk came to shake my hand. I felt an enormous pity for the poor devil.

"Au revoir, Dirk," I said, squeezing his hand for a long time.

His lips moved, but no sound came out.

"Evidence that the day after tomorrow, at 10:35 a.m., you'll already have left my study," the doctor said. "Your visit will be briefer than today's…"

I got to my feet and went out without saying a word. As on every other occasion that I had paid the doctor a visit, I found myself at first in the same state as a compass crazed by a magnetic storm. I no longer knew what to think or do. "Oh, if he thinks that I'll go back, he's mistaken!" I began by exclaiming. To thwart the assault on my liberty, it required no more than that. To start with, I would go away…

Extrapolating the hypothesis of a precipitate flight, however, I asked myself where I was going to go. I could pay a visit to my brother-in-law in Cairo, or go in search of an old girl-friend in Cambo—a souvenir of my last leave—but neither of these prospects seemed very inviting. As for resuming the vagabond life that I had led previously, that would seeking adventures that would certainly be less strange than the one I had found here…

The deluge of rain that began to fall cleared my head somewhat. In spite of its scientific pretensions, this entire story was shady. The fashion in which Dirk was being treated made me particularly indignant. Not that I had any particular sympathy for the poor fellow, but it's difficult to see a human being treated as a guinea pig without raising a protest. I had not been forceful enough. Of all those living in the doctor's entourage, I was the only one who could stand up to him. If I were gone, who knows what his tyranny or influence might do to those who were abandoned to him? But who knew, too, whether he might be using his stepdaughter to lure me into a trap, in order to attempt some other experiment on me?

Well, I would not retreat—and, since I was in the game, he would have to reckon with me. To begin with, would tell him that I would not tolerate a man being crippled in order to make money on the stock market…

I mulled over reflections of this sort throughout the following day. Yvane was absent. Gripped by a fit of energy, she had gone to Marseilles to obtain customs clearance for some packages that had arrived from Holland.

I was ready for anything when I found myself, at the appointed time, in the doctor's study.

The scene was repeated with a haunting fidelity.

"We're going to work, Dirk—will you come down?"

"Of course, Monsieur."

Dirk appeared,

"Bonjour!" I cried.

He did not reply.

"Which shows that your visit will not be repeated in 48 hours' time," said the doctor, mockingly.

Then there was the scene at the window.

"What do you think of the weather, Dirk?"

"Already very hot for the time of year."

"So the weather won't be any different the day after tomorrow," the doctor concluded.

"So you don't see any clouds, Dirk?" I said, glad to find that he saw the sky as blue as it really was—but I had forgotten that he couldn't reply to me, since I wouldn't be there two days later.

The doctor put the Bourse prices into his hands.

No sound emerged from his lips.

"It's Friday," he doctor explained. "Tomorrow, Saturday, the Bourse will be closed—therefore, he can't say anything. I'll leave the paper in his hands, however, in order not to lose the rhythm of our regular employment."

Familiarized with the atmosphere, I was less affected than before. That was the moment that decided to intervene. I took the doctor to one side and began point-blank: "Have you not abused your powers by constraining Dirk to engage in this horrible adventure?"

The doctor raised his head in surprise, to stare at me through the lenses of his spectacles. I met his gaze resolutely. He could see that I was firmly decided.

"I might ask you what right you have to interfere?" he replied, dryly.

"I can't tolerate someone being tortured in front of me, whatever more-or-less scientific motives are invoked."

The impassivity affected by the doctor finished up making me angry. My fists clenched involuntarily. The doctor uttered a sigh.

"My generous impulse," he began, "has betrayed me, as is generally the rule. You want an explanation; here it is, although it will pain me. The man to whose defense you are leaping took advantage of the hospitality that he found at my hearth to seduce my wife. Yes, Monsieur, this young rascal has dishonored me. Not for the sake of love, but out of vanity. Furthermore, he dared to plot my own demise. His criminal conduct was the cause of Gabrielle's death. He knows that one word from me, and he would be in the hands of the Law. Over him, I have the right of life or death, and I could legitimately dispose of him according to my whim—but I have not imposed any conditions on him. He was the one who, in order to redeem himself, demanded that I use him as an experimental subject. I would have preferred to send him away, never to see him again…

"Oh, I don't know whether you have ever loved, Monsieur Delambre, whether your confidence has ever been betrayed. As for me, I have loved, loved stupidly, blindly, faithfully…but let's get on…

"The frightful revelation left me a wreck. It was an internal collapse, a visceral laceration, a desire for oblivion that submerged me. At 40 years of age, Gabrielle had conserved all the naivety of childhood. Even motherhood had not succeeded in weighing her down with gravity and anxieties. She was like an incarnation of eternal youth; her candor was prodigious…that was why I loved her. Perhaps I astonish you. It's extraordinary that the equilibrium of our serious and diligent lives should rest on such slender supports, so delicate that the slightest tempting voice can cause them bend. Conceivable or not, that's the way it is. She…she was not guilty; she couldn't understand; she abandoned herself to some sort of game. When she understood, she died of it. But him, the wretch…

"And at every hour of the day, it's necessary that I have before me the face of that man, the lips that were placed on…the hands that have…oh, it's frightful. In jealousy, the precise images that flesh retains are particularly tormenting. The source of those images is there, constantly before my eyes. Between him and me, the one who has more grounds for complaint is not the one you think. It was three years ago, and I haven't yet forgotten any of it…

"After that blow, what remained to me? My work. My research. I threw myself into it with the ardor of desperation; it was the sole link that attached me to life. And it is also to distance myself from that man, the constant reminder of my misfortune, that I drive him in front of me into the future, further and further still…"

This confession left me nonplussed once more. The entire offensive that I had planned was overturned. Instead of finding myself in the presence of a more-or-less obscure machination, I merely discovered a lamentable and banal story of marital misfortune. For the moment, I could find nothing more to say. But from these confidences, I retained especially, with an egoism that was a match for the doctor's sentimental deceptions, that which concerned the mother of the woman who had captured my heart. In the brief portrait that he doctor had painted of his Gabrielle, I was surprised to find the moral equivalent of her daughter, and even more astonished that the reasons that had motivated the doctor's attachment—the charm of a certain innocence, a certain candor—were the same as those that had seduced me in Yvane. Such an identity of sentiments prevented me from smiling at an unfortunate and rather comical coincidence between the two experiences. More than that; in that replication, produced over successive generations, and in that commonality of instinct which ensures that men are always moved by the same thing, I found a certain mechanical, obligatory quality that diminished, it seemed to me, the scope and value of my inclination toward Yvane. Whereas I had believed, naively, that I had chosen her because of what she was, and because of what I was, and our meeting had appeared marvelous because she seemed unique, I had only been yielding to the obscure solicitations of heredity and general instinct that govern the heart of every male. I had been nothing but a plaything, a cog-wheel. Was the doctor right, then, when he claimed that everything is ineluctably inscribed in advance in the material depths of the flesh?

It also seemed to be a kind of rule that, after each of my interviews with the doctor, the feelings I had for Yvane were seemingly undermined, and that it was necessary for me to see her again, and spent a few days with her, before all the mysterious little threads that attached us to one another were woven together again.

Was she aware of it? Probably. Never was her presence more discreet, more delicate, than at those times when I distanced myself from her in thought—as if she had divined that that was the best means of getting me back.

I had decided not to interrogate her straightforwardly about the doctor's confidences. It seemed to me that precise questions would have broken the charm and delicacy of the atmosphere in which our relationship was unfolding. What happened between us ought only to be concerned with ourselves. I also decided—and perhaps that was my greatest error—to keep our intrigue completely separate from the thoughts that continued to occupy me at other times, which were concentrated on the doctor's activities. When I was with Yvane, I was with her exclusively; I did not want to see in her any but the person that she wanted to be for me, detaching her and cutting her off from her connections and roots—from the entire frame within which she had lived. I regarded her as a sudden apparition, which one does not seek to explain, in order to allow myself to be more completely seduced by the magic of her gratuitous presence. In her, too, it must be admitted, there was something that invited that manner of procedure. It seemed that she demanded, in order to be fully herself, not to be attached in any excessively narrow and precise fashion to the world that surrounded her. It was in her destiny to play the fairy, and one should not lift the veils of mist the float over the heaths of fairyland.

I still had hours of solitude, however, in which to reflect in a more down-to-earth fashion on the doctor's confession. Once the initial surprise was past, it appeared to me that I had only heard his version of events—a version that seemed to me to be suspicious in more than one respect. Another testimony was necessary, and I could only obtain that testimony from Dirk—who had become invisible, maintained in strict secrecy. By dint of thinking about it, I eventually persuaded myself that a meeting with Dirk was indispensable, and I gradually formulated a plan to achieve that end.

CHAPTER NINE

Dirk was definitely resident in the château, since the daily sessions were taking place in the doctor's study. The presence of the dogs forbade any nocturnal investigation. It was impossible for me to trust the Malay servants to take him a note. There remained the simplest solution: to take advantage of an absence of the doctor during the day to reach the place where Dirk was kept, as a more-or-less voluntary prisoner.

It was necessary, however, to discover the location of that place as precisely as possible beforehand. For once, my profession as an architect would be useful to me, in permitting me to reconstitute, from what I could observe of the château's exterior, its interior layout. It had two floors, not counting the raised ground-floor in which no one resided. I knew, from having been here, that the doctor had his study, and the rooms the served as his laboratory, on the first floor. When he had called Dirk through the little door in his study, I had heard the latter coming down a flight of stairs, so Dirk must live on the second floor. On the side facing my summer-house, the façade of that floor had no less than fourteen windows On the other side of the building, the observations that I was only able to make while passing by in the afternoon had to be more discreet. The number of windows was the same, some of them occasionally being open: the servants' rooms, and, perhaps, Dirk's. The difficulty was to determine the situation of the latter, in order not to enter one of the Javanese servants' rooms inadvertently.

The young women lived in the right wing, which was to my left when I was observing from my summer-house; the doctor, on the other hand, lived in the left wing. Dirk had to be lodged not far from him, which left me a choice between seven windows on each façade. The main staircase, which I had taken to go up o the doctor's study, occupied the middle of the building and led to a long corridor on the first floor which ran from end to end, on to which opened, among others, the door

64

of the study. Remembering the colored glass that ornamented the study windows, I was easily able to locate the three windows corresponding to that room on the façade.

The interior stairway that led to Dirk's room had to terminate above those windows, and could not lead to the other façade of the château if, as I supposed, a median corridor ran the entire length of the second floor, replicating the disposition adopted for the first floor communications—which was probable, given the symmetry of the building. That only left me a choice between two windows on the second floor on the facing façade. Supposing then that the stairway leading from the first to the second floor was in the middle of the building, I calculated that, having reached the second floor landing, I had to turn right and walk perhaps ten or twelve meters before finding myself in front of a door opening into Dirk's apartment.

As I carried out this analysis, the house gradually lost its mystery for me, which was a moral advantage for the success of my enterprise. But now that I think about all those calculations again, and all the time I wasted attempting to discover what I needed to know, of which I still had no suspicion, I am inclined to wonder whether, in so doing, I was not the plaything of a superior will. At any rate, let's pass on…

I could only operate by day, of course. From time to time, the doctor had himself driven to the coast, and I was fortunate enough to have a signal of his absence when the Mercedes was not in the garage. Even better, the noise of the heavy vehicle on the gravel of the driveway carried as far as my retreat, alerting me to his departure while I was at home. It only remained for me to wait for a favorable opportunity.

On May 24—that date was to acquire a terrible importance—I was mulling over my plan, lying in a hammock at the entrance to the summer-house, when the characteristic sound of the Mercedes warned me that the doctor was just leaving. I knew that Yvane had gone to Nice to take Narda to see the dentist. The way was entirely clear. I decided to take my chance.

I went rapidly down through the olive grove, in the clothes that I happened to be wearing—a royal blue flannel suit and espadrilles—and then climbed up to the terrace of the château, going around to the right. A passing glance at the open door of the garage confirmed that the Mercedes was gone. I reached the steps of the main façade and tried the door-handle. The door opened. I was inside.

Affecting a casual air, in case I were to run into a servant, I took the large staircase that led me to the first floor. Thus far, all had gone well. I paused momentarily in front of a reproduction of *The Anatomy Lesson*,[5] which decorated the landing. Then, not hearing any noise, I set foot on the stairway leading to the second floor. I began to feel that my state of mind was that of a burglar. The stairway, narrower than the other, was displaced three meters to the left, which modified my calculations. On the second floor, I found myself confronted by a rather narrow corridor, where a surprise awaited me. All the doors opening on to that corridor were on the same side, facing me—corresponding, in consequence, to rooms whose windows were on the principal façade. All my calculations fell into the water.

Somewhat disorientated, I retraced my steps and knocked on the door of the doctor's study on the first floor. There was no response. I tried the handle, but the door was locked. Two analogous attempts on the neighboring doors were no more successful. The doctor had taken his precautions.

Gradually, the anxiety that has accompanied my initial steps gave way to a sentiment of irritation, which gave my actions more audacity. After sitting down in a rattan armchair on the first floor landing, in order to resume my deductions at leisure, facing *The Anatomy Lesson*, I went back up to the second floor, counted out 14 meters—11 meters plus the three meters of the stairway's displacement—along the corridor

---

[5] *The Anatomy Lesson of Dr. Nicolaes Tulp* was painted by Rembrandt in 1632.

extending from the landing, then, facing a partition wall in which there was no door, I knocked twice with my fist. There was no response. The wall sounded solid. I was about to repeat the action when I was surprised to hear a muffled sneeze, and then a second. The noise seemed to be coming from the floor. There was no doubt that someone was there, who could not be anyone but Dirk—but it was necessary for me to be able to enter into communication with him.

I was going back down to make a further attempt on the first floor when I noticed, half-way down the stairway, a door hidden in the wooden paneling. It opened without difficulty to a mildly forceful push, revealing a narrow corridor illuminated at floor level by the tops of the first floor windows. The story had been divided at mid-height over a certain extent, which I had not anticipated, and it was in one of the rooms thus consti-tuted that the prisoner had to be lodged. The corridor ended in a spiral stairway, which, after a few ascendant steps, was blocked by a vault of recent construction. I was able, however, to distinguish in the gloom of the stairway—which was not directly lit—some sort of panel opening in the wall. I opened its battens to reveal a rather narrow opening, like those used to transmit plates from a kitchen to a parlor. I extended my arm, and by groping around found a shutter at the back, which I pushed. A little room, ill-lit, appeared at a lower level. On a corner divan, I made out an elongated form.

"Dirk!" I called.

The form stood up. I recognized Dirk by his silhouette rather than his face, so dark was the room. He came toward the opening and raised his arms, as if to receive something that I had held out to him. It was by this route that his nourishment must be brought to him, and he was repeating a familiar ges-ture.

"Dirk," I said to him, "it's me, Pierre Delambre. I've been looking for you; I wanted to see you in the doctor's ab-sence. Isn't there some means by which I might get to you comfortable?"

His lips moved, but no sound came out. Evidence confuses you by virtue of its evidential character, all the more so when one has not anticipated it. There, I encountered the capital obstacle to which, in spite of all my reflections, I had not given a moment's thought in the planning of the expedition. How could I enter into communication with Dirk, given that the poor fellow's thoughts were no longer occupying the present moment?

I persisted, though. "Make an effort, Dirk, I beg you. Can't I have a conversation with you? I didn't know that you were being held prisoner like this. Whatever wrong you did, the treatment to which you are being subjected is inhuman—worse, of a deliberate cruelty that I find repulsive. I'm your friend, Dirk, ready to do everything I can to help you. Answer me—tell me that you can hear me."

My voice took on a plaintive tone. I could not extend my head very far through the hole, but I could pass my arms through. Dirk, standing on tiptoe, had seized the hand that I held out to him and shook it with an energy in which I thought I could see the mark of his despair at not being able to express himself. The blue sleeve of my jacket seemed black in the gloom. I had the appearance of leaning out of the window in a carriage door, saying goodbye to a friend who was remaining on the platform at a railway station.

The grip of Dirk's hand was sustained for some time, and suddenly, I heard: "My dear friend, you have my every sympathy! Poor Yvane—that strange, atrocious death! Drowned! Drowned in such circumstances…"

At first, I didn't understand. Then, suddenly, I was struck in the heart. I uttered a bestial cry and withdrew my hand brutally.

"Dirk!" I cried into the opening. "Repeat what you said, Dirk. What are you saying? Yvane…Dirk, what did you say? Repeat it?"

I howled, threatened. He did not breathe another word, and even retreated to his divan before my insults.

I fell silent. I was inundated with sweat. Mechanically, I took a few steps along the corridor. No, it wasn't possible; I was mistaken. And yet, with an intensity and a precision that the memory of a sound had never assumed in me before, I heard his words echoing once more: "*Poor Yvane—that strange, atrocious death! Drowned! Drowned in such circumstances…*"

Half way along the corridor, I made a half-turn to come back toward the opening, to try to repair the thread that my cry had broken. I begged again, imploringly, but nothing came of it. Dirk did not even move.

"*That atrocious death! Drowned! Drowned in such circumstances…*" The words were buzzing in my head. My mind still refused to accept their full significance. I collapsed into an armchair in the hallway, resolved to watch out for the doctor's return, waiting for him with an impatience compared with which, the impatience I had put into watching him leave was derisory. What was he doing? I had to see him immediately…

I don't know how much time went by like that. Finally, I heard the car drawing up before the steps. I ran out.

"Doctor! Doctor!"

"What's wrong?" he said, confronted by my haggard appearance.

"Oh, doctor…"

He drew me rapidly into the study, some distance away from the chauffeur, who was unloading the vehicle.

"Dirk," I said, "Dirk…tell me, first…how much time is here? How long is his advancement?

"29 days and six hours," he replied. "Why?"

"29 days and six hours," I repeated. "29 days and six hours…" I cried, in protest: "No, that's not possible!"

"Come on, explain yourself!" he demanded, with understandable irritation.

I told him everything, without omitting anything: the suspicions I had conceived, the manner in which I had spied on him. I told him every detail of my afternoon expedition, hiding nothing.

When I pronounced the words that Dirk had let escape, I saw him grow pale. Without him saying a word, tears began to run from his eyes.

"No, no!" I exclaimed. "Tell me that I'm mistaken, that it's not true! You don't believe it; you can't think it. I have no other hope but you; it can't be true. Dirk is making a mistake; he sometimes speaks at random."

The doctor shook his head. Softly, he demanded: "Repeat the words you heard."

I repeated them.

The doctor bowed his head silently, and hid his eyes behind his hand.

"But after all," I cried, again, "we shall fight, now that we've been warned. Now that we know, we can take our precautions in consequence... The boat, the boat that we were going to buy, I know now what I have to do. I have to keep her away from the coast, night and day. Since we know, thanks to you, thanks to your experiments, we must be able to get out of it."

He shook his head and replied, sadly: "We also know that the world rotates, but we can't stop it, for all that. What you hope to do is as impossible as immobilizing the Sun."

That resignation made me indignant. I got up, and thumped the desk hard.

"Well, as for me," I said, "I don't accept it. I accept the challenge. I shall save her; I have to save her...don't you understand that I love her." I was shouting in the doctor's face, which had become impassive again. "I've loved her since I first saw her. I've never said so, admitted it, either to her or myself, but I love her. I won't allow the woman I love to be snatched away. Yvane, Yvane..."

I no longer knew what I was saying.

The doctor watched me in silence. "Calm down," he said. "You're not telling me anything I didn't already know. But we men ought to be strong. If a physician had told you that a fatal illness would carry you away, wouldn't you be able to control yourself?"

"But an accident can be avoided. Drowned, drowned—her! When I think that, only the other day, leaning over the edge of the boat, she said, with regard to the sea-bed…oh, it's frightful! But I shall fight, I shall fight, I shall get the better of you, of your experiments, of everything…I don't believe it, anyway. I tell you this to your face—I don't believe in what you've done."

He came toward me and took me by the shoulders. "Yes, my poor friend, don't believe it—I might have been mistaken."

It was obvious that he as only saying that to allow me some hope. I let myself fall into an armchair, repeating: "But I love her…I shall fight, shall fight…help me…"

"Yes," he said, "I'll help you. But don't warn her—that would be too atrocious. Speak vaguely about a presentiment, if you wish, and then, with her sensitive nature…be on the alert, watch over her. Let's see, this is the May 24. Twenty-nine days—that gives us until…let's see, does the month of May have 30 days or 31?"

With these words, the memory returned to me of her pronouncement: "*You've kissed me in September.*" I couldn't hold out, and let myself dissolve in tears. Eventually collecting myself, a little calmer, I murmured: "Perhaps I'm mistaken; perhaps I was misled by similar sounds. What if you were to try to bring me together with Dirk again?"

The doctor seemed to be reflecting.

"The scene that you've described, during which a connection was formed between the décor and Dirk's mind, in an entirely fortuitous fashion, obviously reproduces a farewell scene on a railway platform. At this moment—which is to say, in 29 days' time—you're in the train; you have left Dirk, and are far away from him. It's therefore impossible for a new connection to be forged between you and him, for the time being."

The calmness and lucidity with which I could see that he was reasoning made me indignant, and restored all my feverishness. "But we have to do something, even so! Don't accept, search!"

"You see me as crushed as you are, my friend. Yvane is the sole affection that remains to me on Earth, the last link that still connects me to my poor Gabrielle. When I look at her, I think I'm seeing her mother alive again...you love her, you couldn't find a more delicate and more precious individual....I'll think about it—but I confide her to you, Pierre..." And he added, pushing me gently toward the door: "Who knows what love can do?"

CHAPTER TEN

I didn't want to lose a moment. I went to take up a position next to the gate to watch out for Yvane's return. Anxiety was gnawing at me. Who could tell? Perhaps, already…

When I saw the little car appear on the road, I hurried out in front of it.

"Yvane! Yvane!" I shouted.

I leapt on to the running-board, took hold of Yvane and threw myself upon her cheeks, covering them with kisses. I had got her back—she was alive, really alive! My behavior contrasted so strongly with my habitual reserve that she was utterly nonplussed.

"What's wrong?" she asked, her voice as calm as ever, but nuanced with surprise.

"What's wrong?" I said, collecting myself. "Nothing, nothing—it's just that I'm so glad to see you again!" Turning toward Narda, I added: "You too." And, to put Yvane off the scent, I tried to take her in my arms and kiss her too.

"No, not on the cheek," she said. "My tooth's still hurting." She turned her head to get away, and my lips brushed hers.

"Come on, Pierre, why these sudden manifestations?" Yvane demanded.

"It's such a long time since you left—I've had a frightful dream. Yvane, come with me immediately—Narda can put the car away."

As soon as the car had gone, I put my arms around Yvane again. I didn't let go, in order to assure myself of her presence, to touch her body, her muscles, to feel her next to me, robust and full of life. There really was no affection in the gestures.

"One might think you were a puppy greeting its master," she said, in an amused tone.

"Yes," I said, "that's it. That's it, exactly."

I didn't want to waste another minute before putting her on her guard, but I hadn't prepared any lie.

"Yvane, promise me…or, rather, I beg you to promise me…It's a favor that I'm imploring of you…listen, it's very serious: you must promise me on everything you hold most dear…so much the worse if it seems bizarre…"

"What a preamble! What's up with you this evening?"

"I want you to promise not to leave La Colle for a month, not to go near the coast, and not to take a boat out for any reason whatsoever."

"How bizarre! Why?"

"You mustn't ask me for explanations. It's very serious, I assure you…very serious for me."

We were walking along a side-path; gradually, I recovered my composure. The little smile that she had had on her lips during my demonstrations was frozen into a slight grimace that seemed to have been forgotten on her face by her preoccupied mind. I didn't want her to reflect—it seemed to me to be so easy to deduce. I wanted her to accept my conditions as a bizarrerie of my character.

"It's a trial that I have decided to impose upon you—but I beg you to grant me what I ask of you, stupid as it might seem."

At the tone of my voice, which must have seemed quite anguished, her beautiful face became grave.

"Yvane," I continued, "all that I'm shutting up in my heart, all that I cannot bring myself to say, but which is as plainly visible as the sun in the sky…Yvane, since you know that you are the only thing on earth that counts for me…"

She put a finger on my lips. She was right; it was better for me to shut up. I stammered another: "My love"—or, rather, my lips articulated the syllables on her lips. We were standing in the midst of impassive cypresses. My two hands were sustaining her shoulders. From head to toe our two bodies were touching. For the first time, I held her against me, no longer like a large flower found by the roadside, but as the only creature in the world. I hugged her to my breast, like the other half of my heart—the heart that I could feel beating through the light fabric, the heart which, perhaps, was already counting the beats that separated it from silence…

Then began the most agonizing and the most marvelous days that I had ever known.

While I was with Yvane, touching her with my hands, never taking my eyes off her, discovering in her adorable face a thousand hidden retreats into which I went to lose myself in dreams, wandering amid all the secrets of her nape and her hair, testing with my lips the caress of her lashes, the cool corners of her eyelids, rediscovering on her cheeks the perfumes that allowed all the flowers of May to escape into the air, I forgot…I forgot everything.

Having spoken, having put an end to my stupid hesitation, to my internal reticence, I had opened the way to a tide of affection, which escaped me in torrents of joy, causing me to shiver with happiness, giving me an infinite confidence in the forces of love.

But when night came, and I found myself alone with myself, the atrocious anguish gripped me again. I saw her under the atrocious threat. Thinking that the greatest regret of the living is not to have loved enough, not to have told those who have departed that they loved them often enough, I wanted, at least, to escape that remorse, to tell the living Yvane over and over again of a love so great, so immense, that it could overwhelm her eternally.

Then, insomnia developing, I forged insensate grievances against myself. "Coward," I said myself, "you didn't speak, you only committed yourself because you found out that she's going to die. That love isn't the kind that can vanquish death. It was before you knew that you should have declared yourself. Don't hope to snatch her away from the destiny that awaits her."

At dawn, as soon as the last demands of convention permitted it, I ran to Yvane's windows. I didn't want to lose a single minute. Still entirely possessed by my nocturnal errors,

I thought her dead, and every time, my first kiss was like a kiss that one deposits on a lifeless face in a mortuary chamber. And I had the indescribable joy of seeing that face come back to life, of feeling two arms of flesh entwine around my neck, of finding Yvane as true as ever.

She had meekly given in to my demand that she not stray far from La Colle, and not to approach the coast on any pretext. No more excursions by boat, no more sea-bathing. I pretended to be jealous; I wanted her all to myself, to be with me every moment of the day.

One night, I woke up covered in an anguished sweat; while half-asleep, I had just remembered the reservoir that I had forgotten. Level with the ground, it was a permanent threat. I got up immediately, went to open the drainage tap, and did not leave the place until the reservoir was dry.

To be sure, it's commonplace to associate death with love. But in this instance, it wasn't a question of literature, and never were those two divinities interlinked as intimately and as authentically as they were for me as the days went by. The thought of death stirred in my heart as if to extract, with an unexpected intensity, all the passion of which a human being might be capable. I was in love, so much in love that I might have died of it myself.

Gradually, the days were passing by, and I recovered hope. As I was distanced from the moment of the horrible confidence, as I saw Yvane, happy and very much alive, trusting in the infinite affection that I evidenced for her, I began to doubt, to forget. All my precautions had been taken. I mounted a vigilant guard. The nightmare became less painful. I maintained a strict consistency, striking out each passing day on my calendar, the bearer of a black accolade extending from the May 24 to June 22. The days passed without incident. The month of June was delightful, in its light and coolness.

"Will you hold me prisoner much longer?" Yvane asked me, during the long pale evenings when the Sun seemed unable to decide to disappear.

To tease me, she proposed a little excursion by car on the coast road, but when confronted by the effect that any such proposition immediately had on me, she did not persist, only murmuring: "A bizarre trial, like no other…"

I only lived for her, and with her. I refused to see any other resident of the château; I did not want anything to disturb the dream in which we were taking refuge. Forgetting the external world gave me more confidence in the powers of the heart. Yvane was there, always there. Her supple figure, which I felt like a firm and living liana at my side, was a certainty that helped me to chase away the somber torments of the night. Calmer, less anxious regarding the immediate, I could watch her live, with more curiosity about her mind. It appeared to me that her thought-processes, which had always been rather mysterious, did not allow themselves to be enveloped in the immense affection that I draped around her body and her heart. On the contrary, as if assured that someone— who was partly herself—was standing guard over her flesh, freeing her from the concern of maintaining everyday contact with reality, she seemed to be using the possibilities of her leisure to extend her dreams toward more distant horizons, where I had difficulty following her. Silently, I remained halfway to those heights, like a shepherd who allows his flocks to frolic on the summits, sure that when evening comes he will find them again on the path to the valley.

"Is happiness—the thing is more mysterious than the word—a closed shelter or a trampoline that facilitates bouncing?" she mused, aloud. "Being happy, I never felt so light, so disposed to bounce…beyond my happiness, if I might put it like that. As in dreams, I could almost believe that it would be sufficient for me to extend my arms to fly like an arrow into the sky, to become a skylark, or a cloud…" Meanwhile, her hand was playing with my hair. "Pierre, Pierre, with a name so hard, how can you be so tender?"

The strange thing is that it was necessary to hear that, the significance being in the intonation, almost as a reproach, as if the word "affection" signified carelessness or laxity…

In the course of one of the walks by means of which I tried to make her forget our seclusion, I sat down on the side of a hill. She came to wedge herself between my knees, lying back against my breast—in her armchair, she said—and I inclined my head over her neck, tasting in the cleavage of her blouse the savor of her warm and supple flesh. My arms were folded around her breasts.

"Nothing, nothing can tear her away from me," I whispered, in the shadow of her hair.

After a long silence, I heard her murmur: "It's beautiful, beautiful—as if I were about to die…"

I cried out in protest.

"Why?" she went on. "Happiness is so much greater than life, that when one confides oneself entirely to someone, one surpasses life, and death no longer has any meaning."

"No, Yvane, that's a blasphemy. You mustn't tempt the gods."

She reflected for a while. "You value my flesh more than I do," she said. "Isn't the person who loves the most the one who goes furthest, driven by happiness?"

So great was the power of the spell that several times, on the evenings of those days, I forgot to strike out the elapsed day on the calendar. The second fortnight of June had begun. We decided that we would make an ascent of a neighboring mountain on the day of the summer solstice. On the longest day of the year, we would see the last sunset of spring, and we would walk all night to reach the summit and see it reappear at dawn: the summer sun, already fleeing from us….

Narda drove us in the car to the foot of the mountain, treating us as lunatics because we had refused to take anything with us.

"I want to walk with my arms free, aware of nothing but my own weight," Yvane had said. "Every precaution, every preparation, is an insult to the landscape, a weapon against nature…"

We started along the path at 8 p.m. The day was still warm. I let her walk ahead of me to set the pace, which was more than slothful, and to keep her in sight, like a spectacle of which I never wearied: the sway of her figure, the play of her long bare arms, naïve in design. Sometimes, she passed over an obstacle with a rapid bound, revealing a pale calf beneath her short dress, chaste and hollowed by the effort. With the hands that she had wanted to liberate she caressed the berries of arbutus trees as she passed by, or tested the tips of aloe-leaves, turning round abruptly to reassure herself of my presence, and replying with a smile to the smile with which I accompanied her every gesture.

The last lizards were abandoning the place; the vegetation was becoming sparser, the path narrower. With our backs to a section of a wall of rock, still warm, we watched the sunset. The view extended through the depths of the valley to the sea, grey and shin in the distant mist: the sea, my secret enemy, sullen within the décor illuminated by the red earth of the mountains, as if I had snatched away the prey that it hoped to claim. With the satisfaction of a victor, I took the bare arm of that prey, who was standing silently beside me. It had been grazed in places by the dry branches of juniper bushes. To erase the white marks are restore its natural polish, I caressed it with my palm, as one does an object made of precious material.

"So you, too, don't think it necessary to consent to the marks imprinted by life?" she asked.

I took time to reflect before replying: "The same life that inflicts them also erases them, better than our ministrations."

She had tilted her head back toward the zenith, which was already turning a dark violet. "The clouds don't soil the sky," she said.

Darkness rose in the east. There were no more birds. A belated sparrowhawk passed below us, fleeing toward the valley.

"Well be the only two living, thinking beings on the mountain this evening—that's a great responsibility," she said, ironically. "Here's the night—I can feel it coming, warmer…" She turned toward me and added: "The first night when we shall be together." Then, abruptly: "I'm glad; there'll be moonlight."

A pale clarity became visible on the peak facing us.

"You divine everything," I observed. "You see everything before me. For myself, I only want to see you…but it's as well that you're in advance, interrogating things, like my infinitely sensitive watchman."

She put her arms around my neck and laid her head on my shoulder. "Carried by you, I see better and further—alone, I would never have come so far. And everything here is so calm! What are we going to find at the top of the mountain? What if we meet angels?"

"Are you happy?" I asked.

"Enough to forget to live," she replied.

We resumed our march. Our mountain had nothing immense or painful about it, but it had a peak, and its inoffensive slope brought us closer to the stars. The air became still and the rocks retained around them a little of the warm atmosphere of the day, impregnated with thyme. Little by little, in the lunar light, forms lost their excessive precision. The world of the night was born around us.

She put her mouth close to my ear to murmur: "Listen—in its progress over the earth, the night is marching from summit to summit, and I'm sure that we're going toward the place where its bare foot will rest…"

I knew that in her, excitement took the form of a return to childhood. I too felt myself gradually entering into the enchantment. A diffuse fatigue inclined me to follow all the solicitations of the imagination, and I was able to see the elves gliding between the pools of moonlight, in good faith.

I proposed a halt.

"No, higher up," she said, "higher still."

I followed her white shadow, which scaled the final scree-slopes at a run.

"The summit!" she said, stopping suddenly, open-mouthed before the fantastic décor of standing stones that crowned the plateau we had just reached. She was breathing hard. A moonbeam, catching one of the crystal buttons of her dress, shimmered like a pale star.

"You'll have a heart attack, child," I said, placing my hand on her breast.

"It doesn't matter. Poor heart, it's carried me this far. It's yours, keep it. Me, I belong to the night."

The night surrounded us with its infinite silence. Very close to my ear, a murmur became audible: "I shall never consent to cease being happy. Now, I'm so happy, so intoxicated to have come so far, so high, that I'd like to dance, to dance solo for the night."

I scarcely recognized her voice.

She tore herself away from my arms, bounded a few paces away, and, abruptly taking off her dress, seemed to flee into the starry sky.

A white form in the moonlight, leaping from stone to stone, momentarily motionless, slender beneath the immense sky, then bounding through the shadows to reappear at the far side of the darkness beneath the dark blue vault, sometimes pausing on an altar of stone, sometimes gliding more smoothly between the grey monsters of crouching rocks…

One might have thought her the priestess of some strange cult, understood and celebrated by herself alone. What spirit emanated by that antique earth had taken possession of her body thus? What sacred flame, reborn from the ashes of the past, had returned to life in her? A chaste Bacchante, in love with the great secrets of nature, she seemed to be offering herself to the caress of the heavens…

The queen of the elves danced on the mountain that night. A spark of flesh bounded within the confines of the earth and the sky. My eyes saw her, beneath the stars that cannot see at all.

I dared not intervene. Something there surpassed me, whose gravity I felt more than understood—something, however, of great and profound significance.

I received in my arms and rested on my knees an exhausted form, half-unconscious with fatigue, streaming with perfumes of the earth and juices distilled by her flesh.

Like an obscure acolyte of some great mystery, I piously gathered from her temple, amid her sticky hair, the sweat poured out by that body as a libation to the spirit of the night. The heart that had been abandoned to me was still palpitating with the emotions of an excessively mad endeavor; I cradled its repose gently, until the return of the dawn.

By the light of the paling sky, mauve rings were visible around her closed eyelids. Her hollowed cheeks took on ivory tints. The new day revealed to me another face, which I scarcely recognized: a perishable face, but one whose very frailty made me love her even more than hers glorious image even more. I loved her in a way that touched the utmost depths of human affection, delirious with joy.

She opened her eyes, and, confronted by the silvery, more distant stars, murmured: "It's ended, already..." before burying her face in my bosom.

I wrapped her in my jacket. The first coolness of the day was threatening us. We began to descend. She walked with closed eyes, leaning on me like a sleepwalker. "How far it is!" she sighed. I wanted to carry her in my arms. To march at dawn, carrying the object of one's love! In my intoxication, I would have lifted up the world...

When the summer Sun rose, I looked at it with pride, as an equal.

I did not leave her until we reached the threshold of her room, in the shelter of the familiar frame. One last time, I hugged her as if to stifle her. Happiness was streaming through me, impregnating me to the most distant fibers of my being. I went to throw myself down on the divan in the summer-house, to resume the dream...

Later, while I was half-asleep, I heard a voice calling: "Pierre! Pierre!" I sat up. It was Narda's voice. I raced to the threshold. Narda was running up the slope toward me.

"Pierre!" she cried. "Come quickly!"

"Why? What's wrong?"

"Yvane—come quickly! Yvane, in her bath—she's not moving. She's very cold."

Dream or reality? I tottered. Abruptly, facing the midday sun, I understood, and collapsed, unconscious.

CHAPTER ELEVEN

The medical examiner requested an inquest, which returned a verdict of accidental death. An electric hair-drier dipped into the bathwater had provoked an initial electrocution, whose work had been completed by a prolonged immersion of the body in the cold water. On emerging from my faint, I had not wanted to see the woman who was no more. No image of death ought to tarnish her memory. I didn't want to see anything or hear anything, but to continue to dream.

I decided to go away, to leave the summer-house forever. I was taken to a railway station. I got on to a train. When the train stopped, I got off in a city. For two days I lived in a world that I no longer recognized. There was nothing; nothing remained. I could not extract myself from my hallucination. I said to myself: "Do I need to eat? Oh yes, I need to eat. So what? I need to eat." Or "Sleep? Do I need sleep, then?" But slumber would not obey me. If, by chance, I succeeded in becoming drowsy for a few hours, my awakening was all the more atrocious. "What's wrong, then?" I asked myself, for long minutes, having lost all memory. Then I remembered the horrible appeal; I thought I heard Narda's cry for help. Every time, there was the same shock to the heart, the same fall into the void, the same gulf to the bottom of which I was precipitated. The broken thread could not be reattached. My mind remained astray. An individual is measured by the void they leave behind. With Yvane gone, the void was so great that it swallowed the world.

I could not continue to live like that. I returned to the summer-house. There, at least, I recovered memories; there, shadows were still floating beneath the branches, with which I could hear myself, and which might perhaps invite me, little by little, to accept that to which, with all my forces in revolt, I still refused to submit.

I rarely went out, awaiting the hours disdained by humans, the hours of complete darkness, or dawn, to deliver myself to pilgrimages of a sort, in the course of which I reshuffled dreams endlessly. I feared no ridicule. I went to find the dogs in their kennel to talk to them about Yvane. Those animals, which I could scarcely go near before, now accepted me as their companion, as if they understood.

I slipped into the garage to revisit the little car in which I had seen her for the first time. I caressed its seat and its steering-wheel, pressed my lips upon the handgrip of the gear-stick that had been polished and worn by the palm of her hand, and, with my eyes closed, clutching that cold, absent hand in mid-air, I worked my way through the rosary of memories associated with her: her tanned hand on the table of the inn; her movement, always with the left hand, to push back the rebellious wisps of hair behind her ear; her hand on the tiller of the boat; or, again, her fingers extended as if to catch hold of the distant notes of a keyboard, gripping her forehead—that was the day when we went up on to the *loggia* that revealed the red mountains...

At the turning of a pathway, a gust of honeysuckle stopped me in my tracks; I thought I heard her voice again, saying: "I prefer it to all the orchids on Earth." She was about to appear, her white socks rolled down over her ankles, well-secured in large yellow shoes, her blonde curls escaping from her headscarf to float over her sunburnt nape, all of her beautiful face bright, transparent, illuminated by her pale blue eyes...

On finding a glove that I thought was hers beneath a garden table, I thought I would faint, and my distress as so visible that Narda, whether it was true or not, protested loudly that the glove was one of hers.

I recreated her, initially determined to add nothing that did not belong to her, but also not to conserve anything of her but that which we had in common. A form lighter, more diaphanous, easier to manipulate in my dreams, with which I could continue to pursue the dream in which I had lived. Thus a sleeper snatched from slumber tries, with all the resources of his awakened imagination, to reconnect the broken thread of the dream that had enchanted him. Fragments of our conversations came back to mind. Little by little, I invented others, imaginary ones, in which I asked questions and made replies, guiding myself by the intonations of her voice remaining in my memory to find the words that she would have pronounced. It often happened that I cursed the makers of legend, but I was forced to recognize that certain individuals compel legend-mongering.

On seeing my dream-Yvane develop, I understood a little better that she had been unable to live in a real, complex world, demanding too much calculation. A certain physical awkwardness (what would have happened, the day of the tricycle, if I had not turned up?) a certain forgetfulness of her body, a disgust for its activity, the versatility of her moods—in brief, everything that made her a delightful and charming individual—was out of step with the world. Too delicate to live. Who knows? Perhaps, even when she was alive, I had already loved her as one loves a dead woman, ideally. But what good was this world, then, if the only precious individuals that one meets here are also the only ones who cannot live in it?

I knew full well that the first distraction of my thought, the first relaxation of my effort of will, would bring me back into contact with the reality: "She's dead"—and the aerial phantom into which I was trying to breathe life would collapse. The frailty of my dreams by comparison with the implacable density of the real was thus a constant reminder of the harshness of the world. And the doctor's arid philosophy, the implacable aspect of destiny, gradually imposed itself upon me. He was right; everything was written; nothing could be done about it. Had not Yvane been conscious of it herself? Did not her passivity in confrontation with things, and her refusal to take decisions, demonstrate submission in advance to an invincible fatality?

Gentle summer rains accompanied these reveries. The château's residents respected my solitude and my follies. For my part, I had developed a complete indifference with respect to the doctor and his research. So far as I was concerned, it

86

had exhausted its possibilities at a single stroke. The future was of no more interest to me than the present.

One day, I spotted my host at a distance in the grounds. I noticed that he had become more severe—more careworn, it seemed—but I made a detour so as not to meet him. From various symptoms, I deduced that there was a great deal of activity in the laboratories; the windows remained illuminated for much of the night and sometimes, the howls of martyrized animals reached me. It was of little importance; I was a stranger to the universe, as far astray in my own fashion as Dirk might be in the future, thanks to the effects of the doctor's magic. In my case, there had been no need of any scientific apparatus; the mere memory of Yvane had sufficed to bear away my mind, to carry into the past, leaving nothing in the present but an empty body.

Sometimes, I happened to run into poor Dirk. Although I did not know why, the kind of captivity in which he had been held for a long time seemed to have been relaxed. As he was always mute, he did not disturb me. He fell into step with me, stopping when I stopped, going away when I showed signs that his presence was becoming tedious.

One day, in the pine-wood, we were sitting together on a fallen trunk. In the distance, a crew of woodcutters was working in an area that had recently caught fire, and axe-blows punctuated the silence at regular intervals.

"What a horrible war…" he murmured.

I thought at first that he was talking about a battle between ants that was unfolding at our feet, toward which I directed a vague gaze; then I remembered that his words could not be referring to the present. I had an opportunity to report them to the doctor, who surprised me one morning in the garage. His face seemed fatigued, with a slightly haggard nuance in his eyes that was new in him. A certain abruptness of word and gesture punctured his desire always to seem affable.

"The confidence is interesting," he said. "Dirk is nearly a year in advance at present. He must be referring to a European war. For several days, I haven't succeeded in getting anything out of him, and now I know why: the era in which he's living is disturbed by events, and the possibilities of forming connections with the calm atmosphere in which we live are rarer."

"Oh, a war…" I said.

I said it mechanically, fundamentally indifferent. The doctor misunderstood the meaning of my reflection.

"The fact that he spoke to you should reassure you as to yourself, and establishes that, whatever happens, you'll still be alive a year from now."

I made a gesture of detachment. The logic of the deduction irritated me—and I thought all these more-or-less obscure pronouncements about the future rather childish. They reminded me of the predictions of fortune-tellers, and such tea-leaves didn't interest me any more by virtue of their scientific pretensions.

"Don't be surprised if you hear a certain amount of noise," the doctor said to me then. "I'll probably be obliged, during the coming sessions, to fire a few rifle-shots in order to create an atmosphere."

It was after we had parted that my thoughts returned to the assurance he had give me: "You'll still be alive a year from now." Thus, in a year, I would still be the same person, having eaten and slept regularly, having continued the monotonous game of life, perhaps having forgotten. One comes to love one's pain, to the point of dreading uneasily that it might one day go away. The prospect of eventually forgetting wounded me deeply. Thus, that brief conversation with the doctor had awoken my rancor at a stroke. The same rebellion that had taken hold of me at the announcement of Yvane's death gripped me again. "Oh! I'll still be alive a year from now!" What right did he have to dispose of me thus? And my free will, what became of that? The impression of fatality under which he had made me live had become intolerable. I felt that I was at the limits of a kind of madness, but that it was no longer in my power to command myself.

A chaotic mass of thoughts and feelings was seething within me: my pain, the memory of Yvane, a rebellion against fate, against life. Suddenly, I thought I glimpsed a possibility of vengeance against the universe, against the doctor, against his pronouncements. "You'll still be alive a year from now." It had been a bold move to advance that prophecy. If it was impossible to prevent death from doing its work at an appointed hour, with life one must still be able to act in its stead. Me, alive a year from now—that remained to be seen…

Sliding down that slope, in the atmosphere of semi-madness that was then mine—and the only one in which I could live—I eventually came to think that, if I succeeded in inflicting a falsification upon the doctor, I would ruin his entire theory, and, in consequence, the death of Yvane would be negated. That unsustainable idea nevertheless appeared to me to be more luminous with every passing day. Oh, he would fire rifle-shots! Well, I too had a revolver…

I had been ripened by all the bad habits of solitude…now it seemed that Yvane was appealing to me. If, in creating her legend, I was not obeying a pure fantasy, but yielding to her invitation, was it not the case now that she was inviting me to join her, in the indescribable places where her memory was perpetuated? Yes, it was really her that was calling me…

From that moment on, threatened on the one hand by an implacably progressing universe, and solicited on the other by the most gracious phantom ever borne aloft by the light air of those summer nights, could I hesitate much longer?

When a warm and placid evening arrived, so similar to the evening on which we had left together for our last excursion that I thought I could hear the sound of the car that had taken us outside my door, I could resist no longer; I slipped my revolver into my pocket, and I set off for the mountain.

Carefully, I followed in her footsteps once again. I had forgotten nothing—nothing at all. Every pebble, every blade of grass, was etched into my memory. As I passed by, I caressed the same leaves that she had stroked. At the first halt, beside the wall of rock, the same Sun plunged into its bath of molten gold, and in the empty space my hand passed back and forth for a long time over the arm that was no longer held out to me. A final hesitation still gripped me, but when the same sparrowhawk, recalled by the evening to its nest on the plain, plunged into the valley in front of me, I no longer doubted what awaited me on high. The meaning of the strange scene, in the course of which she had escaped from my arms to bound into the night, now seemed clear to me. With a marvelous prescience, while alive, she had arranged a rendezvous with me in these mysterious places where life overlapped death. Her phantom was still dancing; I only had to go to meet it.

I could have continued on my way with my eyes closed. I went up the scree-slope again and reached the summit. The rocks were there, standing to attention, faithful to their strange forms. I sat down at the place where I had taken her in my arms and awaited the miracle. The Moon was slowly following its path through the stars; my eyes grew weary interrogating the reflections and the shadows; my heart was crying out within my bosom, but there was no reply in the silence.

I understood the meaning of that heartbeat then: one last step remained to be taken. I breathed in deeply, inflating my chest to the maximum for the last time. I closed my eyes, greeting with a welcoming smile the other night that was already descending within me, which a radiant apparition was about to illuminate. I put the barrel of the gun to the very skin of my breast, and pressed the trigger.

There was a click; the weapon had jammed.

I swore, and threw the revolver to the ground. Thwarted! I had been defeated. The doctor had won. Even the right to kill myself had escaped me. Yvane was dead, really dead. I had advanced to the very threshold in the attempt to rejoin her, in vain: the ultimate door remained closed. I remained alone, sober now, on the rim of the abyss, and I felt the long crisis of dementia, in the course of which I had attempted to bring her back to life, unravel within me.

While recognizing the insane aspect of the adventure, however, while now understanding with perfect lucidity what crazy reasoning had driven me to want to kill myself that she might live, I still would not consent to be dominated by fate. Undoubtedly, nothing could make destiny turn back on its past decisions, but if I had not been able to kill myself for Yvane, I could at least kill myself to prove that I was, in spite of everything, free.

It's strange to commit suicide twice for entirely different reasons. Groping about, I searched for the revolver in the heather. Very deliberately, I dismantled the loading-chamber, replaced it and cocked the hammer to arm the weapon. I smiled again, but out of hatred for the doctor.

"You've won twice—now it's my turn!" I cried. I put the barrel to my temple this time, and even more deliberately and more determinedly than before, I squeezed the trigger.

Revolvers don't jam twice.

CHAPTER TWELVE

It was white, brighter than white, like a star of silver or polished metal. Blue glints were woven into the rays that emerged from the thing for me, guiding me to the crossroads of light in order to permit me to reach the thing itself, the silver star that also seemed to be a diamond destined to serve as a lodging for my gaze. I had never seen such a marvel, brilliant, suspended, motionless, attractive. Never had any rising star or crystalline drop surprised in the morning dew shone with so pure a gleam. My indolence, wandering in dark space, escaped the darkness in which it was content, and in that dazzling and icy flame that I had suddenly discovered at the limit of my vision, I witnessed that extraordinary miracle, the revival of my curiosity. Light, true light, caused the rebirth within me of the glimmer of intelligence; the one gave birth to the other, and my consciousness, reanimated by that spark, which extracted it from limbo, discovered itself at the moment of its awakening, to lend its unreal magic to the magic of reality. I remained in suspense for a moment, as if at the confluence of two worlds: that of things and that of their comprehension, immobile on their sparkling frontier, hesitant to choose, to renounce the pure and simple marveling of the conscious gaze alone—but an already-awakening intelligence did not leave me any further leisure, pushing me into the infinite network of its mute interrogations to capture the object of my initial surprise, which, amid a thousand memories of anterior experiences, asleep and forgotten, scattered in the debris of my memory, it was finally able to recognize and to identify as being a nickel-plated tap.

The magic ceased abruptly with that realization, but the repose that followed the seething activity thus regenerated was no less delectable for that. In order to savor it, I closed my eyes, returning momentarily to darkness. When I opened them again, there was an angel on the wall. Perhaps I was waiting for him.

The angel did not say anything, paying less attention to me than to a young man who was clutching his arm. He was an extremely handsome angel, in truth, whose harmoniously-formed wings descended to the ground, and I admired the way that he bore them with such ease, like the tails of a coat put on for eternity: an angel with long blond hair, too long for my memories…yes, definitely too long…

At the same moment, thanks to that exaggeratedly-expansive hair, I understood that I wasn't dead, and that the angel was part of a picture hanging on the wall of my room.

I wasn't dead, and the colored plate above my bed told the story of a young man miraculously saved by his guardian angel, whose apparition was holding him back from the edge of the precipice. I had already encountered the engraving in the books of my childhood. Here, more pretentious in its gilded frame, it participated in the strange charm of aperitif advertisements on the walls of village cafes. But I wasn't dead. Why, then, had I to make that observation, which is not usually one of those that imposes itself on awakening?

A woman in a nurse's uniform came in, bearing a break-fast-tray. She seemed surprised to hear me ask her questions, and came back in company with a man in a white smock, whose face brightened when he heard me. My very ordinary reflections were, however, solely concerned with the fine sun-light that was shining that morning. They withdrew to let me eat. Later, the door opened again.

"Narda!" I exclaimed.

I watched her coming toward me, as brunette as the angel was blond. She took one of my hands in hers. "Pierre! How glad I am! You recognize me! You recognize me!"

The sound of her voice completed my return to myself, and permitted me to reconnect with memories of the past. In a flash, I reviewed the château, the summer-house, my depar-ture, the night on the mountain.

"But where am I?" I asked.

"In a hospital in Switzerland, near Lausanne. We brought you with us."

"But why? What's happened, then? How long have I been like this?"

"Tomorrow, it will be six months since the day when you were found on..." She stopped, fearful of bringing back painful memories.

"Six months!" I exclaimed, unable to believe my ears. "What? I've been in this state for six months!"

"The wound healed quickly, but the rest took longer to put back in order," she explained, with a discretion of expression that was touching. "When they telephoned this morning to tell me that you were talking, I didn't want to lose a minute, I came right away. I never lost hope, but the doctors didn't want to give any guarantees..."

The novelty had not yet passed, and in my confusion, it was a very trivial thought that came to my lips: "For once I get a year's leave, and I spend six months unconscious—just my luck..." But I was still in need of explanations. "Who takes care of me?"

"We do," said Narda. "My uncle, the doctors..."

"Has your uncle been looking after me?" I asked, suddenly anxious.

"No, don't worry," she said, laughing. "But we didn't know who to inform. I've written to addresses found in your papers; we've had a reply for Cairo, from your sister. She offered to accommodate you out there, but the climate..."

"Why, in fact, am I in Switzerland?"

"One of my uncle's ideas. The sojourn in Provence had ceased to please him. You'll never guess why—he's afraid of a war. We've moved to Switzerland, lock, stock and barrel—and you came with us."

"I see, I see," I murmured, having become pensive since mention of the doctor had entered into the conversation. "I owe you an infinite debt, my dear Narda. It's truly admirable that a solitary individual always finds, in his hour of need, devotion at his service..."

An interval of forgetfulness that lasts six months, even when one has not been conscious of it, creates a situation in which one looks back the man one has been with new eyes. I recovered possession of myself as if of an abandoned apartment; I recognized the general disposition of places and objects, but the affective links that bound me to them had changed. I was a stranger in my own dwelling. On passing my hand over my forehead, I encountered a scar near my temple, the first new thing that I had found within me. It was also the last of the man that I had been. There, in fact, was the junction between my successive selves. In the old me, that scar had had a profound spiritual significance, but I no longer acceded to its gravity. Now, for the new me, it was no more than a little sinuous line, losing itself in the roots of my hair, and I limited myself to following it with my finger, with an almost amused curiosity.

In a few days, I recovered full rational possession of myself. I was able to leave the clinic, to go out for walks in the town, and, after the brief intoxication of convalescence, to retrieve the petty annoyances of life. Politeness, for want of any other sentiment of gratitude, obliged me to pay a visit to Dr. Mops. I could not make up my mind to do it—not so much, I thought, because of memories of a past that was well and truly dead, but because it displeased me to present myself to him in the somewhat ridiculous role of a failed suicide. Day after day, I put off my visit, letting myself drift, in the mild Swiss ambience, from breakfast to lunch, and from lunch to dinner, without making any decision.

In the course of the visits Narda made, I expended treasures of diplomacy in declining the invitations she addressed to me on her uncle's behalf.

"We're living not far away," she told me, thinking to soothe me. "Nothing has changed—you'll see."

"Yes, yes," I said, distractedly, knowing very well for what reasons nothing had changed. Giving in to the succession of memories, I added: "By the way, what's become of Dirk?"

"Still the same, still just as mad. He doesn't talk anymore, so to speak. He hasn't forgotten, but he gets everything mixed up. A little while ago, he greeted me with a 'Bonjour,

Madame Delambre'—which surprised me greatly. I hardly expected to hear your name emerging from his mouth."

In spite of myself, I let the impact show.

"What's wrong, Pierre? You're very pale."

Immediately, I felt myself blushing and tried to turn away to avoid Narda's gaze.

"I'm sorry," she said. "I'm too stupid. I didn't intend to remind you of the past—but the harm's done now; don't hold it against me. And since I'm so awkward, I'll leave you…"

It was obvious that she attributed my distress purely to the memory of Yvane. As for me, my emotion did not derive so much from Dirk's new prediction—which I felt capable of falsifying, now that I was strong from top to toe, no longer paralyzed by any sentiment—as from the idea that the experiment, whose interference with my life had already had such consequences, was still going on, and that it was threatening to draw me in again.

The decision that I had hesitated to take was immediately set aside. Utterly resolved to draw a line under the entire story and not to set foot again in the doctor's home, who could think what he liked of me, I would leave for Paris the following day.

The next day, with my bags packed, I was about to have them transported to the station when a note was handed to me. It was from Narda.

Things are happening here that are making me anxious. I need someone to help me, but I don't know who to turn to. Could you possibly ask one of the doctors who has cared for you, and in whom I can have confidence, to come here on some pretext or other? He must ask for me first. Sorry to inconvenience you by asking you to do me this favor. It's rather urgent.

I had ten minutes to think about it before the car left for the station. My first impulse was not to modify my plans at all. Then it seemed to me that I had time to telephone the chief physician of the clinic in which I had been looked after, to pass on Narda's request. However, I did nothing. Was it not cowardly on my part to abandon a young woman of 18 to difficulties that I sensed to be rather acute, since I was fleeing them myself? Not to mention that I owed her my life, since she was the one that had directed the search for me toward the mountain...

On the other hand, it was also too stupid to start playing the St. Bernard dog again, and I had had it up to the ears with this whole story, and that entire family. I had decided to leave, and I had only to do it...

I re-read the letter. It was not a call for help; at any rate, it was indirect and very discreet. In spite of its brevity, it contained several spelling mistakes, which touched me.[6] It was those spelling mistakes that made me put off my departure to the evening train...

A little later, that same morning, I rang Dr. Mops' doorbell.

---

[6] As rendered in the text I am translating, Narda's message does not, in fact, contain any spelling mistakes. It is possible that they have been corrected by an editor. At any rate, I decided that it would be inappropriate to introduce any, in spite of the inconsistency.

CHAPTER THIRTEEN

"Bonjour, Delambre—glad to see you again."

The doctor had come into the room while my back was turned. He came forward. I scarcely recognized him, so much older did he seem to have grown. His voice, harsher still, broke on the final syllables. His tone was still trying to be patronizing, but it was forced, and missed its effect.

As Narda, to whom I had asked my arrival to be announced, opened the door in her turn, he said dryly: "Give us a moment, my child—I'd like to talk privately to Monsieur Delambre."

Narda obeyed without any response, but before disappearing she shot me a glance whose meaning I could not quite decipher. She seemed to be begging me to be circumspect.

The doctor's abrupt manners were perhaps intended to get the upper hand on me, but no longer having any need to be wary of him, I felt myself ready to respond tit for tat.

"Would you care to follow me?" he asked. "Here, I mistrust the walls."

We found ourselves back in the eternal study, where the right hemisphere of the brain was hanging in its accustomed place. The old décor no longer impressed me, but it had an unexpected effect on me: for the first time since consciousness had returned to me, I started thinking about Yvane again. Not that I had forgotten her, but her remembrance occupied a region of my memory that I had forbidden myself to revisit until that day. But now, solely as an effect of the disposition of the furniture, that entire voluntarily-obscure zone of my memory lit up, became animated—not, as before, as a life that was bound intimately to mine, but as an image lit from behind, whose outline revealed a familiar face. It was no longer the living Yvane, but a portrait of Yvane, awakening more curiosity than profound distress. A portrait that made me think, all the same…

"My dear chap," the doctor began, having given me a long time to install myself, "you see before you a man who is finished, empty, clapped out. The mainspring has broken, a few days ago."

In truth, his voice had become miserable; the mask of authority with which he had greeted me had fallen away, leaving a flaccid face with distressed features, and a dull, weary gaze. Far from feeling pity, however, I experienced a slight repulsion instead.

"I'm not exaggerating," he continued. "Dirk is dead."

"Ah!" I said, slightly disconcerted by this news. Aside, I thought: *So that's what has troubled Narda.* Aloud, I continued: "And you probably fear annoying inquiries—but I imagine that you can easily find explanations."

"I've killed the goose that laid the golden eggs," he continued, ignoring me.

I should certainly have anticipated that he was not a man to be moved to it by the death of an experimental subject, and that he was only deploring the loss to his interests.

"Anyway," he said, getting to his feet, "you'll see."

"No, no," I protested. "I don't want to." I preferred not to get mixed up in the affair, which might become awkward— but as he did not seem to comprehend my refusal, I added a vague explanation: "The sight of dead bodies, you know…"

"What? The sight of dead bodies? What do you mean?"

"Well, you've just told me that he's dead."

"You've misunderstood," he said. "He's dead, but he's as healthy as you or me."

Bewilderment must have been painted on my face.

"I thought you remembered," the doctor explained. "I was pushing Dirk into the future. He was eight years ahead when, suddenly, within the last week, all possibility of communicating with him was broken off. I tried everything before giving in to the evidence. He fell silent because, in eight years, he will quite simply be dead. But while waiting for the eight years to elapse, he's here, solid and very much alive. You can judge for yourself."

He got up then, went to the little door, and the scene I knew so well began again.

"We're going to work, Dirk—will you come down?"

On hearing Dirk's footsteps on the stairway, the indifference that I had felt until then gave way to a vague anxiety. What was the phantom that was about to appear?

Dirk came toward me, his hand extended. I had to vanquish a slight hesitation, but I shook the hand. It was vigorous and warm, like a true hand.

"Come on," I said, turning to the doctor. "Are you sure that he's..." Dirk's presence prevented me from pronouncing the word.

"Alas," sighed the doctor. He went to tap Dirk on the shoulder; then, without any inhibition, he said: "Dead, dead—he's really dead, I assure you. In the long run, it was certainly to be expected, but who would have thought that that, in eight years, this stout fellow would already be clapped out? He's solid, though—look at him. I thought he was good for another thirty years, and I continued fearlessly, gaining several future weeks every day. With an advance of only eight years, I thought I still had a healthy margin in front of me, but *crack!* He's come apart in my hands..."

A sort of despairing wrath returned some animation to the doctor's face. He strode back and forth, while continuing his lament.

"At the very moment when I was in the process of learning, thanks to him, some astonishing things about the treatment of cancerous tumors by cosmic rays! As you can imagine, with an advance of eight years, I was no longer playing the stock market—a mere initial amusement; in any case, there were difficulties...

"No, what interested me was deciphering the science of the future. I was directing the experiment to its true goal, realizing the dream of all scientists: to know the next episode of the great serial of discovery, the state of science for future generations. You'll recall the words of your Renan: 'I would give everything that I know to be able to read the little textbook that will educate the schoolchildren of the next century!' And now the dream that I was in the process of realizing has suddenly collapsed, because of the death of this imbecile. It's my entire life's work that's come to nothing…"

Dirk was listening, as if it were happening to someone else. The scene was curious. Ever suspicious, I ventured a few objections. "What tells you that he's dead? He isn't talking to you anymore, but perhaps it's you that will be dead in eight years?"

"I thought of that, but I have irrefutable counter-proofs. The microphone installed in his room continually records on tape, day and night, everything that he lets slip. What he says in his sleep, take note, is independent of the external surroundings, since every night resembles any other night in the past or future. Until the last few days, the tape recorded fragments of nightmares, but for three days, there's been complete silence, after one last night that it isn't difficult to recognize as a night of death-throes. Look, I'll play it for you…"

"No, no—I believe you. There's no need."

My eyes never left Dirk, who seemed to be following the entire conversation, turning his head from one interlocutor to the other, smiling, and sometimes passing his hand distractedly over his cheek. An interested movement had made him sit up when the doctor proposed that we listen to the night of his death-throes—but more sustained attention permitted the recognition of the automatic nature of these gestures, and a certain absence in his facial expression might have revealed the living dead man.

In spite of my determination to stay out of the whole story, I could not help being affected by the interesting nature of the scene. Beads of sweat formed on my forehead. I mopped my brow; in fact, I felt very ill-at-ease. With the insensitivity of an executioner, the doctor continued to give me details in a loud voice. I wondered whether, in spite of everything, Dirk did feel and understand something.

The doctor only felt sorry for himself. "Twenty years of study, ten years in the laboratory, two years of daily cares devoted to bringing a marvelous subject to perfection, an experiment to which I have sacrificed everything—much more than you can suppose—and it all disappears at a stroke! What do you think I can do with my life now? All that work was my reason for living. I have nothing left—nothing! Start again? I'm too old, and one doesn't find such a subject every day. I thought I had reached the extremity of distress once, with my marital misfortunes—today, it's even worse. I've fallen back to zero, with nothing to hold on to. All hope has left me. The real dead man, in this story, is me. He's all right—look at him…"

The scene was becoming painful. The doctor was getting carried away, and his face was going purple. As I made no response to his plaints, he was raging in a void, like a damned soul.

"This central heating is truly pitiless!" he suddenly exclaimed. "It's stifling in here."

Marching toward one of the stained-glass windows, he opened it wide with a single thrust. A gust of fresh air irrupted into the room, and a marvelous mountain vista appeared in the window-frame. Beyond Lac Leman, the view extended to the great chain of the Alps. Above the lake's mists, in the clear pale blue sky, the dazzling whiteness of snowy peaks rose up, seemingly suspended miraculously in space. It was a magnificent winter day, illuminated by a low December Sun, cutting out the contours so clearly that no detail escaped the gaze. One might have believed that one could touch the summits by reaching out an arm. The large surfaces of glaciers reflected the sunlight in places like convex mirrors. Elsewhere, light translucent clouds rose up over the eastern slopes, toward the shadow. The entire panorama of the high mountains was empty, devoid of dwellings and human beings, as immense and pure as a gigantic snow-crystal, in which nature seemed to be contemplating itself. The icy air that came to bathe the temples drew thoughts irresistibly toward dreams of altitude. The doctor had stopped speaking; a release-valve had been opened in our minds. I took refuge in the contemplation of the landscape.

"Whisky?" the doctor suddenly proposed.

He handed me a glass of whisky and soda, offered one to Dirk, and let himself fall into the depths of an armchair, holding his glass in his fist and agitating a piece of ice. In the silence of the room, nothing was audible but the crystalline sound of the ice knocking on the wall of the glass.

It was then that something extraordinary happened.

"Hosanna! Hosanna!" said a loud voice.

I turned toward Dirk; his mouth was still open and the liquid was swaying in the glass that he was holding.

Startled, the doctor dropped his, which broke on the parquet. "Did you hear that?" he asked me, in a low voice.

"He can speak, then," I said.

Without seeming to attach any importance to our stupefaction, Dirk drank a mouthful of whisky, put down his glass and then, gripped by a frisson, cried: "Hosanna! Hosanna!"

"You see, he's not dead!" I exclaimed, triumphantly, glad to score a point off the doctor for the first time.

My triumph was facile. The words "stupefaction" and "bewilderment" were insufficient to describe the doctor's expression. Mouth open, his eyes quite round, fixed on Dirk, his intelligence seemed to have quit his face conclusively. In a low voice, he murmured: "He's dead, dead—I'm sure that he's dead."

An idea suddenly crossed my mind, and I exclaimed, on a whim: "Well then, he's in Heaven!"

I expected a burst of laughter on the doctor's part. I saw him go green.

"In Heaven?" he said, in a pitiful, stammering tone. "No, that's impossible. There is no Heaven. There's only death, nothingness, oblivion…"

As in the course of a combat in which one is mysteriously alerted to the adversary's secret weakness, I sensed at that moment that the moment of my revenge had come. I took full advantage.

"What do you know?" I proclaimed, drawing myself up to my full height authoritatively. "The décor, always the décor—that snow, that purity of atmosphere: he's found him-self at home. He's in Heaven, in Heaven... This is the moment when the experiment will become truly interesting, and we shall learn what no one has ever been able to learn. At this moment, he's singing the praises of God..."

And for the third time, Dirk uttered his double "Hosan-na!" I was almost convinced by it myself. Excitedly, I turned back to the doctor, and cried: "Do you understand? He can see God!"

I did not have to go on. The doctor's eyes turned up, his upper body stiffened in shock, and then he collapsed like a dead weight on the floor.

CHAPTER FOURTEEN

I lifted him up again, laid him on the leather-clad divan and bathed his temples with whisky. Dirk continued drinking, as if nothing had happened. I was looking for a hand-bell to summon help when the doctor came to.

"The fresh air caught me unawares after that heat," he said. "Will you close the window, please?"

His speech was slurred, and the pallor of his face against the background of brown leather was striking. A continuous tremor shook his right hand, which was extended alongside his body.

"Who should I call?" I asked.

"No one," he replied. "I'll be better momentarily."

"Nevertheless," I persisted, "A physician…"

"I know what it is." He tried to raise his left arm to the back of his neck, which must have been causing him pain.

I slipped a cushion under his shoulders.

"Awfully sorry to put you out," he muttered. With all his might, he tried to collect himself. "Take Dirk back, I beg you," he asked, then.

When I returned, I found him sitting on the divan. He had made an effort to get up; he was still grimacing.

"Danger of hemiplegia on the right side," he murmured. And he gave voice to a little click of the tongue to emphasize the gravity of the diagnosis.

"I'll ring for someone to carry you to your bed," I decided.

"Never, never," he protested. "I don't need anything; I don't trust anyone. It will all be better momentarily. If you want to oblige me, sit down. Let's have a chat to try to see things clearly. You'll help me to think—my head still feels heavy."

He closed his eyes and passed his left hand repeatedly over his face, which was creased like the skin of a pachyderm.

"You said something very stupid in speaking of Heaven just now, Pierre…"

I knew full well that that was the irritant point, but I wasn't going to abandon a dominant position out of pity for his condition. He had taken a beating, physically and morally, but I sensed that he was still tough.

"How, then, do you explain that Dirk is dead, but that he can speak?" I asked him.

"I can't explain it yet; that's why I need to think." He laughed mockingly. "Heaven! But that's the opposite of what I've thought my entire life. I've never ceased to turn my back on it, on Heaven—and I won't, for the sake of a few exclamations let slip…"

"But the experiment," I persisted. "Your experiment…people find what they weren't looking for—that's almost the rule in any scientific investigation."

When I pronounced the word "experiment," he opened his eyes again and fixed me with a long round-eyed stare. He wanted to see whether I was speaking seriously, whether I might be seeking to deceive him by latching on to his weakness. He was committed to his "experiment," the old fox, and he found himself caught in a dilemma: either cease to believe in his experiment, or accept its conclusions.

He shook his head. "It's scarcely probable that I shall ever believe in Heaven. I make mock of it, of Heaven—it's the Earth that interests me."

He was, however, far from presenting a fair countenance to the Earth.

Forthrightly, with an authority all the more definitive because it was a matter of indifference to me, I declared: "Then the experiment is concluded."

A twitch ran across his face. His heart must have been hurting, for he raised his good hand to his breast to forage inside his waistcoat. There was some cruelty on my part in torturing that old man with diminished power of thought, whose pride was—I sensed rather than thought—suffering, because he had become my plaything, and saw me adopting a casual attitude toward him. I was about to stop exploiting my success and abandon the game when a sharper stab of pain caused his head suddenly to jerk backwards.

He began: "Yvane. It was…" Then a second fainting-fit caused him to lose consciousness for a few seconds.

"A drink," he said, on coming round.

I filled a glass, which I had to hold up to his lips.

"The tablets in the little box, there on my desk."

I followed his indications.

"Two," he said.

He took them, and swallowed them with a mouthful of water. His eyes never left me, staring at me in a jaundiced and malicious fashion. He resented me more than ever; I could feel it…but of what was he resentful? Perhaps being able to move freely, being healthy, and fundamentally indifferent to his physical and moral torment. The most curious thing was that he still refused to let me call anyone, and insisted that I remain alone with him.

The tremor in his right hand, which he had concealed in the pocket of his jacket, was incessant. It had even reached his head, even though it was supported by the back of the divan, and a slight periodic creaking of the leather broke the silence of the room, like a cricket in the woodwork.

"How droll life is," he murmured. "One gets used to things, to people, without perceiving them. Through the house runs a little animal, lively, amusing, silent, a well-behaved child, whom one suddenly sees coming to a halt in doorways, wondering if she might come in. Once, going along a corridor, I stood on her doll's plates. There was a flood of tears; I picked her up and put her on my knee to comfort her. I caressed her head, her fine hair, tied up in a red ribbon…that must have been when it all began."

He was mumbling, in a thick voice that I had difficulty following. I thought he was becoming delirious, but he opened his eyes and he gaze fell upon me, harsh and very keen—a gaze that made no appeal for pity, and before which I instinctively put myself on guard.

"Yvane," he said, without taking his eyes off me. "It was me who killed her."

I succeeded in remaining impassive. The hostility of his gaze had warned me that it was necessary to expect a direct blow. Not one of my eyelashes quivered. To tell the truth, I didn't understand immediately, and before the full meaning of the confession got through to me, I only realized why I was still there, what obscure force had kept me in the presence of that half-dead old man. Now I knew, and my first impression was almost one of relief.

He had closed his eyes again before my impassive face. He went on, stammering, searching for his words.

"A rival is born—that's something from a novel. It doesn't matter—there's truth in it. The same image revives, fresher and younger, next to the old one, which fades away without one being aware of it. The little hand that disappears into the large paw that one holds out grows bigger day by day. The voice becomes nuanced, the mid becomes more precise; something entirely new is there, in a bud that will blossom. It's a recommencement, one is gripped again by things that one held fifteen years before. One is unaware of one's own aging—and then, one asks for nothing, save for a presence, and that diffuse impression of contentment, of lightness, that the mere sight of a gracious face procures. One is also without suspicion.

"She lifted up her hair to braid it in spirals behind her ears. It was her first grown-up hair-do; she asked me if it suited her. Everything suited her; my smile was my reply. That was in a boat; we were coming down the Rhine during the holidays, leaning on the rail. Her ear, bitten by the cold wind, went pink. We were making the voyage together, a philopena that I had lost.[7] I'd bought a large umbrella, of which she made fun.

---

[7] Philopena (*philippine* in French) is a question-and-answer game in which the loser must pay a forfeit.

"One doesn't know, one never knows anything of what is happening, fundamentally. What was I searching for in books, in the laboratory? I forgot to live in trying to divine the secrets of life. But others were living in my stead, and to watch others live, when one loves them, is sufficient. We had our first secrets—it was me who covertly gave her money to buy her first car. One day, when she was preparing for her baccalaureat, she came to ask me to explain the nervous system to her, in a few words. She was preparing for the oral, and was afraid, so timid was she. The nervous system, in a few words!"

He opened his eyes to say: "She was sitting where you are, listening with a touching good will to explanations that had never been so confused. It pained me to see her forehead furrowed attentively because of my clumsiness in expressing myself. Those wrinkles hollowed out between her eyebrows were still child-like; that was the only sign that my words could awaken in her face...

"When death determined that we remained alone, I kissed her through the veil of mourning, I knew the taste of her tears. For myself, I didn't weep, I wasn't in pain. I wasn't aware of a displacement of affection. Life went on. Every day I was struck by the increasing resemblance to her mother. It wasn't only her arms and her gait, but the expressions on her face, her little habits, the way she threw her hat aside when she came into the hallway, the same musical intonation in long words, her liking for the same flowers, the same delight punctuated by hesitations and reticences, and an occasional bizarre sadness in her gaze. The woman I had always loved was still present. She kept the house with a touching application. We scarcely talked to one another—I didn't know what to say to her. Certain attentions, filial in inspiration, charmed me. When you appeared, I hated you immediately, for it was only at that moment that I began to understand. It was necessary for me to fight; I fought.

"I fought. I never recovered from finding the sickness so profound and deep-rooted for such a long time. I employed every possible means: reasoning, moral rigidity, obsessive work; I went so far as to treat myself, in order to sterilize certain zones of my sentimental imagination! Why did I continue to refuse to accept the inevitable? Without mentioning insurmountable obstacles, I was old, and my prestige was too fragile by comparison with a single youthful smile. I fought. Nature laughs heartily at our determination. The more I shut myself up in the laboratory in order to forget, the more the sickness tormented me. What miseries are hidden beneath the most indifferent appearances! An old fool with the soul of a child! A horrible jealousy devoured me. My last chance in life was escaping me without my being able to prevent it. It was necessary. I had to consent to it. Why, then, did you come to tell me what was going to happen?"

I listened in spite of myself, sickened and as if crushed by a particular kind of horror. With the pronouncement of Yvane's name, I had felt all the memories engraved in my mind come to life again. The image that I had believed dead, or distant, regained its presence, the flesh of my flesh. And if I still did not react more extravagantly, it was because my whole mind and body were no more than a confused and dolorous mass, and because the awakening of that pain occupied me entirely.

"I fought. In doing so, I came to consider you as a savior. You were helping me, without knowing it, to fight the good fight. I encouraged your meetings. I hoped that things would work out, that, sensing that she was more attracted to you with every passing day, seeing her acquire from someone else a happiness that I could never hope to give her, I would get used to it…

"I didn't get used to it. The jealousy, far from being extinguished, became even more unbearable. I was not so much jealous of you, nor of her, but of the youth that you both had, of the youth that authorized you to show your sentiments in broad daylight and without shame, while at my age, under pain of being an object of repulsion and disgust, they had to be buried.

"Yvane no longer even saw me; I bored her; she scarcely appeared at meals. She withdrew from my life. I could not reconcile myself to that void. I came to think that I would have preferred to see her die...why, then, did you come at that moment? Why did you notify me that it was going to happen? You revealed to me what I was going to do, which I didn't yet suspect myself...and once I knew, what point was there in fighting? What was the point of my anguish? I was marked for the frightful task,[8] I had to succumb. There was nothing to divert me, to tempt me. From that day on, I stopped fighting. It was you who pushed me over the edge, you who pronounced the sentence of destiny upon me."

So, not content to display his ignominy, he was claiming...

"You're vile!" I shouted at him.

"I know," he said. "I don't care." And his half-paralyzed face creased into a sort of smile. But why was he smiling?

He had succeeded in plunging me back into a nightmare. I was the one who, horrified in the face of his monstrous calmness, at the idea of a possible culpability, felt a criminal anguish squeezing my heart. He was humming now, and, believe me, his voice took on a near-triumphant tone.

"I loved her, I killed her, as they say in the assize court. "With a few nuances, I could say as much—and you, too, could say as much. Our means were different—but dead, she belongs as much to one of us as to the other. She belongs to anyone who can evoke her memory, and I hold a trump card that you don't have. Dirk is dead—in Heaven, you say; well, my dear Pierre, he'll give me news of Yvane before you..."

I could not restrain myself. I passed from horror to disgust, from repulsion o the desire to use both hands to wring the wrinkled neck from which that frightful confession had

---

[8] I have translated this phrase literally, but it is worth noting that the French *tâche* [task] is phonetically identical to *tache* [stain], a tacit double meaning emphasized by the use of the term *marqué* [marked].

emerged, with rattles in the throat and expulsions of phlegm. I got to me feet abruptly. For an instant, I hesitated. Then I slapped him twice, with all my strength. His head wobbled from right to left and from left to right against the back of the divan. I marched to the door. Behind me, a raucous sound rose up within the room.

He was laughing.

CHAPTER FIFTEEN

I slammed the door, and fled into the corridor. I no longer wanted to see anything or hear anything. The mud that had just been stirred up never ceased to give off noxious poisons. It seemed to me to be saturated with them, to the utmost depths of my being. That which I had treasured more than anything else in the world would henceforth be utterly soiled. When I had believed that I was living on a level a little higher than the ordinary, I awoke floundering in a muddy pool and nameless horrors.

A hand was placed on my arm; I shook it off.

"What's the matter, Pierre?"

Narda was trying to stop me as I passed by. "Where are you going? I was waiting for you—I wanted to talk to you…"

"I'm going away," I replied, brutally. "I'm going away—don't ask me for anything more." And almost running, I went out on to the road beyond the gate, in order to flee as quickly as possible.

She followed me. "At least tell me what happened! One would think that you were afraid."

"I'm going away. I don't want to have anything to do with this place any longer. Your uncle is a monster. If I have any advice to give you, it's to do as I do. Find relatives or friends to take you in—don't stay in this house for another hour."

I spoke without turning round, as if I were being pursued. She trotted along beside me.

"Come on—I need an explanation," she declared.

It was difficult for me to give her an explanation as complete as was necessary. I could at least say something, though. While striding on at a rapid pace, I told her the whole story of Dirk, the roulette, the Bourse, the doctor's experiment, everything that I had seen and everything that he had told me.

And then a sentence emerged from that naïve mouth which brought me to an abrupt halt.

"And you believed him?" she said, ironically.

"What?" I stammered. "Did I believe him? I had to…" At the same time, though, for the first time, doubt sprang forth in my mind like a lightning-flash. Why had I not asked the question that Narda posed so candidly before? Had I allowed myself to be deceived, like the worst of imbeciles?

"I'm almost sure that he's never won at roulette or on the Bourse," Narda went on. "I receive the mail, and I've never found any evidence there that he's acquired the fortune you attribute to him. Without being constrained, our situation is far from being as brilliant as one might believe."

That simple factual information, given in a frank voice and with a smile, shook me again. I had never actually witnessed the gains that the doctor had told me he had won at roulette. On reflection, however, the hypothesis of a deception was impossible. "But after all," I protested, "there are other things. I've witnessed experiments. I've seen your uncle operate. His knowledge and sincerity are beyond doubt."

"Oh, I've had abundant opportunity to observe that he doesn't doubt it," Narda went on. "I believe that he's sincere, but he's deceiving himself. That's what I wanted to discuss with you, and that's why I asked you to come. Gradually, he's convinced himself that he can know the future. The future! Come on—that's impossible! I don't understand all the scientific explanations at all. That he's rendered Dirk stupid is certain—but what's also probable is that the ease with which the poor fellow is amenable to suggestion has done the rest, and has permitted my uncle to delude himself. The interest that you've appeared to take in his studies might also have provoked him, with all the sincerity in the world, to deceive you. He's been acting out a comedy, and he's ended up believing it himself."

"But then…" I said.

"Yes," she said, "I think he's mad, possessed by a curious folly. He's become the prisoner of his simulation—or, if you prefer, he's gone mad by virtue of being able to believe in his experiment. I wanted him to be examined unawares by a specialist physician. You could have introduced, as one of your friends, a doctor in whom we could have confidence."

I stood there, by the side of the road. The doctor was mad. That seemed almost obvious now. By the same token, that madness removed any value from his frightful confession, and his accusations. He had been delirious while speaking to me a little while ago. I began to breathe more freely. At the same time, listening to Narda speak procured me a curious impression of relief. Her common sense brought me back to reality. It was admirable that a head not yet twenty years old had seen clearly at first glance, which such convincing lucidity, in a situation in which I had sunk into the mud.

"In truth, Narda, what you say would explain many things. I should have thought of it sooner. But what led you to think that...?"

"It seems quite natural to me. While you were ill, I talked to the physicians that were in charge of you. I also saw other patients. I noticed that mad people almost never appear to be mad...and I made the connection."

It was, however, necessary to make sure. Now I was the one who wanted to proceed urgently to the psychiatric examination that Narda had suggested. I didn't lose a moment. I took one of the doctors at the clinic where I had been cared for to one side and explained the case to him. That afternoon we returned to the villa, on the pretext of paying a friendly call on Dr. Mops.

A strange noise greeted us at the entrance. One might have thought that it was an accordion of harmonium. The servants seemed to be absent. I took Narda's place marching at the front and headed for the first floor. The noise became clearer: music composed of percussive notes, a sort of brisk dance, wild and refined at the same time, evoking the spirits of the air: a ballet of sparks. Where had I heard music like that before?

Without knocking, I opened the double door of the study, and a gust of incense hit me in the face. The room was full of thick white vapor. Gradually, the air current dissipated it. In one corner, two Javanese men were crouching in front of their xylophones, tapping out as hard as they could the Balinese tunes with which the cremation of cadavers is accompanied out there. But a large organ was suddenly unleashed in the smoke. A voice, in which the doctor's timbre was recognizable, began to sing:

"*Au ciel! Au ciel! Au ciel!*
"*J'irai la voir un jour....*"[9]

Then we perceived Dirk in the midst of the smoke, sitting in front of a bottle of whisky, and finally, the doctor himself. He had turned up to the maximum a gramophone that was playing a record by Franck. Having put on a long white smock over his clothes, with his head tilted back toward the ceiling, he was reeling off all the religious songs he knew:

"*Esprit sain, descendez en nous…*"[10]

As the Javanese had ceased striking their instruments at the sight of us, he noticed us, and aimed a revolver at them. "In the name of God, play!" he roared.

The *Béatitudes*, howled in a furious fashion, continued to rend our ears. The odor of incense was unbreathable.

"There's no need to see any more," the physician whispered in my ear.

---

[9] This is the first couplet of a popular French religious song; the person that the singer is looking forward to seeing in Heaven is the Virgin Mary. The song's composer is unknown; its accompaniment here by the music of César Franck is presumably cited in the interests of deliberate incongruity.

[10] This is a deliberate misrendering of the first line of another French religious folk-song. The actual version begins "*Esprit saint*" [Holy spirit], but omitting the t renders the phrase reminiscent of the common expression *sain d'esprit* ["of sound mind", or simply "sane"]. The subsequent reference of the beatitudes (the blessings contained in two speeches by Jesus recorded in *Matthew* and *Luke*) is not to the words of the song; Mops is mixing up lines plucked at random from various sources.

I exchanges glances with Narda. The expression on her face was striking. It rendered the sentiment I inspired by the scene exactly: a resigned sadness. Her calmness had not been mistaken; she had found the right note instinctively.

It was necessary to draw closer to the maniac, whose back was turned to us. Suddenly, he perceived me. "No, no" he cried. "No murderers in Heaven!"

The words were lost in the brief struggle that followed. Soon, a special vehicle took Dirk and the doctor away.

After that abrupt denouement, I found myself alone at the hotel where my suitcases were waiting for me. The thoughts that had inevitably been displaced somewhat during the afternoon's comings and goings return to assail me. The doctor's insanity threw glimmers into the past that completely altered its lighting and significance. If he could be regarded as an irresponsible madman, the measure of involuntary responsibility that I had had in the events increased in proportion. "Murderer"—the last word that he had hurled at me, echoed for a long time within me. In that horrible adventure into which I had been dragged without understanding any of it, my role was revealed as frightful. I had been lacking in judgment and suspicion, to the point of directing the maniac toward his victim. Of what blindness had I given proof! I had seen nothing, sensed nothing of everything that was happening between the individuals with whom I had lived for weeks. Like an ignorant child, I had passed by the frightful secrets resident in other hearts without being aware of them, without being alerted to them, too egotistically wrapped-up and sequestered within my own sentiments. I had not wanted to see anything other than Yvane; I had only had eyes and thoughts for her; now I had to pay the price.

It was around Yvane that all those obscure forces were gravitating, to her that I returned again. Her phantom pressed me more closely than ever. And more than anything else, the thought broke my heart that, while I believed I was giving her all the love of which I was capable, I had only marked her for death. I horrified myself. The significance of my sentiments, the very ones that I had thought the noblest, appeared to me to be deceptive and frightful.

In spite of everything, it all remained obscure, as if too complicated for me. What parts of truth and falsehood were mingled in the doctor's words? Had he wanted to avenge himself on me by torturing me with terrible confidences invented wholesale, or had he confessed the truth in one last fit of lucidity? His madness did not explain everything. In the play of secret powers that we had all unleashed—me in allowing myself to be guided by my heart, the doctor by his mad research—Heaven and Hell seemed to lose their colors, to play their parts indifferently.

The fact also remained that certain predictions made by Dirk were strangely verified. Was it not to escape a new prophecy that I had decided, the previous evening, to flee? Might not Narda's rectitude of thought and cold lucidity, which had pleased and reassured me, be one more trap? Why had I promised to help her? Where was the error? Where was the truth? The excessively clear explanations that she gave left out too many things, too many nuances to which, in spite of everything, I felt attached. And was she not prowling around me like a new threat? I no longer knew what to think; I was frightened. Living in that atmosphere, I felt that I was in danger of ending up like the doctor. It was necessary to abandon everything, to renounce seeing clearly, to leave, to have a change of scene, to forget.

CHAPTER SIXTEEN

Three months passed; my leave was coming to an end. After a few days in a rest home, where inactivity had done me more harm than good. I embarked on a tiresome winter crossing to the Canaries, then accompanied a friend I had made on an automobile journey across the Sahara. I saw many faces, many horizons, deserts and seas, but I could not forget. Remorse pursued me incessantly. The entire human race seems always to be carrying out a duty of expelling from its bosom that which honors it. But even I, no more than anyone else, in spite of all my love and what I thought to be a sophisticated understanding, had not been capable of saving the most delicate and most marvelously sensitive creature that had ever seen the light of day. More than that, I had been chosen, as if by the gods, to be the instrument of her annihilation. I could not get over that.

Although, with time, my despair had taken on a less precise and lees acute form, less attached to those details that the memory retrieves to pierce the heart, and I had moved on to vaguer, more abstract considerations, the memory of Yvane still occupied my thoughts fully, like an infinite chain of mountains, so imposing that no matter how far one moves away from them, they nevertheless mark the entire landscape with their character.

I had anticipated that a certain pride would enter into that desire to compose a great dolor for myself, but taking account of it did not signify any progress toward a cure. Whatever attitude I took, the fact remained that I had met the most exquisite of creatures, and that I had killed her. I was infinitely guilty. A certain dread of life, and a certain mistrust of myself, still paralyzed me. Every action seemed to engage my beyond my intention. I would have preferred not to leave the desert or the four walls of a room.

It was, however, necessary that I return to Paris in order to make my return journey to the Far East. One morning, I was

119

about to collect my mail from the American Express office when a tall brunette girl came toward me in the hall.

"Narda!" I said, surprised at first but then immediately embarrassed to see her again after the abrupt fashion in which I had left Lausanne—but she did not appear to be disposed to hold me to account for that. She accompanied me, chatting all the while, as far as the sidewalk of the Opéra. She explained that she was about to leave for South America, in the company of a Dutch family, and gave me abundant details of her future situation. Discreetly, she avoided any reference to the past, but one question was burning on my lips. I asked her for news of the doctor.

"He's in a nursing home—quite calm, but there's little hope of ever seeing him leave it."

"It's better thus," I said, becoming thoughtful again, "for he might be dangerous."

"Dangerous?" she said, in surprise.

It was my turn to be astonished that, with the sureness of judgment with which I credited her, she had not been alerted to that. After various allusions that, although clear, were not understood, I said straightforwardly: "After all, he was the one who killed Yvane."

"What?" she said. "What are you saying?"

"I'm only repeating what your uncle confessed to me." I added: "In order that Dirk's predictions should not be found at fault, he did not hesitate…" In spite of myself, my voice broke.

"But Pierre," she said, placing her hand on my arm, "what you say is impossible."

"He told me himself, and gave me reasons that I cannot repeat to you."

"His mind must already have been disturbed, and perhaps it was his bad conscience talking. He's a lunatic, but he's not a criminal. I'm absolutely sure that he didn't…"

Blushing with emotion, she could not finish her sentence. In the midst of the noise of the traffic, in the open area in front of the Opéra, that conversation took on a strange character.

I regretted having spoken, having dispelled the illusions of an innocent soul again. Decidedly, everything I did turned bad. But Narda resumed: "He didn't kill Yvane, since…"

"…It was an accident," I finished, evasively.

"No," said Narda, looking me in the eyes. "It wasn't an accident. Yvane killed herself."

A bus could have emerged from the entrance of the Metro and I would not have been so amazed. It required all the credit that I gave to Narda's precocious intellectual maturity, not to believe her, but to be persuaded that she really had pronounced the words I had just heard.

"Killed herself! Come on, that's impossible!"

"Yvane killed herself," Narda repeated, very calmly. "I know that because she left me a letter. The version of the accident having been accepted, I preferred to keep the secret to myself, but after what you've told me, you need to know the truth."

I shook my head again.

"If you'd care to accompany me to my hotel," she proposed, "I'll show you the letter."

I followed her, without seeing or hearing anything. When she said: "Here it is," I stopped, and let myself fall into a chair in the hallway.

She brought out a letter: a piece of white paper, folded in four. The large, irregular handwriting, with exaggerated capital letters, was definitely Yvane's. The sheet trembled in my hands, and I was obliged to lean my elbows on the table.

I read:

My darling, I'm dying because I want to die. I shall never come down from the mountain. When one has reached the summit of happiness, one can no longer accept going back. Don't weep, I have nothing to lament. I have seen and felt everything that it is necessary to see, and it's with an indescribable delight that I depart. Never have I been so happy. Be kind to Pierre. You are both of the race of the living. Yvane.

Facing me, pinned to the wall, was a poster for a shipping company depicting an African woman laden with bananas beside the bow of a ship. Through the open door, in the little street on the Left Bank where the hotel was located, I could see hatless women passing by, all carrying identical waxed-cloth bags, from which vegetables protruded. It was morning; a market must be close by. "It's truly curious," I said, "that all the women in a quarter resemble one another." At the desk, the manageress, a plump blonde, was rubbing the plate of glass in front of the counter with a rag, moving the telephone and a stack of papers from one side to the other in their turn. The bus going past in the neighboring street made the electric light-bulb hanging from the ceiling vibrate. I raised my head; fortunately, it was not directly above me. I uncrossed my legs, and the wicker armchair creaked under my weight. An old American woman presented herself, politely and modestly, and greeted the manageress—who, after a glance at the pigeon-holes, shook her head: there were no letters, no more today than yesterday, probably. Then I heard the sound of a vacuum cleaner on the upper floor, coming down the elevator shaft. The elevator wasn't working, in need of repair. On the rattan table that separated me from Narda, a large yellow ash-tray bearing an advertisement for an aperitif caught my eye. Yielding to the imperious solicitation, I lit a cigarette. Finally, I said: "Yes, yes…"

Thus, in that décor which I had not chosen, which I would never have been able to imagine, but which imposed itself upon me with a reality and a solidity that I had been unable to recognize in the surrounding world for many weeks, I felt the insistent phantom whose company held me prisoner in the past abandon me, at the same time as remorse. What relationship had the present décor of the world to the words of that poor letter, which I read once again? To what point in a vanished past was it trying to attach itself? The mountain, happiness—that was far away, far, far away beyond the sea. The residue of the stormy perturbation was fleeing into my internal sky. A great wind was blowing, bringing with it the quotidian

122

daylight. The familiar, the banal and the ordinary resumed possession of my life.

Narda was still talking.

"...like my Aunt Suyter, her grandmother, who also killed herself—perhaps you knew that? An oppressive heredity weighs upon the family. Poor Yvane, she was already bizarre as a child, and had to be put in a nursing home on several occasions. In her, fits of terrible depression followed instants of great excitement. After her mother's death she gave rise to great anxieties. My uncle had decided to keep her close to him, but his company was not designed to make things better. I had arrived at La Colle too recently to take clear account..."

Her voice resembled the noises of the street. Her hair was as black as the telephone-stand. The cretonne cushion of the armchair also gave the impression of a family-member with a corsage, because of its embroidered flowers. She went on talking. Her common sense was overwhelming and contagious. The clock opposite showed that it was 12:25 p.m.

"Well, shall we have dinner together?" I asked, abruptly.

She accepted without needing any persuasion. At the corner of the street, I took her arm. It was smooth and muscular.

"I know a little Italian restaurant..." she began.

The idea of that little restaurant suddenly illuminated me. I was hungry. I was aware of that for the first time in many months.

"An Italian restaurant?" I said. "I remember, one day in Boulogne...hang on...I ate...what was it called? It was marvelous...a mixture of pasta and vegetables...oh! It was *lasagne verdi*."

"Well, I believe that I saw the exact same thing on the menu!" she said, in a joyful explosion.

I was holding on to that arm very firmly; it was allowing itself to be held. "No! They have it!" I replied, laughing. "Then I love you!"

I was not, however, to marry her until much later, after the war. That erupted so abruptly into our lives that the entire drama that I have just recounted slipped away into the past before I could form a clear idea of it. In any case, I have been trying for a long time not to think too intensely about it, and the war at least had the merit of aiding me in that task. Thus, caught between so many proposed explanations, I have never been sure exactly how Yvane died, and why. Similarly, with respect to the doctor's experiment, I have never been able to determine with certainty how much truth was mixed in with the simulation. All things considered, I prefer not knowing. I've reported the facts; I shall leave to others the pretention of seeing them clearly and interpreting them. For my part, I limit myself to the disillusioned opinion with which I began: everything that happens is of no importance whatsoever, and it is only for the sake of vain mental satisfaction that one imagines a logical sequence in the course of events. There are so many equally plausible ways of representing things that I flatly refuse to adopt any one of them. And what I have seen during the war could not modify my way of thinking—or, rather, of not thinking.

THE EYE OF PURGATORY

CHAPTER ONE

Misfortune is definitely pursuing me. From the series of mishaps that has befallen me, I have even been able to conclude that the world has something particular against me. This morning, again, the vile Gugenlaert refused the canvas that I brought him, which he had virtually commissioned. His pretext: that his clients only like bright paintings. I'll give him bright painting! What does he think I am? Anyway, like all art dealers, Gugenlaert knows nothing about painting. No one knows anything about painting, not even those who do it.

Such blows make you disgusted with the work, and with yourself into the bargain. I came home with my canvas under my arm. Coward as I am, I have tried to do it over, to brighten it, to do what was required of me—but I soon perceived that it is impossible to match the image that others have of you, and I went out for a walk.

I found myself in the Rue de Rivoli, amid the stalls set up for the New Year exhibition. I told myself that I might perhaps find what I needed, among the crowd of hideous and rather grotesque individuals, for my great canvas, my Fairground Burlesque project—and I put on a show of being interested in improved taps, articulated broomsticks, Armenian paper, home-made sweets, glue for sticking plates together, and all the usual trash. There was a reek of acetylene, which was quite pleasant.

I stopped in front of a booth selling visiting cards to look at the display. Some specimens manifested pretentions to humor: ADAM ADAM, Rue de Paradis; MONSIEUR NEMO, Ship's captain; BERTHE LAVENTOUSE, qualified nurse—with a little red cross in relief to the right. In a whimsical vein, one could read in the middle of a frame of lilies, MADEMOI-SELLE L'INCONNUE, Rue de Seine...

The melancholy printer was wiggling his feet on top of an oil stove; from time to time he uttered his cry: "Two francs for 100, not even the cost of the paper!" He stood up suddenly; a client had pointed at one of the samples. It was an old man enveloped in a sort of greasy black overcoat, with a yellowing beard and medium-length hair protruding from a battered bowler hat. I noticed his aquiline profile and his eyes, sunken in their orbits: two veritable wells, toward which the forest of hair extended. If not for the bowler hat, he would have resembled Leonardo da Vinci.

He spelled out his name for the merchant: Christian Dagerlöff.

"Monsieur is a foreigner, I see. And the profession? The profession is 75 cents extra."

"Profession?"

"Men generally indicate their profession on their cards. This card is an instrument of trade."

"Put *génie*."[11]

"Engineer? Military, no doubt?"

"No, genius—man of genius, but genius will suffice."

At that moment, I burst out laughing. The old man turned toward me. His eyes were bright and translucent, an exceedingly pure aquamarine in color, with none of the opacity of old age. His white hair made the blue of the irises stand out. His gaze manifested the candor and vague reproof of a well-brought-up man.

"It's the *genius*," I explained.

"You don't know what genius is?" he said, in a voice that was slow and serious, but very confident.

"Yes, but I'm astonished that one can make a profession of it."

---

[11] There is an untranslatable double meaning here; the French word *génie* can mean "engineer" as well as "genius;" that is why the card-seller mistakes his customer's meaning.

His jaw stiffened beneath his beard. "Can you prove that I'm not a man of genius, young man? No. In that case, kindly refrain…"

The printer had activated the wheel of the press and slipped the cards into a little box with gilded strings. I was about to go on my way when the old man, abruptly pushing down his bowler hat, so that it swallowed up his white hair, said in a very courteous fashion: "Monsieur, to whom do I have the honor…?"

In order not to be wanting in politeness, I told him my name. Then, opening his freshly-wrapped parcel, my interlocutor held out the first of the hundred cards to me, before venturing, with a sigh: "I don't want to keep you, Monsieur Poldonski. Go, and plunge yourself back into the mire of the century…"

A certain curiosity, which I must have inherited from my poor crazy father, determined that, instead of going away, I sought to continue the conversation. There was a café within a few paces—one of those hideous modernized bistros in the vicinity of the Bastille, all ostentation, tingling with the desire to cut off thirst and inspiration. We went inside.

The customers were worthy of the place, as sticky as flies caught in the dirty foam of an old glass of beer. On a seat upholstered in crimson *breitschwanz*, my companion assumed, by contrast, a certain allure. The light filtered through faded lampshades with floral motifs brought out nuances of cobalt blue and carmine in the hollow surfaces of his cheeks. His head might have served as the cold patch that I saw in the foreground in the left-hand corner of my Fairground. Unobtrusively, I weighed him up.

"Perhaps you've categorized me as an eccentric," he said. "In life, I have chosen to think. Men, those animals that think, think so little that anyone who declines to observe such parsimony undoubtedly seems eccentric…"

He turned his head slightly, as if in order to address himself to empty space, and the contours of his face stood out even more clearly against the background of white hair. All things considered, he was less reminiscent of Leonardo than of Albrecht Dürer.

"In what direction does the activity of your thought tend?" I asked, distractedly, in the way that one chats with a model during a posing session.

"In all directions. In consequence of a particularly painful personal drama, however, toward the truth…" He hesitated momentarily before continuing. "My attention is specifically focused on the problem of life and death."

"Ah! The problem of life and death…" In spite of myself, irony crept into my voice.

He must have sensed that I was not taking him seriously, and got to his feet. "Such a conversation is in contrast with the décor that surrounds us. Everything here is in the colors of Pernod and Calvados, which are not exactly those of the mind. You see, by taking an interest in anything but a tin trumpet designed for mustard, or an apparatus intended to dispense mayonnaise, one is making oneself seem a stranger to one's century. Oh, if only this century could, in fact, make us as strange as we deserve to be!"

I parted company with him, a trifle disappointed; I had hoped for more amusement. He left me in an even worse mood than before I had met him, having shown me that I did not have a monopoly on hostility to the world. Is the hypochondria with which I am trying to flatter myself anything but the acrimony of future failure? That is what I am asking myself in my studio, in which the fire is going out, at the moment when, in order to get a better measure of the nullity of the day, I am amusing myself by writing this vain record of it…

Oh, if I could only wake up tomorrow full of enthusiasm for work, equipped with true genius—and not the old man's kind!

Hope is decidedly tenacious within the human heart! It is the measure of its stupidity!

The run of bad luck continues. To begin with, this morning was Sunday, a day of which I have always had a horror.

Then again, to begin the day, there was a letter from my mother, the first in eight months. She's getting married again, out there in Argentina. The change of continent has not put more sense in her head. I wonder how many more she might yet rack up.

When a mother marries again, it is as if one is losing her. Here I am, an orphan. I am so stupid that I cannot rejoice in it. My father must be laughing in his coffin. I imagine that, if he could give some advice to his successor, he would have a great deal to say. Mad as he was, the last time I went to see him in the asylum, he spoke to me quite sanely about his wife. Curiously enough, he did not seem to realize that he was talking about my mother. Perhaps he no longer realized that I was his son? My mother seemed scarcely to be aware of it either; she has never seemed to understand that I might love her…

I wanted to devote my Sunday morning to physical work and bring a little order to my studio. Armande, my girl-friend, soon arrived, taking me by surprise. I had forgotten that it was the day when I was liable to be interrupted by her. Finding me in a bad mood, she talked non-stop, about her workplace, the clothing store, and her customers. Oh, what do I care about her clothing store! I made a semblance of listening, but I was thinking how ignoble the habit is that gives an individual the right to pour out her everyday thoughts in front of you: tedious, monotonous, idiotic gossip that crushes you with its worthlessness. The inside of a head that gets carried away, self-confidently, is much more annoying than a body. That's why I like easy women and brief adventures: such a companion does not have time to paralyze me with her stupidity; she merely delivers a wedge of flesh, without commentary.

We dined in the studio. I only have two knives, one good and one poor. When Armande sets the table, she never fails to giver herself the poor knife. Stupid as I am, I always find that persistent and mute delicacy touching…but it is insufficient to make me tolerate more than two hours of her company. I offered my work as an excuse. She pretended to believe it, picked up her handbag, hat and umbrella. I know she thinks that I never do anything—and is not entirely mistaken, moreover—but, sensing the state of my nerves, she took care not to let on. The tranquility and ease with which she yielded irritated me. All too obviously, she was humoring me like an invalid.

After her departure, I tried to get down to work and make a sketch of the man of genius from memory. It didn't happen, of course. I was suffering from a kind of residual wrath—not to mention the Sunday tedium that was oozing out of the walls…

Chancing to find Dagerlöff's card again, I decided to pay him a visit in order to refresh my visual memory and eventually to be able to make use of him as a model. He lives in the Rue Quincampoix.

"Fifth floor, facing door," the concierge told me, with sufficient astonishment that I gathered that visitors were few and far between.

The staircase gave off an odor that made me hold my breath. On the floor in question, I found one of the visiting cards that I had seen him order pinned to the door. The old man had added a handwritten inscription: "Please knock hard, because of the occupant's deafness."

I acted in conformity with the prescription, and the occupant came to open the door.

"Excuse me…" I began, raising my voice.

"I'm not deaf," he said, immediately. "The instruction on the door simply serves to allow me to estimate, by the manner of their knock, the moral quality of my visitors…"

I pronounced a polite sentence to explain my visit.

"The best way of forgiving you," he said, interrupting me, "is to take up my meditation at the point I had reached, dispensing with the customary banalities. Follow me."

The room was cluttered with piles of books and miscellaneous objects. He went to sit down in an armchair positioned with its back to an old electric standard lamp, set between a table loaded with papers and an empty cage. Laid flat along the wall was a doll: an old doll with soft limbs, sad and out of place. My host stretched out his legs in front of a little cast-iron stove before rearranging an Algerian blanket, in which dust was attempting to conceal the ravages of mites, over his knees.

"What do you think about voyages? That's where I was up to…"

I found myself paralyzed by the dread of knocking over the pile of books that rose up next to me. One of the legs of the chair on which I had sat down was showing signs of weakness. The mute presence of the doll, to my right, also disturbed me.

"Voyages?"

"Yes, in space…" he continued, widening his blue eyes, whose youthful color was not in harmony with the dilapidation of the décor. "Not the voyages of the Cook agency, but those that might be made in three-dimensional space, to the Moon, to Venus…"

"To tell the truth, I don't think about them at all."

"You're right. Such voyages are pure folly. What good would it do to discover new Americas, new planets? Going to Courbevoie or Sirius is exactly the same thing, exhausting in tedium and monotony; pain and death await us there as they do here. There's a passage in the *Imitation* that I could read you if it were the time for quotations… Let's leave voyages in space to the imagination of schoolboy dreamers. Let's pass on to voyages in time. What do you think of travels in time?"

Getting into character, I replied: "Such voyages are pure folly."

"You said it!" he cried, wiggling his toes in pleasure within the old slippers that were caressing the stove. "Voyages in space, voyages into the past or the future, poor human dreams deprived of imagination, deprived even of common sense… As for time, we travel with it, at a speed of 24 hours a day; that's quite sufficient to go toward death. The future can only resemble the past, and the past isn't amusing—our fore-fathers died of boredom with it. Eternal hopeful voyagers that

131

we are, though, are there other voyages we might possibly undertake?"

I looked at the stove, the empty cage, the doll—it had a green dress—and the door to a neighboring room standing ajar, allowing a glimpse of an improbable heap of dishes in a vast sink. Mechanically, I said: "There are voyages around my room."[12]

He uttered a theatrical cry of pain, and a mime of despair appeared on his face. "Stop thinking, I beg you. It would be better simply to follow me. Well, yes, there are other voyages, precisely those about which I was thinking before being interrupted by the blows you struck upon my door. Space and time are the first two categories. You understand me—you've been to school?"

"I'm a painter…"

"Don't say another word!" he exclaimed, in commiseration. "I'll reply for you. School informs us that there is, after space and time, a third category: causality. Why shouldn't one undertake voyages in causality?"

With all the good will of which a voice might be capable, strengthened by the experience of madmen that I had acquired in looking after me poor father, I exclaimed: "Yes, of course! Why shouldn't one undertake voyages in causality?"

"I'm burning my Charentaise slippers, damn it!" he shouted at that moment, abruptly withdrawing his leg in order to rub his reddened toe.

I couldn't help smiling.

"Don't be incredulous. I sense that you're more interested than you're trying to seem… We were talking about causality. What is causality? The connection between cause and effect. There are clouds; it will rain. I go into the water; I'm going to drown myself. The Earth rotates around the Sun, tomorrow will be similar to today. Causal links everywhere around me. The world is causal. No miracles. I enclose the

---

[12] The reference is to Xavier de Maistre's *Voyage autour ma chambre* (1794), a novel parodying early travel literature.

world in the causal vision that I obtain from it...but don't think that the world, the true world, gives a damn about causality. Does the snow care whether it comes from frozen water? And steam would be quite astonished if it were told about its parent, water. One could claim the inverse with as much reason. This world might have an aspect other than the causal. One might dress it in another garment entirely, and come to see it in a whole new outfit, an overcoat, a leotard, a toga— what do I know? That would be making a voyage in causality, an excursion into the 'thing in itself,' as the philosophers say."[13]

My opinion of him was confirmed. Lunatic or not, though, he could serve me as a model equally well. The quasi-lunar radiation that his hair acquired within the rather somber room confirmed my intention. But his honeyed tone, his hammy manner, and—above all—the direct and seemingly-absorbent gaze that he directed at me, gave me the feeling that he was also weighing me up. What, then, did he want from me?

"You doubt the integrity of my faculties," he continued. "All the same, you're an artist. And what is it to be an artist, a poet, if not to escape the everyday appearance of the world in order to attempt to other approaches to reality? After their fashion, men of your type are attempting voyages in causality. They want to escape the prison of the familiar world, but their strength lets them down and they fall back into it. They return to their point of departure; they set forth on the railway of dreams, but the train does not leave the station; the rocket does not get off the ground, the adventure fails... The artistic expe-

---

[13] To be precise, it was Immanuel Kant who drew a crucial distinction between the world of phenomena—i.e. the world as we experience it via our senses—with the world of *noumena*, or "things in themselves." It does not seem to be the case, however, that seeing the world in another guise would constitute an approach to its *noumenal* reality, so Dagerlöff's argument is more than a trifle shaky.

riment has failed, just as the poetic experiment has failed! Artists and poets have not found the means of escape, have not reached the limit beyond which they will escape the glue of the world. They sing of love, the joys of the flesh, life triumphant. A fatal error. Instead of letting oneself fall prey to the attraction of the world, it is necessary to experience a definite repulsion for it."

The inspirational tone that he presumed to be adopting was annoying me. I had had enough of his speeches and of serving as his audience. I resolved to take a strong line with him.

"Everything that you say is false," I declared. "If one were not held to the Earth by the attraction it generates, I, for one, would have taken flight for the stars a long time ago. I don't love anything or anyone—not even myself. Human beings only inspire me with disgust, and I spit on life as we have made it. Nevertheless, as you see, I'm still here, and I'm quite simply going to take the stairs, to take my leave."

He murmured: "Is that really certain? Is that really certain?" I had intended to squash him, but he seemed very cheerful. His blue eyes lit up, illuminating the whole room. In a fit of frankness, I asked him straight out whether he would consent to pose in my studio. He offered the excuse that he was busy.

"Where do you work, then?"

"At the Pasteur Institute."

"A doctor?" I exclaimed, without hiding my rather impolite surprise.

"No." And, after a pause, he said emphatically: "I'm a laboratory assistant." He might have told me that he was a Cardinal, or the President of the Republic, without adopting a different tone.

I came out of his lair with the beginnings of a migraine, which deprived me of any scant appetite for work that I might have had. I had winkled out a great model there! With his stories, he had cut off all my inspiration! I wasted the rest of the day in the neighborhood cafés.

Met Babar, full of his customary aperitifs and projects that never lead to anything. Within two minutes, he proposed to collaborate with me on a poster, to decorate a little bistro, and to form an under-thirty group. Between projects, he dipped his trunk into his perennial glass. Such projects weary me, and if I get involved in them, they always fail. He was surrounded by jokers who gave as good as they got, discussing social influences on the composition of the palette, and telling fashionable tall stories. That sort of herd life sickens me. They're all compressed into a mass, heaped up like lovesick toads. When one picks up one of them, he becomes ten, or twenty. They warm up their mediocrity and future failure by rubbing against one another. I told them so straight out. Babar laughed, and replied: "You have no vocation either. All true painters are optimists…"

"One can't be an optimist when one sees mugs like yours," I retorted, and I left.

Those poor fellows spend their time paddling in saucers. The company of their peers seems to take the place of work, talent, and everything else…

The sight of them annoys me. I don't want to see them anymore.

CHAPTER TWO

This afternoon, a little model came to introduce herself, courtesy of Babar. He told me about it yesterday, but I forgot. The studio wasn't very warm, and I hesitated over asking her to take her clothes off. The poor child was thin: skin and bone. Eighteen years old, though. I made a few sketches of her, but her thinness was scarcely inspiring. "My mother works in a bleaching factory," she told me, "but she's getting old now. The water gives her blisters on her hands." Always these miseries of the life that you pursue…

Like all the rest, she wanted to see the drawings I had made of her. "Really? That's how you see me? How ugly I am!"

"What about you? How do you see me?" I demanded, annoyed by her stupidity—to which I have had, nevertheless, to become accustomed.

She looked at me for a long time before replying: "You lack that little glow of life in the eyes."

Poor mite, she can't see the interior flame that I hide in order not to blind everyone. I can't see it myself, but I sense it brooding there—and look out when my genius bursts forth in broad daylight! At any rate, the chit's reflection has given me an idea for an etching: a corpse drawing a skeleton, a subject worthy of Goya.

I risked a few moves before she got dressed again. She only made a minimal fuss, but I lacked impetus—and the thought that Babar had probably already paraded his trunk over that bag of bones ended up leaving me cold. I even felt a shiver of repulsion, which caused her to say: "Are you cold too?"

I paid her; she left. Immediately, I threw the sketches I had just made on to the fire; even in effigy, I could not keep a pullet caressed by Babar in my apartment.

Stretched out on my divan, dreaming under the influence of what that old madman Dagerlöff had said, I wondered what attached me to the world. The answer came to me forcefully: women! It was by desire that I was rooted in the stinking compost of human beings and life. I had a little notebook, in which I stupidly inscribed the initial of a forename after each new adventure. I amused myself by counting them; I found a total of 299 forenames, and checked it three times: 299. I found that such a herd does not leave much residue in the imagination—and suddenly, that number, that sum of my escapades, filled me with sadness. Summarized in three figures was my destiny as a hunting dog, long dismal excursions in an endless labyrinth of side-streets, all that time wasted in a thousand wakes…

Why that interminable pursuit? Searching for what? For whom? Was it even a search? I wasn't looking for anything. There was no definite individual to find. I was following my instinct, like an animal. An instinct, a thing without a face. And it had me in its grip, rather than me following it. I was being pursued, tracked by an anonymous desire…

To escape the bitter depression of that chain of reasoning, I went downstairs, and at the counter of the first bistro I had a glass of brandy, then another. Then I buttoned up my coat and went out on to the boulevard. The last glimmers of the sunset were passing between translucent motionless clouds, brushing the roofs of the city with the delicacy of an angel's robe.

Instead of going back up to the studio, I wanted to stretch my legs a little, and to soothe my eyes with the translucent mist spreading through the atmosphere. I went through the Luxembourg gardens, from which the last students were emerging, and across the Seine, green, flat and somber between its banks, where the first street-lamps were lighting up. I went as far as the Tour Saint-Jacques, whose gargoyles had been leaning since time immemorial over a swarm of easy girls… It was a diabolical temptation!

On the terrace of a café, I had another drink, on the fringe of a crowd dressed up for a celebration. I was feeling even more indecisive than usual, troubled and depressed by my recent meditation, when, abruptly confronted by a Valkyrie in black satin who was swinging a silvery rabbit-fur stole with the insolence of a winning gambler over a Rubensesque rotundity, a voice rose up within me: "There's the 300th!" The figure 299 seemed as ridiculous to me at that moment as the 4.95s of the nearby bazaar. I needed a round number.

The change of mood that followed was catastrophic. Curiously enough, my resentment rebounded on Dagerlöff. He was the one who, with his speeches, had turned my thoughts toward women; it was because of him that I felt myself pursued by a procession of three hundred phantoms, a cohort of furies who seemed to be calling for help to all their sisters in the world, to destroy me, to extinguish my flame little by little, to end up pushing me, cold, useless and empty, into the Inferno. A disquiet, a fear extending as far as anguish, rose up within me…I sensed the advent of a crisis. At the first pharmacist's shop I came to, I bought my usual drug.

The capsules worked. I took another two, and sleep arrived.

I was still asleep when the doorbell woke me up. I thought that the concierge was bringing me a letter. The old bag rarely came up, and only when she scented through the envelope that it was a matter of bad news: bills, tax demands—she never missed a single one. Ordinary letters she was content to give me when I passed by her lodge. At the second ring, I went to open the door. It was Dagerlöff.

It was 8 a.m. The studio was freezing. I plunged back beneath my bedclothes, sighing: "You're the very last person I was expecting…"

"I know. A person of my age and my sex has lost all hope of being expected…"

"Do you know what time it is?"

138

"What does the time matter! My dear Monsieur Poldons-ki, my genius has finally had its reward: you see before you a thinker at the instant when he has just made the greatest discovery of his career. Have you ever tried to catch a fly?"

Huddled behind the rampart of my bedclothes, my only reply was a troubled stare.

"The threatened fly takes flight ahead of your hand, as if it had divined your intention. An observation so simple and so banal that it might seem trivial, discouraging any prolongation of reflection—but an observation, nevertheless, that contains the seed of the most remarkable discovery to be made in this world…

"Have you ever, perchance, while walking in the fields, caught sight of a crow or a magpie, and made the playful gesture of aiming your stick at the bird as if it were a gun? It takes flight, as if you had just taken aim with a rifle. I could multiply examples, but I prefer to give you the brilliant explanation of all these behaviors right away: animal species do not all live in the same time!"

"Ah," I said, in a perfectly neutral tone.

"Why should human time be that of animals? The crow and the fly, living in advance of our time, foresee our gestures of capture or death, and are able to escape us. The displacement can also be the other way around. The cow watching a train pass by seems stupid to us because, being behind our human time, it only perceives the locomotive at the moment when the rearmost wagon passes before its muzzle. As a general rule, wild animals live slightly in advance, domestic animals with a delay of variable magnitude—hence the difference of fates experienced by a wild rabbit and one fed on cabbages. All the so-called miracles of instinct that confound human intelligence are explicable with the greatest of ease if the time of the ant or the bee, clearly in advance of ours, permits them to see the larva in the egg, the future queen in the larva, the honey in the pollen, and, I dare say, the stupidity in the entomologist's head! The swallow and the sparrow regulate their migrations according to a summer time inconceivable to the

139

ornithologists thinking in terms of winter time. To sum up, as I have told you, living species are not all in the same position on the line of time's flight…"

He paused; as a precaution, I never took my eyes off him. His excitement did not seem dangerous, and even conferred a strange beauty on him. I got up circumspectly and put on my clothes, avoiding turning my back on him. He collected himself, and soon recovered his loquacity.

"It was necessary to identify the situation of different species in time—that was my task. Elementary organisms, less impeded than others by the accomplishment of complex functions, must find it easiest to advance in that race against the watch [14] that is life. Microbes, in fact, have shown me that they are at the head of the troop of species. Other surprises were in store for me. In certain conditions, the characteristic advancement in time specific to microbial species is hereditary, transmitted by addition to the following generation. To put it another way, with each new generation, the advancement in time of a microbial colony tends to increase. It can even be transmitted in the milieu of a culture. I thus arrived at a surprising and enlightening explanation of human mortality by virtue of infectious disease: microbes, proliferating in the patient's blood, communicate to that blood an advancement in time such that the invalid dies of it—the microbes have carried it with them into the future!

"But are you really dead because your blood, your liver or your kidneys, having encountered harmful microbes, are found to have gone through their normal evolutionary cycle at an accelerated pace? Do you not undergo somewhere, with a disconnection of time, the number of years that, all things being equal, remained of your life? Linked as we are to our familiar universe, we see the individuals that precede us dying before our eyes. Mourn them if you will, but recognize too

---

[14] The word *montre*, here translated as "watch,",has a double meaning that is only faintly echoed in English, its alternative significance being "showcase" or "display."

that they are showing us a means of escaping our causal world, in allowing themselves to flow through time along the fourth dimension of the universe…"

Perhaps he believed that he had come to talk nonsense to me. Extracted from my bed, I had no intention of wasting time, and reminded him that he was here to pose.

As I made a few rapid sketches, something curious happened: his face, animated by excitement, appeared in my drawings to be dull and secretly tainted. Depressions and pits of shadow were hollowed out in the planes of the forehead, temples and cheeks. One might have thought that he was sculpted out of a piece of Swiss cheese. Was that his true character, revealing itself in spite of him, beneath my charcoal? When he began to talk again about his causal world, the memory came back to me of the previous evening and the grudge I bore against him.

"Because of you and your forays against the world, I asked myself whether women…" And I told him the story of the 300th.

"The eternal pursuit of a phantom through thousands of feminine manifestations—such is the lot of the male, and such is the principal force that attaches us to this world more than gravity," he said. "We need to understand the deceptiveness of the life that has made us. We need to see the inverse of the tapestry of the world, which seems so tempting, woven of a thousand sordid threads of desire, collectively assembling all creatures! Perhaps then we would experience a redemptive retch, which would permit an escape from its baneful attraction, a removal from the base equilibrium of the causal universe, and a departure…"

Like a cat falling on its paws, he always came back to his hobby-horse. Aggravated, I exclaimed: "Oh, don't pester me any more with your speeches!"

"I'm sorry," he said, without the least hint of regret. Then, he murmured softly: "Did the 300th have such a deleterious effect on your morale, then?"

Scarcely desirous of his sympathy, and out of bravado, I said: "She was a beautiful girl, who pleased me well enough at the time…"

"As she has pleased others."

"Undoubtedly. At the time, one scarcely thinks about that. Retrospectively, the adventure is certainly less flattering. Is that what weighs upon me? I remember that on several occasions, on the point of entering a place of ill-repute, if I happened to see another man coming out, my desire was suddenly annihilated."

"Interesting, interesting," he said, with a little unsavory whistle that made his white beard vibrate. "For the 300th, you too were obviously only a number in a sequence…"

"Given her profession, I don't doubt it."

"Perhaps you were the 3000th or 4000th…"

"What!"

"At three clients a day—that's the minimum required to make a living—we end up with a figure of about 1000 a year, and she would only have to be active for three or four years… You find yourself in the position of having insidiously acquired a kind of link with 4000 of your peers. Doubtless it's the gravity of that burden that oppresses you slightly…"

"A link with 4000 of my peers?" I repeated, a trifle choked.

"Four thousand? Much more!" he exclaimed, scribbling in pencil on his sleeve. "For that woman, the 300th, was preceded by 299 others, each one of whom gave you approximately the same gift, given that you have selected your lovers in the same easy milieu. It's necessary to multiply 4000 by 300—which is to say, 1.2 million—to calculate the number of…"

"You're making fun of me!"

"The million might be surprising, but the arithmetic is correct and irrefutable. And take note that the figure is an underestimate. Indeed, the women with whom you have associated pursue their careers thereafter, and the count of your successors continues with every hour of the day or night, inflating the indicated total…"

Suddenly, I exclaimed in an aggressive tone: "I see what your game is: your age has inspired you with a rancorous jealousy of my libertinage."

"I'm not passing judgment on your lustfulness; I'm dwelling on it because it interests me. Your rebellion is symptomatic in itself, and puts me on the track of new reflections. The cost of so-called amorous relations is beginning to become clear to me. The bond that I have been seeking between the texture of the causal world…"

I had heard enough. I showed him the door, almost brusquely. He left, radiant and satisfied, the bowler hat perched cockily on his rebellious hair. I could see that he was amused by my nervousness.

Letting myself be possessed by an aging laboratory assistant, a loquacious mountebank—that was where my quest for picturesque humanity had led me! He thought I could be influenced; I would show him that he was mistaken. In the meantime, I opened the ventilator to change the air in the studio once he had gone. Alas, it was my brain that could have done with an airing!

Until nightfall, in fact, the old imbecile's words continued to haunt me, preventing any mental concentration on my work. Finally, I decided to go out. It was dark, and it was raining. The agitation of the street, replete with umbrellas and damp reflections, initially had the effect of a refreshing compress applied to my feverish forehead. Passing anonymously, like everyone else, I let myself move with the crowd. On seeing me in my old mass-produced raincoat, who would have suspected that I had a bizarre and secret link with a million men? But the thought that, in the midst of the crowd, I was probably—almost certainly—rubbing shoulders with some of those counted among the million, began to harass me, and would not let me alone. I found those men hideous, stinking, filthy…

In the Metro, the sight of women nauseated me. I saw in my mind's eye the thousands of invisible threads woven on the inverse of the tapestry by the needles of feminine bodies to agglomerate us all, holding us prisoner within the mediocrity of the general design. It was to that glue, I was sure, that I owed my inability to work. The people in the carriage were crowded together, obliged to brush against another. Desire displayed its viscous cloth all around me and I saw men wriggling with the smug convulsions of agonized flies. With a surge, I tore myself free from that magma to regain the outside air.

I found myself in the Champs-Élysées; it was 7 p.m. The blast of anguish that had almost stifled me had given way to the evocation of Armande and the kindness that she strove to show me when she was in a good mood. Was I not in need of sympathy? Of the presence of a creature I could consider to be mine alone? Armande was an oasis. I caught as she came out of her building.

I intended to be affectionate, but I was jealous. At the restaurant to which I took her, the men looked at her with an insolent insistence. I saw the tide of desire flow ignobly around her, ready to submerge my last haven. And far from seeming offended, Armande seemed flattered. I was in a hurry to be able to take her away from their gaze; the waiter hardly had time to fetch the bill. Outside, it was still raining. Several cabs went by without stopping. I had a fit of bad temper.

"Why are you always grumbling?" Armande said placidly, beneath her umbrella. "You said yourself the other day that it makes people…"

"Don't you understand that I'm at the end of my tether? I can't bear it any longer…"

"Bear what?" she said, stupidly.

I shrugged my shoulders without replying.

As soon as I found myself alone with her, at home, I began to get bored. Her presence prevented me from thinking—and by all her gestures and intonations I saw that she was treating me as if I were an invalid child. Finally, she left. I

144

started writing in order to try to understand. I don't understand. This must change, or it will all end badly.

All day, I have tried to work without doing anything worthwhile. Toward nightfall, Babar rang my doorbell, verbose, half-drunk and repulsive. He had come with good intentions: to take two of my canvases to a dealer whose acquaintance he had just made. I raised difficulties, without giving any reason for my hesitation; all the time he was here, I was asking myself whether he too was one of my companions in pleasure. Womanizer as I knew him to be, it was very probable; the women of the quarter are not so very numerous…

Seen from that angle, he appeared to me more particularly hideous, with his absence of chin, his slack lip, his ill-shaven cheeks and his little yellow eyes that disappear into eyelids as sticky as his lips…

How was I able to accept his acquaintance? To allow him the possibility of coming into my home? I steered him gently toward the door.

He wasn't annoyed; he merely said: "It's no better, then."

"What's no better?"

"Your bad mood makes me anxious." A reflection that succeeded in irritating me. What had my bad mood to do with any of them?

He adopted a sympathetic tone, with smiling eyes, which set vulgar wrinkles upon each of his temples. I couldn't stand it anymore. He's gone now, but the obsessive thought continues to assail me with even greater force: is Babar one of my companions in pleasure?

I'm giving up work. I've spent all day at home, thinking and doing nothing. The doorbell rang twice. I didn't open the door. No human contact; I'm sterilizing myself.

I had to go out to buy something to eat. Result: having seen an African in livery barking at the entrance of a cinema, I asked myself whether, by chance, he too might not be a colleague. After all, it's quite possible; women are such animalistic creatures. It's insane to entrust them with—how shall I put it?—a part of one's dignity. Even the Vestal virgins were not up to the task of keeping the sacred fire…

There must be some truth in what that scurvy old Dagerlöff says: women weave the tapestry of the world. They gather the human herd, debasing it, eager to maintain it in mediocrity by inculcating within it the sordid concerns of the stable and its litter. They find it quite natural that the world rotates around their sex. The bees in a swarm attach themselves together by the legs and the wings, which is already not very pleasant to see—but what can one say of humans, who are attached to one another by their pubic hair? Heartsick, I can no longer paint landscapes.

The sunset, seen from my window, was very beautiful this evening, with those pale wintry colors, milky and diaphanous, which contain a part of infinite space without letting it appear. There, the skylight opens on something else. One could breathe, and perhaps live happily, if one's gaze never quit a winter horizon, pure and naked…

Someone rang the bell, and shook the door. Stretched out on the divan, I didn't budge. I expected the door to open of its own accord, but it held firm. It understood; it's a friend. Later, in an hour or two, I'll go see whether the visitor has left a note on the mat. I'm not in any hurry. It's no bad thing to put a little distance between myself and humankind. When one wants to do great things!

How much time one needs to think when one is alone for a while! Time to figure out what one is doing. The unfortunate thing is that, instead of thinking, one becomes bored. That's the way it goes! One expects thought, and it's boredom that arrives. Tedium must have the ability to paint itself. That would be an appropriate extra-human subject for me. Boredom in a winter landscape: an opaque patch in the middle of an opal, enclosing infinity, of course.

I wipe my brushes with pages torn out of an old book. Just now, I lifted up a leaf spotted with ochre and vermilion, and read: "*If you are at odds with this world, you are not obliged to remain a citizen of it.*" I looked at the author's name on the back of the book; his name is Plotinus.[15] I was wiping my brushes on Plotinus. He thanked me with a piece of advice: why remain a citizen of the world?

Everything depends on the way things are said. That advice, offered in such a calm and amenable fashion, has insinuated itself into my thoughts much more profoundly than a brutal invitation to suicide. Not to remain a citizen of the world is not to deliver oneself to death but to change nationality, to accomplish a formality, to leave the city with the disgusted expression of a well-bred man who has gone astray. To depart in those conditions would be almost pleasant. Discreetly, one offers a lesson in good taste to others, to those who remain and gorge themselves to the full with the coarsest of spectacles...

On impulse, I tried to read some of the pages that remained in the book, but it quickly became incomprehensible. My Plotinus only wrote one good thing, a single sentence. That's not bad, though. They won't be able to say as much for me after my death.

Curiously enough, I am more at ease when nothing is happening in my life.

One has very few things to do, once one reduces oneself to the essential. I would not have thought, before this cure of solitude, that one can take up so little space in life, and that life can take up so little space in you. It is as if I were seeing my life shrivel up a little more with every passing day, beneath the magnificent foliage of boredom. I interrogate my past, seeking memories, and find ashes: a dull grey powder. There is certainly more to pile up in the building's dustbin.

---

[15] The third-century Neoplatonist philosopher whose essays and aphorisms were collected as the *Enneads*.

My past, the residues of my life, defy the sieve of memory; nothing remains of it. So much the better.

My gas heater is out of order.

I was beginning to think that my disappearance had provoked little enough concern in the circle of my acquaintances when the doorbell rang. For a change, I went to open the door. It was Armande.

"What? You're here!"

"Why did you think that I wasn't here?"

"I ran into Babar; he told me that, having knocked on your door several times, he thought you'd gone away."

"Ah! You've run into Babar..."

The color of her lips had faded to the cyclamen red that gives her complexion a sallow, almost cadaverous tint. She was wearing a hat that I did not recognize, mauve and grey, whose fabric was so skillfully tormented that it had to be elegant. All that was revelatory, but the astonishment she experienced at finding me at home was even more so. Of course! She had only come as a precaution, in order to go find Babar again in full peace of mind. So it was through her, my titular girl-friend, that I must share a confraternal relationship with Babar!

Under this new blow, I stammered: "Why Babar? Why the vilest of all?"

She looked at me in surprise, pretending not to understand. "I was going past the Dôme, unaware of anything. He was on the terrace—he beckoned to me. What did you think, then?"

Crushed by disgust, I replied: "I believe in God, the Father almighty..."

"So that's it!" she said, with a theatrical sigh.

"Yes, without a doubt, that's it," I went on. "You've deceived me with an animal that a zoo wouldn't want. That's what you mean, isn't it?"

"Jean, my dear Jean!" she sighed, adopting an imploring expression. "How can you..."

I had decided to throw her out if she mentioned illness. For once, I was thinking clearly and rapidly; I didn't want anyone to question my mental balance. I told her what I thought of her, with irony and detachment. She became angry, and launched into a torrent of reproaches: that I was leading an impossible life; that I would try the patience of a saint; that I always attributed to others the falsest and basest motives, although, even while I claimed to be a painter, I was never capable of seeing anything, just as I hadn't even noticed her new hat; that she sacrificed herself for me without getting anything in return; that I took her to eat in wretched restaurants when she could be going to Fouquet's; that everybody told her that she was an idiot to attach herself to a phenomenon like me…

She went on like that for a quarter of an hour. She got carried away by her own words and her eyes gradually began to protrude from her head. They became grey-mauve, like the hat she had accused me of not seeing. A toad's eyes, they disgusted me. The last effort of good will I was making in order to listen gave way, and my attention wandered in order to study the bizarre texture of a patch of damp on the studio ceiling. By looking at it hard, one could imagine it as a horse that was rearing up in front of an egg-cup. The stain had intrigued me before, but never as much as at that moment.

Profiting from a moment when she was drawing breath, I said: "There's no point continuing; I'm not at home."

"You're not at home?"

"My mind has gone out."

Bewildered, she said: "Where to?"

Then, to finish it off, I replied with the utmost seriousness: "I'm voyaging in causality."

She shot me a glance as concentrated as a searchlight. Her head remained motionless for a moment, like that of a chicken which, while scratching the earth, has found a garter. Then, picking up the gloves she had thrown on the chest of drawers, she exclaimed: "Oh! You're voyaging in causality? Well, send me a postcard." And she fled down the stairs.

So, at the very moment when you're wondering whether one ought to remain a citizen of the world, look what surf the world throws up at your very feet, in the attempt to retain you! Oh, misery of miseries!

Everything down here is intent on deceiving me: men, women, not to mention myself. Men are sad puppets, women funereal whores, and I, devoid of talent and greatness, am a coward for having condescended to live for nearly thirty years in such company.

I shut myself up again. What, then, is this fate of ours, and which dictates that to accomplish anything, anything at all, even the most elementary actions, it is necessary for us to struggle painfully? So, to say that the world f***s us over is a vulgarity that has not even the excuse of being exact. I know full well that I'm in a bad way, but if that's the solution…

A note from Dagerlöff asking me to go see him! These laboratory assistants have a nerve, haven't they? Anyway, he wearies me with his inept old codger's verbosity. Every time I've seen him, I've come away with the impression that he has been shaking a dusty rag in my brain. He ought to get his ideas in order! Mine are clear, and sufficient; I'm waiting for my decision to finish ripening.

I've sorted out my canvases and brushes. I shall leave my palette tidy. The palettes of great painters—those who are exhibited after their deaths—always resemble a plate abandoned by a lover of Camembert. I shall spare my problematic admirers that nausea. Instead of distressing me, the thought that I will never paint again gives me pleasure. I found a new tube of chrome yellow. I squeezed it out until the last drop, with a sort of sadistic intoxication; I imagined that I was strangling light.

I wonder whether I should sweep the studio one last time. What does a little more or a little less dust around my own matter?

To open one's veins it is necessary to have a bathroom. A bottle of alcohol and opening a gas-tap are the preferred means in California according to Davys, an American college friend who had as much talent as a postcard. The rope has its adherents and, for that matter, a certain tradition among painters…

Men are as lacking in originality when it comes to dying as they are at living. Evidently, only the result matters—but one would like to have a choice of means at one's disposal as varied as that of *hors-d'oeuvres*. Nature has more imagination than we do when she's the one delivering the final blow. To list the infinite diversity of diseases and fatal accidents on the one hand, and the few means of suicide on the other, and to draw conclusions as to the poverty of the human mind from the disproportion of the two columns, would be a pleasant occupation for someone who is determined to die…

I know full well that they think I'm mad, But what does that facile word "mad" mean? That I don't conform to the idea they have formed of me? Then they're right, since that's why I'm dying. I refuse to resemble that which they want to see in me: a satisfied swine made in their image.

What irritates me is that I would have been able to love this world with a little more…

Then again, these thoughts weary me. I don't know what to do with my time. The moment has come to make a decision.

I've made my decision; it will be tomorrow.

At dusk, the hour appropriate to the semi-ghost that I am, I took one last turn around the quarter to satisfy yet again the ambulatory mania that has devoured so many hours of my life. The gloom was cold and damp with rain. The trees on the boulevard extended black skeletons over the hurrying passers-by. Montparnasse cemetery had closed its gates, imprisoning its dead for the night. On the wet roadway the cabs, fearful of skidding, were moving slowly, as if following a funeral convoy. The entire city was like a vast burial vault with streaming

151

walls, where those who thought they were still alive seemed to be pursuing some posthumous activity. I was walking in the midst of that décor, slightly haggard, like a condemned man walking to the guillotine, when a shadow that had taken refuge between the porcelain forget-me-nots and silvered pots of a memorial mason's window-display grabbed my arm as I passed by.

It was Dagerlöff. "Where are you going?" he asked.

"To my death."

"That's not very original. Instead, help me to stop one of these cabs, which refuse to see my signals."

To be obliging, I hailed a few drivers, without obtaining any response but mocking laughter. Vexed, I turned toward him. "What possessed you to come to this wretched quarter?"

"My sainted Apolline, the daughter I lost…the drama of my life, around which my thoughts have turned for 20 years. Not that she's there"—he gestured toward the wall of the cemetery—"but every anniversary…"

He was going to subject me to the confessions of a inconsolable father. I extended my hand to him, brutally. "Goodbye—I'm in a hurry…"

"To go your death?"

"Yes—I'm killing myself tomorrow."

He didn't blink, but his blue eyes, like those of a kitten, settled their gaze upon me in mute interrogation. By way of diversion, I laughed. He's more intelligent than I thought; my attitude didn't put him off. He knew immediately that I was serious.

"Permit me to take my hat off to you," he said, baring his head in spite of the rain. In response to my protests, he went on: "No, no, you're heading for a coffin, and custom obliges me to receive a little water on my skull. Why should I not render to the living man the homage due to his corpse? The man who is not going to die salutes you, Monsieur Poldonski. You have decided to plunge head first into the world behind the great blackboard of death, on which we, the living, continue tremulously to write and erase the insoluble equations of

152

mystery... Were it not for the duties that I owe to my discovery, I might allow myself to be tempted by your example—but why consent to precipitate myself into darkness when, with a little more perseverance, I am assured that..."

The animal! I had just told him that I was about to die, and still he saw in me, as ever, nothing but an audience. I had no discretion to maintain.

"You know, words, phrases...I'd rather be left in peace."

"Peace? But you're going have it so soon, and eternally into the bargain, that you can surely tolerate me a little longer."

The fact is that he didn't want to let me go. He started trotting along beside me like an old black dog. Perhaps, after all, the buzz of his speech rendered his presence less burdensome than that of a silent creature.

We arrived at my apartment. I threw myself on the divan. In my habitual surroundings, I was able to recover a few thoughts to offer a few comments to my final interlocutor on the decision I had taken. It was strange to take for a confidant an old lunatic with whom I had no connection. The mania of explanation definitely only leaves one along with life...

Afterwards, a headache, more violent than those I usually had, was hammering my skull. I complained of it loudly, and an idea struck me. "Wouldn't you, a laboratory assistant, have a drug that would permit me to end it all immediately, painlessly?"

"It would be better to cure your migraine."

Cure me! So he hadn't understood anything of what I'd tried to explain to him! It was enough to drive one to despair. Anger took old of me. "Get out!" I roared.

"I'll come back, I'll come back," he said, to save face, as he took flight.

There you go! Is it possible to find anything more inept than that last interview with one of one's peers? Decidedly, I would not succeed in anything, not even death. Oh, no one could write a dialogue in the manner of the *Phaedo* [16] about me! My death will be considered, if it is ever considered at all, as that of a poor cretin. I hoped, I confess, in company with that old madman, to find an opportunity to suspend a few pleasant nihilistic garlands around my passing. Instead of that…well, let's say no more. That which I have within me, and what I have to say, will remain unknown to the end.

To settle the last echoes of the scene, I am confiding them to paper—and, in so doing, recovering a little of my serenity.

Without any sadness, without pity for my fate, in the silence of the night, I coldly run my gaze over the wall, as bare as my life would have been, the dirty plaster ceiling that separates me from the celestial vault….

In the lamplight, the horse rearing up in front of the egg-cup becomes once again what it is: a patch of damp. Let us apply ourselves to seeing everything as it really is: a practically inoffensive nothingness. And to begin with, let us not see in our head, in the very thoughts and that pain lancing through it, anything more than the displacement of particles among nervous filaments confused to a greater or lesser degree. An electrical current stops when one presses a simple switch. Do I think that I am killing electricity when I turn a commutator? No. No more stories, then, to make up in my head, with all its ideas…

I must…

The animal came back! I hoped that, full of repentance, he was bringing me the pill I wanted. He came back with a damp compress! To soothe my headache! He tried in vain to put it in a good light, to play the hypocrite.

"So, the man who has decided to kill himself cannot bear an insect-bite. You have need of all your strength to take the plunge, and your struggle against physical illness is getting

---

[16] Plato's *Phaedo* includes a classic account of the death of Socrates.

in the way. This compress on the forehead, properly applied, directly over the eyes—the eyes that are the origin of all irritation of the nervous system…isn't the first instinctive movement in the struggle against suffering to lower the eyelids? Keep it over your closed eyelids for as long as possible…"

I remained mute. My gaze cut through him. He finally understood, and went away, abandoning his compress. That ultimate intervention ought not to trouble my serenity. A sleeping-powder. The compress, since the compress is there. A few more hours' sleep. And, looking things squarely in the face, tomorrow morning at dawn, I shall boldly open the gas-tap.

CHAPTER THREE

Something extraordinary has happened to me. I woke up cured!

My resumptions of consciousness on emerging from sleep are always immediate. When I woke up, this morning, I initially experienced a diffuse sensation, a sort of internal inflation of unknown nature, which surprised me until—at the moment when my misty gaze, encountering a pool of pale sunlight displayed on the wall facing my divan, recovered therein the magic of color—I recognized the sensation that is inflating my bosom as happiness: the happiness of which I had lost even the memory, the very idea; the joy of existence, quite simple, quite bald, given gratuitously, without cause or reason, accompanied by an appetite for life that multiplied my strength tenfold and made everything appear to me with a stupefying facility.

I got up—no, I leapt up. My body anticipated my intention; I felt nothing but the freedom of an indescribable lightness. I felt strong, irresistible. The universe around me offered a smile of infinite indulgence, full of inexhaustible future promise. An incredible adventure! Was that still me?

I had to look at myself in the mirror. I recognized myself—who would have believed it?—with delight. My tousled hair had taken on a Venetian blond tint; my stubble-blurred cheeks made the smooth hauteur of my forehead stand out; my gaze met itself, as limpid as a deep pool. Dare I confide it to this piece of paper? There was a powerful genius there! Then I thought: "It can't last…"

It did last, and full consciousness didn't diminish any of the magic of that Thousand-and-One-Nights awakening.

I opened the window. For a long time I contemplated the view over the roofs: that magical universe made of bricks, zinc and slates, lacy, bristling and eccentric, full of unconscious humor, beneath a spring-like blue sky through which regattas

156

of little white clouds pass by, arriving on a light easterly breeze that flattens out the plumes of smoke, transmuting them into an impalpable duvet charged with caressing the cheeks of the sky. The dome of the Val-de-Grâce is refined by the effects of a hem of sunlight. The unfinished parking-lot that raises its concrete carcass above the neighboring hovels is a gigantic open cage for chirping sparrows. The chimneys rise up like hollyhocks; I almost expect to see them flower! I have become stupid. And to think that I was to die this morning!

How can this transfiguration be explained? I have found my way back to reality. Instead of seeing things from the darkroom of myself, I see them as they offer themselves to clear and naïve eyes. It's good to be alive.

I made haste to go out, to expose myself to the smile of the universe.

That was an exquisite stroll, in which there was nothing other than pleasure to assure me of the amicable presence of things. I saw houses, streets, dogs, carriages, people—and I found them all admirable! The ground was admirable for being hard enough to sustain my footsteps; the air was admirable for being keen enough to invite me to hasten my pace; the cornering cabs were admirable for not running me over, the people for putting movement and color into the décor of the world. The entire mechanism ran without a hitch, with an accurate sense of value, without the need of any orchestra-conductor. And what can I say about the warm croissants dipped in coffee with cream! I need to put the brake on my enthusiasm, or I will no longer believe myself...

I shall write to Armande, make overtures to my friends. By way of an *ex voto*,[17] I will paint in large golden letters on the wall of the studio: *Life is admirable*.

---

[17] An *ex voto* is a votive offering to a saint made in fulfilment of a vow.

The enchantment continues. I might have dreaded that it was a matter of an unstable impression, of a peak moment, but when one grasps the truth, or is grasped by the truth, one does not let go of it again.

I met good old Babar at Gugenlaert's. He was a trifle deflated—he had not been given the commission for the fresco in his local bistro—and I was obliged to cheer him up. I did so with such vigor that he seemed surprised.

"Painters—the true ones—are optimists," I said to him, clapping him on the shoulder.

He had a boil; he roared in pain. I jollied him along more forcefully, recommending the inoculation of sulfamides in large doses—elephantine doses! In the face of my exaltation, he found nothing to say other than to repeat: "You're making me anxious…"

"Oh no, old chap! Change the record—you're behind the times!"

I didn't want to depress myself, and I left him with a long face on the sidewalk. There are people who are never content. They either find you too miserable or too cheerful. For them, everything is always excessive. Personally, I'm very fond of excess—it's the sign of a rich nature.

Calmly, I'm preparing my canvases in order to get back to work. I shan't paint the "Fairground Burlesque" but a "Hymn to Joy," to make a pictorial pendant to the symphony of the old. Painters are optimists, for God's sake!

Obviously, one cannot expect to live in a perpetual euphoria. Minor snags are inseparable from existence. For example, this morning I opened the tap on the wash-basin; the water came out yellow and dirty. Accustomed to drinking it, I didn't even dare wash my face in it. The City would do well to check the pipes.

I've written a careful letter to Armande. I'd made many mistakes—was totally wrong, if she wishes—but let's leave reproaches to commonplace lovers. Then again, I need her. The kind of hymn that my heart sings to the recovered world awaits an echo, a response that she alone can bring me. Tenderness is the complement of happiness.

Never have I felt so tender, in spite of my frowns when the little snags I mentioned crop up: no matches with which to light my gas; the cupful of water that I warmed up to make coffee had nearly evaporated when I came back to it, because I had left it on the boil for too long; for my aperitif, the waiter brought me an ice-bucket whose pieces were almost all melted...

I'm ashamed to report such petty details, but everyone's mood depends on trivia of that sort. A succession of minor hitches, and the equilibrium of happiness tilts...

Some malign genius seems to want to deflate the balloon of my new enthusiasm with pinpricks. I've come to wonder whether things are not expressly designed to repel anyone who shows too much interest in them. Love makes them afraid, as it does to humans, and they slip away...

To begin with, the water ran yellow and dirty all morning. There are certainly leaks in the pipes, and I'll have to complain to the concierge. When I tried to shave, the mirror was so dirty that I couldn't see the stubble on my cheeks, which felt fearfully rough to my hand. My shaving-soap refused to do its job, only spreading a sort of molten cream over my skin instead of the "ample and soapy" foam promised by the advertisement. I set to work and found the hairs of my new brushes agglutinated, as if they had just been used. I bought a newspaper and unfolded it; it was crumpled, as if I had already read it three times. The virginity of their appearance is, however, the only interest of these daily rags.

Yet another incident: I took out my watch on the boulevard and noticed that its glass is broken. Being superstitious, and finding myself directly outside a watchmaker's shop, I went in to have the damage repaired. I held out the object, and heard someone say: "But, Monsieur, the glass isn't broken."

"The glass isn't broken?"

The watchmaker caressed the face with his thumb. I leaned over in order to look. At that moment, a slight crack was audible.

"Oh yes—it's just broken."

Could I have had a presentiment?

At any rate, I didn't foresee the arrival of Armande late that evening. She came into the studio like an apparition. My heart leapt. She fell into my arms, without a word…

Let us follow that example; bliss is mute…at least as mute as great anguish.

I am the victim of a "something" whose nature I don't know—and as my thoughts turn incessantly, in spite of myself, around that problem, my good will and good mood are beginning to be painfully influenced.

I shall pass over the annoyances already cited, even though their persistence is troubling—the water that is still dirty; the soap that doesn't foam even though I've changed the brand; the bad luck that dictates that a newspaper, picked up at hazard from a seller's pile, is always one that has already been read—and come to an inexplicable scene.

Alone in a café, I was waiting for Armande, at the back of the room because of the cold. The clientele was sparse. Not far away, an old bachelor, who had nothing of the humorist about him, was drinking an aperitif with the placidity of an ox in the byre. Having nothing to do, I began observing him. At one point, he took out a packet of cigarettes—already half-empty, to tell the truth—and extracted, not a cigarette, but a butt. How far can the parsimonious sprit of the French extend? But I was even more surprised when I saw him take, from a nearly-new box of matches, a blackened stub, strike it gravely on the side of the box and put it to his butt as if to light it. To be distracted to that extent was implausible. The man had the appearance of someone smoking: the hollowing of the cheeks when he breathed in, the movement of the mouth to expel the smoke, but I saw no manifest puff of smoke escape his lips—a light mist at the most. Was he a clown miming a scene? A smoker trying to give up his tobacco habit?

I was sufficiently intrigued by the spectacle not to notice Armande right away when she came in. Her arrival naturally directed my attention elsewhere, but when I left her, preoccupied with the incident of the smoker, I remembered that a lack of matches had obliged me to light my gas with a cigarette-lighter. I went into a tobacconist's shop. In front of me, a customer was choosing a cigar, and I swear that I saw him take a cigar-stub from the box, which terminated mid-band in a cylinder of ash, as if someone had already begun smoking it.

What does it mean? Should I already be seeing the repetition of these strange scenes as a mysterious warning?

A hard day.

As soon as I woke up, the alarming details began to multiply: my hand-towel was wet through when I picked it up to make use of it; in a new packet of Gillette razor-blades, the first one was covered in rust—although it didn't shave any worse than any other. But let's pass on…after what happened later, those annoyances no longer count for anything.

Having worked quite well during the morning, I decided to go and eat at Ballard's, the restaurant on the corner of the boulevard, a place where one was once able to eat quite well at affordable prices. The soup was a funny color, but I drank it down. I'd ordered a Chateaubriand steak. The waiter brought it, swimming in an unidentifiable sauce, a kind of magma resembling in color and texture the vile pulp that badly brought-up children spit out on the edge of their plate.

"What's this?"

"Chateaubriand, Monsieur."

"I didn't know they serve minced Chateaubriand here. Take that horror away!"

"Would Monsieur like a cutlet?"

The cutlet is approved. I wait. He brings me the same magma, in which he has merely disposed a bone—a cutlet indeed—but a bone already gnawed, to which nothing is ap-

161

pended but the debris of muscle. What a way to make mock of people! I looked at him. He met my gaze with an astonished insolence. There were people around; I dared not kick up a fuss. I had ordered—in advance, unhappily—a half-bottle of red burgundy. It was uncorked in front of me. In order not to suffer a total loss, I poured myself a glass; out of the bottle came a yellowish liquid resembling cat's-piss. Immediately, I summoned the sommelier, who struck a pose in his black apron.

"Look!" I said, with concentrated fury.

"Is it corked?"

"I ordered red burgundy, and you're serving me cocoa."

He looked at the label and the glass, poured out a few drops, drank them, and looked at me in bewilderment. "But Monsieur, it's an excellent burgundy…"

Anger took hold of me. I threw my napkin on the table and went out, regretting that I couldn't slam the door, which was glazed. I marched along the boulevard like a madman, talking to myself in a loud voice, in search of a possible vengeance. Indignation had prevented me from seeing anything, when I came to a halt in front of a florist's window near the Coupole.

Instead of the sparkling array of fresh flowers that was normally offered behind the curtain of streaming water, I saw nothing but dilapidated azaleas, blackened mimosas and withered carnations, giving the impression that the contents of a waste-sack had been exposed. Was this a new kind of advertisement?

An old woman, like those who sweep churches, stopped beside me and murmured delightedly; "How beautiful they are!"

In a flash, the truth struck me: I was afflicted by a visual disorder.

The window-display of a fruit merchant furnished me, alas, with irrefutable proof. On their bed of wadding, I could no longer see anything but the stones of cherries; the grapes had shriveled like raisins in the bosom of an old pudding, and the pineapples resembled the charred heads of Indians!

A visual disorder! In a painter! A cold sweat ran down my back. I needed an optician, an immediate eye test. Having never worn spectacles, I did not know where to go. I raced to the Optical Institute. The concierge snorted with laughter. "Get a telephone book—there's no shortage of opticians..." From among the names, I chose the one inscribed in the largest letters. It was near the Place de l'Etoile. I hailed a cab; I was no longer alive...

At the optician's, I read letters of all dimensions, I sat in all the armchairs, placed my head in the strangest apparatus, analyzed the threads of cloth of every color. After an hour, the practitioner told me: "I can't find anything. The cornea, the lens and the retina are faultless..."

"Then, if my vision is intact, they're hallucinations?"

He made no reply, but he gave me a funny look.

That's how things stand.

As soon as I woke up, anguish took possession of my mind. Where are you, recent delights of the first contact with reality? The joys of living, working and placid meditation were out of the question. I paraded a fearful gaze around my room, not in order to see things, but to check the condition of my eyes. Everything had its usual appearance.

With the intention of obtaining a few books on visual hallucinations, I then set off for the bookshops in the vicinity of the School of Medicine. The sky was the slightly greyish blue of spring, but as I went through the Luxembourg gardens a fine rain began to fall on my hands, so surprising in that bright sunlight that I thought at first that I was within range of a sprinkler. The strollers were opening their umbrellas, however; it was a shower. In the shelter of a kiosk, I raised my eyes to the Heavens to see how long the rain would last; there was not a cloud in sight. I thought it very strange, but I would have thought no more of it had not a rather elegant lady, who had taken shelter alongside me, been holding a little dog on a leash, in a state of indescribable physical distress. It was not pitiful, it was atrocious, its flanks flattened, its jaw hanging down, its eyes almost out of their orbits, its legs twisted: an ambulant cadaver.

"Poor little beast," I could not help sighing. "What happened to it?"

The dog's owner shot me a suspicious glance, pulled on the leash to draw the animal closer to her and took that living wreck in her arms, without manifesting any disgust. I was feeling slightly sick when anxiety took hold of me. Was I seeing the dog as it really was?

Then the kind of panic that had gripped me the day before in the restaurant took hold of me again. I fled from the dog and the gardens to take refuge in the flowing crowd on the Boulevard Saint-Michel. I avoided looking at the passers-by for fear of finding opportunities for hallucination there, but my eyes encountered, involuntarily, a blackened façade, a curtain of twisted iron and a shop-window displaying charred shoes. Curiosity immobilized me on the sidewalk. People were entering and leaving the shop as if it were still open.

"When did that catch fire?" I wondered.

"Catch fire? What's that?" someone nearby replied.

Prudence advised me not to reply. No doubt was any longer possible; I understood that I had to consult a psychiatrist.

Alas, I was all too familiar with torturers of that sort, from having seen them work on my poor father. Curious about your illness, but as far as caring for you is concerned, that's another story: smooth talk that has no effect, or torture by electric shock…

Even if one detests firemen, though, one calls them when one's house is on fire. Once, I had seen the name of Professor Adhésin at the clinic where my father was being cared for. He lived nearby, on the Boulevard Saint-Germain.

A nurse opened the door of the waiting-room. Scarcely had I entered than I jumped: there was a cadaver there, a cadaver sitting patiently, holding a copy of *L'Illustration* on his

164

knees. Some old men can look like mummies, but this one was dead, I would have bet my right arm on it. His skull was yellow and striped with mold; his lowered eyelids left nothing visible of the eyes but white lines; his lips were bloodless, his features expressionless; his skeletal wrists were sticking out of his sleeves—the rounded sleeves of a corpse. My gaze searched for the wax candles and the crucifix…

The door opened slightly; the cadaver got up and disappeared into the consulting-room. I only got my breath back by slow degrees. I had scarcely recovered when my turn came to go in.

The white-coated professor was waiting behind his desk. He looked like a butcher in his Sunday best. With a condescending hand-gesture he waved me to a seat. He was trying to strike an imposing attitude, but one of the lenses in his spectacles was broken and starred, giving his globular eye the appearance of an exploded bull's-eye. In a weary voice, he said: "Have I seen you before?"

"No…I'm not mad…" I began.

He smiled. I immediately understood the classic ineptness of my opening, and promptly added: "I've come about visual hallucinations."

He affected to scribble on his notepad. In a tone of voice intended to signify a provocative superiority, he said: "What sort of visual hallucinations?"

Desirous of explaining things methodically and giving recent examples, I began with the first symptom that had struck me earlier that morning: "I can no longer see clouds…"

In an acid voice, with the incredulous condescension of a superior person talking to a poor specimen, he said: "You can no longer see clouds?"—giving the question an irony so stinging that my blood ran cold. Facing that chattering head, with the accompaniment of a blow of my fist on the table, I roared: "No, but I can still see cretins!"

With which I went out of the door without looking back.

My opinion is confirmed: a quack will always find that you have the illness in which he specializes; if you haven't, he lashes out at you. It's necessary to make one's own diagnosis, to care for oneself by oneself.

All the same, what a disaster!

First of all, I must try to understand what has happened to me. Thus, I have carried out various sorts of experiments all day long.

The illness is real; I am the victim of visual disturbances.

All nourishment appears to me in a rotten form. For example, at the stall of a wholesale butcher near Les Halles, for some time I watched the delivery of sheep arriving straight from the abattoir, having been freshly slaughtered. I saw nothing but collections of bones, like the carcasses of camels in the desert. For me, the croissants on all the counters of the bars take on a viscous, grey appearance; one would think that they had already been eaten and half-digested. Wine, beer, lemonade and everything else has the same color of piss. To the touch, even to the taste—I had the courage to eat a croissant—nothing is changed. Thus, fortunately, only sight is affected.

The hallucination does not stop at foodstuffs, but extends to anything perishable. In spite of numerous attempts—I went to the Madeleine market especially—I have not been able to find a single intact flower in all Paris. There are also the newspapers—more perishable matter. Those that I picked up today were almost unreadable, so crumpled and creased were they. One might have thought that they had served to wrap up God knows how many parcels.

For the rest—people, houses, carriages—nothing is altered in appearance except for the cadaver seen in the professor's waiting-room and the dog in the Luxembourg gardens, which I had forgotten. They were perishable too, evidently, but no more than the others—unless their deaths were closer at hand? Might I be having presentiments of the future? If I interrogate myself, that's not the impression I get. I see what I see, without any suggestion of the future being added to it.

The proof of that is that Armande came to surprise me in the midst of these reflections, without my having the slightest presentiment of her approach. She could easily see that I was preoccupied. I talked about my work…

(My poor work! Can I continue to paint? For the moment, the mental effort that seeks to understand occupies me fully, but in time…)

In any case, I refrained from telling Armande about my condition—but I have to be careful. For instance, Armande's dress was frayed, and I remarked upon it unthinkingly.

"What?" she replied, mechanically smoothing the fabric over her thighs. "It's fresh from the dry-cleaner's."

I blushed, and changed the subject. I'm going to have to keep watch on myself constantly, in order not to give myself away.

I don't believe that it's a question of hallucination, strictly speaking. Hallucinations have an episodic, fortuitous, vaporous character. They appear and disappear, rather like ghosts. Now, I see things distorted, or rather modified, in a constant fashion, as regularly as if it were a matter of an ordinary phenomenon. My vision is naturally altered, if I might put it thus, and it seems to me to be difficult to incriminate my mind, which has never before furnished such loyal and seemingly-sincere efforts.

To say that I have become accustomed to my condition would be an exaggeration—at noon, again, I recoiled before the sight of the rabbit casserole that I was brought—but, in sum, I'm getting on with things. I empty my plate, looking elsewhere so far as is possible. My mind is sufficiently occupied in reflection not to linger on the repulsion that the new aspect of things inspires. I must first succeed in defining clearly what had happened to me. A little while ago, there was an instructive incident.

It was while taking an aperitif, for which—for the sake of prudence and to avoid running into any of my friends—I had gone to the Lion de Belfort. As on previous days, the ice-bucket that had been brought to me contained nothing but water. Instead of grumbling, I picked up the kind of perforated shovel or ladle that serves to pick up ice, distractedly, and extracted a piece of water from the bucket! I mean what I say: a *piece*, resembling transparent frost and clinging miraculously to the shovel, without flowing. At first I sat there, nonplussed, and then I understood that where I saw water, there was in reality a piece of ice that naturally stayed on the shovel. Therefore: *I see things in the location where they are, but in the state that they will be in subsequently.*

I no longer see the clouds because they have already condensed into rain. This morning, I could not see the stubble on my cheeks because I was about to shave it off. I see the tapwater yellow and dirty, as it will be when I have washed my hands. I see the dog in the state in which it would be after being run over, the shop as it will be after the fire, and so on.

With this principle, everything becomes clear. For two pins, I'd say that the anomaly has re-entered into the order of things, and man is a creature so stupidly attached to reason that I have am almost calm this evening. A curious virtue of explanation…

Well, no! That attachment to rational order, which resembles that of a dog to its master, has something servile and revolting about it. No, I won't be satisfied! My indignation remains intact. How have I deserved what has happened to me? And why has it happened?

I've been trying to work, but it's literally impossible. When one is prey to an unknown malady—and what a malady!—it occupies you entirely. Sitting before the blank canvas, palette in hand, I said to myself: *I see things in the location where they are, but in the state that they will be in subsequently. Why then, can't I see my canvas finished? I'd have nothing to do but paint over it!* But I continue to see it as white, perhaps a little greyer than is natural; what does that imply? Of course! It's because, continuing to see things where they are, I continue to see the colors that will cover the canvas on the palette where they still are. It would have been too convenient if my malady had been able to help me out!

Unless, as I remain incapable of work, the canvas only remains blank because I shall never begin the painting! My own deductions are thus blocking my activity…

Oh, my head!

I had to go out, to see an intelligent optician, if the species exists. Knowing that it was no longer a matter of hallucination, I ought to have been calmer—but all day long, a new thought tormented me: I'm seeing things in the state they will be in subsequently, but how much later? In order to try to find out, I had an idea.

Before dinner, I returned to the Boulevard Saint-Michel, to the shoe-shop. People were stopping to look at the window, where the charred shoes were no longer on display. The debris of ruined furniture was being brought out. So, my vision must be one day or two in advance.

An unhealthy curiosity made me stare at the passers-by as I went home. In the crowd I counted three cadavers.

A brief moment of hope: the tap-water was running clear. Was I cured? Alas, it was impossible to make the soap foam, since the foam has been long dissolved at the moment when I see it. Why the clear water, then? Because, collected by the filtration plants, gutter-water becomes limpid again after a few days…

But in that case, my vision is making further progress into the future.

I remain pale and panting.

After an examination that seemed conscientious, Quirinez, a professor of ophthalmology at the Faculty of Medicine, certified that my eyes are in perfect order. It's true that, in fear of being sent to Saint-Anne, I did not give him any explanation. Eyes perfect? Then it must be hallucination. I no longer understand…

I no longer dare go out. Anxiety grips me at the thought of the unknown spectacles that might perhaps be offered to me, and before which my surprise might betray me. For appearing normal for as long as possible is the absolute condition that must be observed, if I want people to leave me in peace. I can no longer offer myself that luxury of the normal person—being eccentric! It's necessary for me to hide from human beings the fact that I am not like them, since that is now true. Look out for myself! If not, the herd will take its revenge! It seems to me that they're already suspicious of me. I'm not so stupid as to say to one of them, while tapping him on the shoulder: 'You, old man, have no more than 48 hours to live!' They haven't stopped burning witches!

But the walls of the solitude, within which I was once complacent because I knew that I had built them myself, resemble those of a prison now that they are imposed upon me. Universe, resplendent universe offered to my window, what did I not tell you, only a few days ago?

I just re-read what I said, in this very journal. What burning straw my enthusiasm was! With a bitter smile, I turned the pages in reverse order, going back through the days. I wanted to kill myself—what a silly idea! I arrived at Dagerlöff's chatter. What has become of him?

Oh! An idea crossed my mind like a lightning-flash! A mere hypothesis, but my brain has been on fire ever since…

When he brought me what was needed to cure my migraine…

I can no longer remain still. I must see him, this very night.

The animal was not at home. I waited on the landing for an hour. I shall go back tomorrow morning in order to set my mind straight. Will I be able to sleep?

At 9 a.m., I bruised my fist again, fruitlessly, knocking beneath the visiting card that read: *Christian Dagerlöff, genius*. Battle-weary, I went to question the concierge.

"Would you, by any chance, be Monsieur Poldonski?"

"Yes."

"Monsieur Christian told me about your visit before departing on a voyage, and asked me to give you this letter."

"On a voyage? For how long?"

"He didn't say. He doesn't talk much, you know."

This is the letter:

Dear Monsieur Poldonski,

The custom is to surround death with mystery. One does not advertize it. At the most, it is insinuated, in heavily veiled words, to the moribund questioner. Since the departure for the great voyage has always been thus vested with a somewhat clandestine character, it is necessary for me to respect that tradition when it is a matter of another great voyage—I mean the voyage in causality.

I have told you in passing, to the extent permitted by your anxious levity and your ill-concealed incredulous irony, something about my endeavors. They have concluded; Parabacillus Dagerlöff, *obtained by the growth of selected species cultivated in the marrow of Siberian hares, has adapted itself to human myelin.*

In this bacillus, the advancement in time—the same one that confers upon the Siberian hare the presentiment of the boyar shotgun or the muzjik snare, and ensures its salvation by flight or a clever detour—is a few seconds. In the improved conditions of culture that sufficed to secure the glory of the all-too-mortal Pasteur, the gene corresponding to the specific character of advancement is transmitted to the next generation in such a way that the advancement in time of the microbial colony increases with every generation. It must be added that the proliferation is particularly rapid in living myelin, and that the cultural milieu is then sufficiently impregnated to participate in the temporal advancement of the bacilli...

A life's work is summarized here in the space of a few lines, but these lines have an importance that has scarcely ever been equaled: they bring the means of the great escape! To the overturned imagination of the perceptive reader, they offer the view, as far as the eye can see, of a line of flight, as material as it is ideal, by which to escape the causal universe. They open the door of the fourth dimension! Time is vanquished!

But it is not the time that is multiplied by the imaginary of the mathematician—that irremediably fictitious and abstract time—which has been put in our possession; it is biological time itself that it will become possible to command in its guise, as if to lift a lid of the universal box, in order to offer life, until now prisoner of bleak and dismal causality, the key to the fields of infinity!

What good, however, would it do to quit this world if one could not retain a point of contact permitting the transmission of the impressions sensed in the world beyond? The dead, who undertake that voyage in their radical and inept fashion, departing in their entirety, never come back to tell the tale of their adventure. It is therefore necessary only to depart along the line of time's flight in detached pieces, so to speak, risking no more than one finger, one hand, or one sense: one gaze...

Parabacillus Dagerlöff, *which can only live in the neurons, offers precisely what is required in this regard. By accentuating its vegetative character, one can maintain it in the vicinity of the location of its seeding. Instead of spreading through the entire nervous system, it will remain localized...in the optic nerve, for example.*

For this, I needed an experimental subject, a man who was not, if I might put it thus, cold-eyed: a young man free of attachments, sufficiently alienated from the world not to oppose injurious resistance to the adventure; a man whom desire no longer attached to the flesh. I needed a man, in a word, already brought to the frontier of life and death, for whom a light push would suffice to send him sliding forth in the toboggan of the unknown. A man disposed to suicide would be very well suited to my project.

Ought I to warn the man? To offer him the bargain frankly? Fearful of last minute changes of mind, I preferred to act with more discretion. The experimental device was, shall I say, hardly evident—so mere a matter as a simple compress to place over the eyes...the contamination of the optic nerves would begin immediately...the bacillus would proliferate at its ease...and slowly, without any noise or fuss, the gaze would set off toward the new horizons of a infinity unknowable until now...

To you, the first voyager departing into causality, I, who remain on the departure quay, wave my checkered handkerchief, that of an inventor and forerunner. You are going into the future, entering into History, and if I add that, nevertheless, you will not be leaving the present, I shall have achieved that temporal salad from which I anticipate the ruination of familiar causality...

The impatience that I experience to discover your impressions has given way, for the moment, to a certain prudence, which, in anticipation of the possible fits of an irritable character, commands me to put a little ordinary space between us. Given that I am only taking a brief excursion to the suburbs, while you are setting out boldly for the most open sea of all, I humbly abdicate all superiority in your regard, and declare myself, my dear Monsieur Poldonski, your admiring servant...

The letter is here, on my table. I sense that I have not finished re-reading it. It is written with a goose-quill on exceedingly silky Chinese paper.

Is it him or me who is mad?

CHAPTER FOUR

For two days, I have been hesitating over the best course of action to take. Go to see a doctor with Dagerlöff's letter? He would laugh at me. Go to the Pasteur Institute to obtain information about the bacillus? The Institute isn't far away...in fact, it's so close that I might decide to go there. And that box, seen from without, with its little brick outbuildings, doesn't look very threatening...

A little while ago, haggard and disorientated, passing in front of the terrace of the Coupole, I was caught by Babar. He had a Rumanian friend with him, a hospital intern, a typical block of Oriental grease. I slipped unobtrusively into the flow of the conversation: "And, is one able to disinfect the optic nerve?"

The other blew into his cheeks. "It wouldn't do you holy daubers any harm, and perhaps you'd paint us tits with something other than Camembert!"

He thought he was being funny; I was obliged to smile for politeness' sake. And this was the response of life to the anguish of the invalid!

To live with that poison! And what a poison! Just now, in the short journey from the bistro to the studio, I had crossed the path of a dozen cadavers! The bacilli filtering my vision must be communicating to it an advance that has already reached several weeks—for that much time must surely pass before all those people die...

I can see the shadow of a padded cell projected on my walls...

On awakening, I resume a life akin to a nightmare. For a moment, I still hope that I might find myself cured. Oh, I demand no more of my guardian angel—I only want to be a man like others, like the most stupid of those who, without knowing it, simply enjoy the pleasure of seeing the world as it is. But no, the malady is still there.

I was ruminating in this fashion, sitting on my bed in a state of bleak stupor, when Armande arrived. Was it Sunday already? As, above all, I don't want her to suspect anything, I pretended to be jovial and exuberant, but my cheerfulness rang false. I joked about my worn pajamas and the untidiness of my increasingly sordid apartment as I set the table for us to breakfast together. Before spreading out the tablecloth, I noticed a small patch of dust on the table, and tried to blow it away.

"Is that how you treat 100-franc notes?" she said—and I saw her bend down to the floor, pick up the rectangle of dust, which miraculously held together, and set it down delicately on my plate. My surprise only lasted a second—the time to recall that banknotes are incinerated on their return to the Banque de France, and that I was seeing that one in the state in which it would be in a few months' time. I shall have to be careful if I want to preserve the last of my money, preferring payment in coin.

"It's only paper, after all," I said, casually, so as not to alert her attention—but my precaution was unnecessary; her thoughts were elsewhere. I saw her making little gestures, striking poses in front of the mirror, studying herself carefully. And to tell the truth, I thought that she was dressed less elegantly than usual; her jacket and skirt were stained, her blouse yellowed by the smoothing-iron, and the ladders in her stockings were plain to see. Suddenly, she turned to me and asked: "What do you think of my little outfit?"

"Is it new?" My voice choked as I posed the question.

"I wear it for the first time in your honor, and you don't even notice!"

Tears came to my eyes. The incident was especially telling. If I could no longer see the efforts that anyone made on my behalf, that was yet another part of life that had escaped me. I buried my head on her shoulder and, recovering her scent, keeping my eyes closed in order to caress her with blind hands, I assured myself that she was intact, fresh and firm. She declared with a joyous laugh that spring had made me very affectionate. I then leaned out to look at the spring—we were at the studio window. On the far side of the parking-lot, the branches of the plane-trees were decked with little withered yellow leaves, like debris on the end of a broom.

"One scarcely notices spring in Paris."

"And those buds bursting forth in glossy little leaves!" she exclaimed.

I had not yet realized that the spring greenery could only appear to me in the colors of autumn…

It is necessary to fight. Not so much against the microbe as against depression. A painter I am, a painter I remain. I shall work through and against everything. I begged for an original point of view from which to see things, and I have it; involuntarily, but I have it. I shall paint it, this world, in its colors of decomposition and death—and I shall force my peers to proclaim my genius. Genius imposes its own vision. It only needs to be powerful—and mine is powerful enough, since I am its first victim. This neglected butcher's stall, this stinking refuse-tip, which is nature in springtime for me, people shall see with my eyes. I shall force them to recognize the verity of the future. To work!

The malady must make frightful progress from one night to the next.

To reward myself for a morning's work, I allowed myself a walk in the "rich neighborhoods." Well, staring at the male and female passers-by, I saw nothing but a procession of tatterdemalions filing along the most aristocratic avenues. Flabby felt hats, jaundiced and singed jackets, greasy and wrinkly trousers—all the men were dressed like tramps. But was I say about the women? Bundles of rags, drawers full of old clothes, protrusions of ambulatory mites! The most curious of all were the hats, like old lampshades quivering with innumerable tawdry ornaments, such as one sees on the heads of madwomen. I could have imagined that the city had been invaded by an army of scarecrows, but I knew that I alone was guilty. To confirm that, it was sufficient to look at the shop windows, where the same tattered and shredded assemblies were on display, which obviously could not be on offer in any but brand-new condition.

Sometimes, the contrast between the rags and the measured deportment of the wearer, the "donkey bearing relics" attitude of a woman showing off a new dress, even drew a smile from me. Confronted with a tramp kissing the hand of an escapee from an asylum, who was getting out of her rattletrap like an empress, I could not restrain myself. They must have thought me a madman. I was inventing nothing, however; I was merely seeing things in the state that they would subsequently be in, and, thus bringing them back to their true value, I could judge them more sanely. What are these rags, these trappings, to which one pays respects, and of which one is so proud? What are these customs, this civilization, built on the crease in a trouser-leg and the carnation in a buttonhole?

The art-dealers of the avenue were exhibiting their traditional little women ticking the breast of a spaniel or a parrot, all painted in white lead without their darker shades surpassing a sugary pink. Well, these St. Honorés of painting had taken on a certain patina—not a Rembrandesque patina, to be sure, but a veil of shadow that attenuated their processed-meat vulgarity. I drew closer. Cracks in the varnish like those I saw appearing could surely only appear after of a year or two? Was I already that far ahead?

I saw my first naked lady yesterday—in the street, I mean. It was warm, but there was no mistake. She was walking without any inhibition, with a slight grey shadow floating about her thighs. I had already understood: a woman whose dress, destined to be burned, was already reduced to ashes in my eyes; a woman too mature, at any rate, for the vision that she offered me to be a compensation for my woes.

I no longer count the cadavers I encounter. Yesterday evening, it was my concierge who passed into the ranks of the

177

walking dead, the first familiar face to be attained by cadaverous rigidity. That, so close to me, gave me a shock.

Are you unwell, then?" I could not help saying to her.

"On the contrary, I'm very well," she replied, cantankerously.

"So much the better—but watch out for draughts, all the same."

On reflection, her lodge is such a dungeon that I'm only astonished that she hasn't kicked the bucket sooner.

One can have plenty of warning, but secretly refuse to accept that one is subject to a state of affairs oneself. This morning, while cleaning my teeth, perceiving a discolored—almost black—premolar, I raced to the dentist with the utmost conviction, only to hear him tell me: "But, Monsieur, the tooth is perfectly healthy."

"Perfectly healthy?"

Of course! Only then did I understand. Negligently, I asked: "Is there a means of inhibiting decay in advance?"

"Regular dental hygiene…but you have the teeth of a film star."

Even so, I could see the still-healthy tooth in a parlous state. Then, I looked at myself for a long time in the mirror, and found myself aged. To be sure, why should I be an exception? I don't know whether I ought to attribute it to the state of anxiety in which I exist and will exist, but I'm aging badly: a facial appearance more tortured than brilliant…

For the moment, though, others see me still young. I ought to take advantage of that…

There is nothing but the faces of cadavers, clothes turning to rags, dead leaves in midsummer; the entire shiny surface of things, which renders them agreeable and flatters the gaze, has disappeared for me. Not a single varnished carriage, not a single sparkling window-display, not a single piece of shiny nickel-plate, not a single polished banister—everything that ought to reflect light is, to my eyes, already corroded by rust. It seems to me that the very stones are wearing away. In a word, I no longer see anything new. I can no longer see it because, at the very moment it appears as such, I already see as it will be God only knows how many months or years later.

Everything that renews itself, which embodies the youth of the world, is already old for me. I have to get used to that, by dint of looking at things and by dint of reasoning too, of repeating to myself untiringly: "You see things in the locations they occupy, but as they will be subsequently"—and yet, I have never been as deeply affected as by the story of the hyacinth bulb that Armande had put in a jar on the window-ledge of the studio.

The bulb appeared to me to be black and decomposed, and I was no longer paying any attention to it when she arrived the following day and said: "Oh! My beautiful hyacinth!"

"What hyacinth?"

"Eh? Come on, Jean—there, in the window." Oh, that mania people have for continually saying *come on!*

I looked at the window. Above the dirty jar fully of murky water, there was nothing—nothing at all. Armande's hand as caressing the void. Sharpening my gaze, I was able to distinguish a sort of grey mist, a fog perhaps having the shape of a hyacinth cluster, which represented all that would remain of the flower long after its withering, long after its decomposition.

In becoming concrete in the formula: "You will never see flowers again," the representation of my condition stabbed me in the heart.

I had known for a long time that flowers appeared to me withered, but I had vaguely thought that new buds might, at least for a brief interval, appear to me as flowers. Not at all. I was obliged to take full account the fact that *I am not seeing the future, but the present grown old.* I am, let us say, three years in advance. In three years, where will the bud be that is about to blossom? Returned to the earth, in the form of humus. I cannot, therefore, see anything but that earth, scattered like a slight shadow, following the contours of a flower. And I can't see future flowers, since they don't yet exist...

Thus, between that which is and that which I can see, a great void is opening up as I advance further. Into that abyss everything is disappearing that comprises the beauty of the world and the youth of life: clouds, flowers, fresh colors, brightness, the initial splendor of living beings and objects. Death is raising his grey shroud on the horizon. Twilight is extending over my vision. A great void is being hollowed out, as between a ferry-boat and the departure quay the beginning of the voyage—the voyage into causality, as the other put it.

If anything could soothe the rage that takes hold of me at certain times, at the injustice of the fate that has me in its grip, it would be the sight of this world: this world that has rejected me, wounded me and refused to recognize me, turning before my eyes into squalor and decrepitude; this world, which, with all its facades sparkling with brightness and pride, insulted my obscurity, no longer holds together beneath my gaze. I can see through it, all the way to the bottom. Its deceptive luxury, its peacock pride and its paste-jewelry insolence have been stolen. I only have to raise me eyelids to pulverize it. I witness its death-throes. The death-throes of the world: nothing grandiose and apocalyptic, but a miserable décor falling apart, tawdry frippery hanging in a plaza the day after Mardi-Gras, an old worm-eaten domino crumbling in a dusty loft...

It is not Rome that I am reducing to ashes, it is the entire universe—and it is dying without grandeur. I sometimes grind my teeth in pleasure, prey to a kind of cosmic sadism. Such a vengeance is worth the price that one pays for it: the loss of one's eyes.

Having made the observation that the slippage of my gaze into the future is producing nothing but darkness, I forbade myself sleep for several days. To keep my eyes open without interruption, it was sufficient to make use of a Chinese method: one places on one one's table a plank studded with nails, on which the head falls as soon as the threat of sleep looms…

My forehead is covered in scars, and my mind is like marmalade…

Futile efforts—the advancement is still increasing. It's the Sun that needs to be prevented from setting!

CHAPTER FIVE

A discovery! Perhaps a rope-bridge thrown across the abyss, to permit a backward glance! God bless human industry! Who would have thought that I would ever utter such an exclamation? But let us start at the beginning.

Armande arrived yesterday afternoon: the holiday had liberated her, and she immediately took me to task. The poor girl complained that I had been looking at her severely for some time. One looks at people as one can, as I know only too well. We had been friends for too long for me to give her any great credit of indulgence. I did not intend to be severe, but merely sincere. At any rate, she brought me, as a gift, a portrait of herself, taken by a photographer: "a real one," she said, "who has a studio in Passy." I don't know exactly where she had met him—I preferred not to ask questions. I stripped the object of cardboard and tissue-paper, the wrappings of every sort in which it was enveloped, finally to discover an Armande in a scintillating evening-dress with a flower on her shoulder, all smiles. Her forehead smooth, her cheeks full and velvety, her hair freshly permed, her eyes keen and full of brightness—in brief, everything that the camera-lens and posterity required.

"The portrait has been retouched," I murmured.

"Retouched? Never in this life! He has a horror of the retouching that provincial photographers do. You're behind the times—a professional, a contemporary artist, no longer retouches his photographs. He knows how to take them, that's all."

"But…"

I had mechanically transported my gaze from the portrait to the original; she appeared to be at least five years older than her photo. And I slapped my forehead: the Armande that I saw was Armande aged, but the photo brought me—probably, in truth, without any retouching other than ordinary make-up—the present Armande, as I might have been able to see her. The photographic paper had borne the five years of aging on her behalf: the print seemed yellowed to the point at which I had thought it an artistic impression on amber paper, when it was actually the most ordinary monochrome. But, in spite of the aging of the supporting medium, the subject—or, rather, her image—was still there, just as the moment had fixed it…

But in that case, in that case…in order for me to see my present—to see it once again—did I only have replace my eyes with a photographic lens?

That same evening, I bought a Kodak. I took photographs of the view from my window, the murky jar, the parking-lot, my own head. I took photographs without pausing, like a machine-gunner. And the prints that I have just gone to collect are on my table. I can see the hyacinth that I ought never to have seen again, the crowns of the plane-trees decorated with all their summer plumage, and, finally, my own face as it appears to the gazes of others…

Flowers, greenery, my youth—it's all before my eyes. I am weeping affectionately over the photographic film, and my heart is singing a hymn of gratitude to Nicéphore Niepce[18] and Daguerre!

Poor amateur photos, all yellow and creased, you bring me the vision of the moment, of the ephemerae that make up everyday joy! I shall go and photograph Paris: the gardens, the avenues, the passers-by, the sky and its clouds. I no longer want to do anything but take photos—let no one ever talk to me about painting again!

I have procured the red lamp and the necessary equipment, and I develop the photos taken during the day myself. Thus, I learn in the evening what I saw in the afternoon; I renew the elegance of the world from which my eyes are distanced; I rejoin the present and its ephemeral grace. A voyager departed for the unknown, I am haunted by nostalgia for the

---

[18] Joseph Nicéphore Niepce (1765-1837) produced the first photographic prints.

183

world I have left behind, and, setting aside the new horizons that are revealed to my gaze, it is the views of the countries I have left that I record avidly on the photographic film...

From the depths of the abysm of time, beyond the years, the voyager in causality turns toward his native planet a telescope that is nothing but a Kodak!

I look at myself in the mirror for a long time, comparing myself to my own photo—an ample and fine enlargement of the face, taken with the intention of this confrontation.

In the mirror, my face is as I see it. In the photo, it is as others see it.

I am thinner and more wrinkled in the mirror. My temples are more hollowed out there. The corners of my eyes are more creased; my eyelids are marked with nascent stigmata; dark shadows are eating into the flesh of my cheeks. The mirror is aging me by at least five years—but my face there has something harsh and strong about it, my gaze a depth that reveals an uncommon inner fire. It is, in sum, a face that reveals a personality.

On the photo, I am fuller in the face and my cheeks are more rounded. I am more ordinary: it is a face not much different from others, even a trifle reminiscent of a prosperous and self-satisfied shopkeeper. The people who see me thus, reckoning by my apparent mediocrity, obviously cannot understand me. Am I not something else, such as I see myself— in progress toward my genius?

Which is the true me? Is it the me of the passing moment, that of the photo, or the me that will be, that of the mirror? Why have confidence in the darkroom rather than my eyes? Is not my gaze more piercing, as it cuts through the layers of appearance to seek out the underlying depths—that which can survive, and, in consequence, is truer? I lose myself among these question marks.

Considering things more attentively, my image in the mirror is not so much a more aged face as a face from which health will be absent. Will what I call my genius be no more than an illness? In five years, will I, for example, be eaten away by a cancer?

By devoting myself to this anguishing problem, I arrive at another interpretation. The body's cells renew themselves. I can see those in my face that are five years older, but I cannot see the new ones, those which are going to substitute for the old, since they are not yet there—which explains that appearance of wear in the texture of the tissues, the lack of matter that causes the shadows in my cheeks, and also the slightly disquieting aspect of my genius!

All these chains of reasoning give me a terrible migraine. They are, however, necessary to permit me to live like everyone else. In effect, it is as if I am being torn apart between that which is and that which I see. If I followed my gaze, I would be irresistibly drawn out to sea, as Dagerlöff put it. I can only resist it by using and abusing the thought-processes that are my only anchorage in the world of flowers and the moment. A frail mooring, submitted to a rude proof. At every moment, it must restore the wholeness of the staff that my gaze sees broken.

Beneath the feeble light emitted by the red lamp in the studio transformed into a darkroom, I was reveling in the midst of the developing basins when the doorbell rang. I was not expecting anyone, especially at that hour. Anyway, given that I had adopted the habit of not opening the door, my friends had gradually forgotten the path to my studio…

The doorbell rang again, more insistently. Determined to give the unwelcome visitor a piece of my mind, I went to the door and opened it abruptly. Standing out against the dark background of the staircase, a skeleton was standing on the landing.

After a start of surprise, I vaguely supposed that the medical students of the floor below were playing a joke, but then the skeleton took a step forward, came in, and walked toward me as I recoiled mechanically toward the halo of the red lamp. Was it a hallucination? A fantastic vision? White hairs were suspended around the skull. Was it Time that had materialized? Was it Death, come already to pluck me from my domicile? I looked for the scythe, the hourglass

Fear made my teeth chatter, and I felt myself bite my tongue.

"Don't you recognize me?" said the skeleton.

Amazed to hear sounds emerging from that empty and darkly-hollowed skull, I didn't recognize the voice. The skeleton posed its coccyx on an armchair and stretched out its tibias. The jaws moved again. "I promised that I would come to see you." At that moment, I identified the timbre of Dagerlöff's voice.

"What has happened to you, then?" I stammered.

"I ought to be asking you that question."

I noticed then that the rib-cage was rising slightly in a regular manner, and that one of the femurs crossed over the other was agitated by a slight periodic swing that extended to be tibia. The movement of these bones was not accompanied by any grating sound. I understood that he was breathing, that his heart was beating—in brief, that he was alive, although I saw him dead and reduced to a skeletal state.

He was caressing his knee with a cautious fingertip. His skull adopted a slight complacent inclination above the cervical vertebrae—rather surprising in a skeleton, in which one expected less expression. That macabre mime had a vaguely comical aspect. With some adventure with X-rays vaguely in mind, I asked him: "What experiment have you carried out, then?"

"Yours is sufficient for my glory. I'm eager to know. Talk. Where are you?"

Only then did I recall that he was the origin of my atrocious adventure—that I was face to face with the monster who had spoiled my vision, the unscrupulous torturer who had used me as a guinea-pig. I clenched my fists, but his skeleton still frightened me.

"Where am I?" I repeated, in a hesitated voice heavy with implication.

"Yes. Speak. At what stage is the most fantastic experiment ever attempted by human science? Has the veil of causality been torn away? Bold voyager in the beyond, are you approaching the secret of the thing-in-itself? What does the other side of the world look like? Tell me everything. I await your report more impatiently than an emperor awaits his crown."

By virtue of a stroke of genius, I found my vengeance instantly.

"But I have nothing to tell…"

"Nothing?"

"Nothing in my life has changed. What experiment are you talking about? What do you think has happened to me? I used to paint, now I take photographs—that's all…"

His lower jaw remained suspended, and the empty orbits of his skull seemed to be staring at me fixedly.

"You've surely received my letter?" he said. "You recall our conversations?"

"One receives so many letters…and one also has many conversations…"

"Even…when you look round, how do you see things?"

"As I see you."

I had never seen a skeleton manifest amazement before, and then pass from amazement to irritation. He was now stirring in his armchair like a hanged man in a strong breeze. He spread out his humeri, fluttered his shoulder-blades, drummed his phalanges. I was slightly surprised to find him so well-articulated.

"That's impossible," he declared. "I couldn't have been mistaken. Is my entire life's work slipping away? To be thus frustrated of my glory? You surely made use of the compress? I inoculated your optic nerves with a bacillus progressing in time…"

The worthless individual was indicting himself before my very eyes, shamelessly. He was glorying in his crime! It seemed to me that I could see hatred emanating from the orbits of his skull. When he cried: "I'll have to do it all over again, doubling the dose…" I could not retain myself any longer.

For some time, I had been nursing a desire to seize him by the throat, and only the sight of that unbreakable, unstrangible vertebral column was stopping me—but my fist unclenched. I encountered, with some surprise, a soft but resistant mass, in advance of the hole of his nose. The skeleton collapsed on to the carpet with a dull thud.

My anger gave way to a mad rage. I wanted not only to kill him, but to see him die. But how can one see a skeleton die? It's necessary to break it, to tear that heap of bones and vertebrae to pieces. I ran to the lumber-closet where my tools were kept. When I came back with a rusty hammer and a chipped saw, the skeleton had disappeared…

It had got up by itself, and the studio door, still open, showed me which way it had gone. I stood there breathless, leaning into the darkness over the stair-well…

Had the wretch simulated the fall in order to create an opportunity to flee? Had he divined from my behavior, in spite of everything, that my sight had been affected? At any rate, given how inept I had been, he now knew my intentions in his regard…

But why do I see him in a skeletal state? A cadaver, like the others, fair enough—but a skeleton? Is it because I am going to kill him?

No. It's simply that my malady has made more progress, and the apparent erosion of the world has been further accentuated for me. I encountered several skeletons in the course of a walk through the poor neighborhoods. Dagerlöff was merely the first that I saw, that's all.

I said the poor neighborhoods, on the fringe of the fortified zone—where, departing from the most sordid present, my eye is able to encounter the image of the most advanced decrepitude. Doubtless, people die in Passy as well as Belleville, but all the ambulant cadavers I encountered in the vicinity of the Etoile were the cadavers of the rich, cadavers who will be placed in oak coffins or leaden biers, defended for a long time against the worms—while the cadavers of poor people, ill-protected by pine or buried directly in the earth, attain the purity of the ossuary more rapidly, and my advancement is sufficient already to see them in a skeletal state.

The first one that I saw was moving alongside the ditches of Vincennes with a slightly limping gait. Fortunately, Dagerlöff's visit had prepared me; otherwise I might have thought in terms of a fantastic resurrection, the commencement of the Last Judgment. I had to say to myself: "If he were dead, he would be in the cemetery, underground; I wouldn't see him. So, since I see him here, upright and walking, it's obviously a living being with which I am dealing." My criterion for distinguishing the living from the dead could no longer be based on their external appearance, it had to rest solely on movement. When it moves, it's alive; when it no longer moves, it's dead. Noble simplicity!

I stopped to speak to my first skeleton, to chat with him. He was a former mechanic fallen into poverty, a rag-picker, a street-singer, something of a jack-of-all-trades. I don't know why he inspired more sympathy in me than an ordinary living person—and I found it amusing to converse with a skeleton who joyously raised an ulna over a bar. By force of habit, I spoke to him in the imperfect tense, as if he were already dead. He was not offended, thinking that I was alluding to the times of his splendor, when he earned 100 francs a day working for Renault. I cannot describe the color of his eyes or hair, but one of the fingers of his right hand had been cut off—one bone lacking on the glass he was holding. I wondered whether he was fat or thin, and, not daring to touch him, I asked him the question indirectly. He passed his phalanges in front of his iliac bone, like someone thumping his chest.

"Life makes one thin," he said.

Never had a skeleton seemed to me to speak so truly. We parted as good friends. Appearances did not put the usual obstacles between us.

On the return journey, I encountered two more of them: one fishing with a line in the Saint-Martin canal, the other running for a bus. I experienced no surprise; at the end of the day, it's a habit I'll acquire. Skeletons appear to me to be simpler, nicer lads, poorer chaps than the others. They wear their destiny with a humble dignity of which I would not have thought humans capable. They reconcile me to some extent with the human species.

This evening, reflecting on all this, I said to myself: "When you no longer have a *sou*, you can get a job with a medical radiographer!"

The number of skeletons is increasing. I study them curiously. They are now appearing in the privileged quarters. Yesterday, in the Rue Royale, I couldn't help laughing: a skeleton walked toward me wearing a sumptuous sable cape over its shoulders! The animal-fur had lasted longer than the flesh of the beautiful woman, that's all—but the contrast was irresistible. I was face to face with a fashionable lady.

In the new state in which I see them, it will be necessary for me to learn to distinguish men from women.

I also see the skeletons of dogs, a trifle hairy—which confirms that hair maintains its integrity longer than flesh.

In front of me, in the Rue la Boétie, walked a skeleton whose bearing and urgency I honestly admired. Gradually, I have become a connoisseur. The play of the joints was supple; the curvature of the vertebral column rose up faultlessly; a binocular-case beat his side: a handsome sportsman. Momentarily, he turned his head and I uttered a cry. In its orbit one eye—and one alone—was gazing at me: an eye in which, naturally, all the expressive power of the individual was concentrated. It shot me a cold, icy and penetrating glance, making me shiver.

"What's the matter with you?" an insulting voice said to me.

My gaze could not tear itself away from that cyclopean eye. Finally, a tip of the hat freed me from the mutilated glory. There went a man who does not suspect that the most durable part of himself is the glass eye that he encloses within his eye-lid!

On examining them more closely in bright sunlight, a light mist, as transparent as gelatin, surrounds the skeletons, marking the location of their actual flesh before it becomes that God-knows-what which has no name in any language, but in which guise I see it.

By their shadows on the sidewalk, I can distinguish men from women.

Taking the Metro to come back from Dagerlöff's lodg-ings—I wanted to settle his account, but he wasn't at home; he was suspicious—I had to spend an hour crowded in a com-partment where there were already four skeletons and a rather large number of cadavers. Instinctively, I maneuvered in order not to be pressed up against one of the skeletons—a legitimate apprehension and an instinctive repulsion, also a vague fear of catching something...but the cadavers with the mingled debris of clothes, corsets, suspenders and the ribs of umbrellas into the midst of which I was plunged were even more repulsive. I was obliged to make us of my usual means of defense: I closed my eyes. Then, through the medium of my other senses, I found myself immersed once again in the warm, fra-ternal human bath of bodies, whose existence I had forgotten. A kind of blissful languor took hold of me. I found life that was softly upholstered, in harmony with my own flesh...

Why had I cursed it before?

From time to time, however, it was necessary for me to open my eyes to read the names of the stations. Then, I found the dead who encircled me, level with my face. A shiver of horror ran through me. Where was the truth?

There were no living beings except for me and a little girl of 14 or 15, with a frightful woman's face. All things considered, I'd prefer to see nothing but skeletons. They're more sterile, more chaste, more British than those who are still meaty.

I'm starting to wish for an aggravation of my curse!

It seems to me that an eternity has gone by since I could see my acquaintances in the neighborhood; that's not true, but, at the same time, it's perfectly true. I was passing the Dôme at the hour for aperitifs, and I didn't recognize anyone. Someone called out to me, and I turned round: a skeleton was waving to me. Who was it? How does one recognize the skeleton of a friend?

In order not to give myself away, I shook the handful of bones that was held out to me. "You're a prize fool!" By the banal vulgarity of the exclamation, I recognized Babar—a Babar who had lost his trunk, whose nasal bone was no longer a sufficient signal. He attacked me amiably: "Solitude doesn't suit you. Your face is dirty."

"If you could see your own as I see it…"

I had the advantage, but he didn't know it.

"It seems that you've taken up photography?"

"How do you know?"

He could only have found that out from Armande. Curiously enough, though, I didn't feel any jealousy. To avenge myself, it was sufficient to look at him, to see his skeleton. He was dead—what did it matter what his flesh might have done? I chatted to him, as with a shade in the borderlands of the Elysian Fields, about facts and memories, the trivia of the terrestrial epoch that was being disembarrassed of all noxiousness. Had Armande deceived me with him? The matter only retained a vague anecdotal interest, affecting me no more than the infidelities of Cleopatra.

The revelation of my sentimental indifference calmed me down so much that I drank my aperitif in long draughts, like a glass of the water of Lethe. Thus, without being aware of it, I had taken a decisive step in the direction of detachment and serenity. I had raised myself above the stupidities of sentimental life. The ordeal I had undergone had had its good side; if my gaze had grown distant, by the same token, my mind had been purified. I floated far above the wretched pettiness that occupied the lives of the occupants of the terrace, whose hearts and kidneys were sounded by my gaze only to encounter nothingness. In all those cranial cavities, the brains might be racked to boiling point; nothing remained of them, and I could now reduce all those turbulences to their real structure: in a vague décor of rusty chairs, pulverized marble, beneath a tattered canvas awning, future candidates for the ossuary were frantically agitating their humeri and tibias with the incoherence of poor optical telegraphs with broken arms, and that was all…

Will my mind attain the altitude necessary to the blooming of its genius?

There was another skeleton with us who addressed me informally and accompanied me to my door; I didn't know who it was.

This morning, my face in the mirror frightened me. I had to take a photo of myself to reassure me: I'm a little thin, and my eyes are sunken in their orbits, but no grave symptom is visible in the snapshot. In the mirror, however, what a sight! I could believe that I'm looking at a mummy. The skin is clinging to the bony structure; the hair is sticking to the temples; wrinkles are hollowing out multiple parentheses on both sides of my mouth. At frequent intervals, I interrupt my work to go look at myself. It seems to me that, from one minute to the next, my condition is getting worse. Evidently, the microbes are proliferating incessantly and my vision is not progressing in fits and starts but sliding in continuous fashion toward the future. On a familiar object, as on my face, I can follow that progression; I can see myself aging with the naked eye, as in a speeded-up film.

Horror! I can see myself not only getting older, but dying! I only understood that a moment ago. The alteration of my features is getting worse at too rapid a pace, I am certainly reaching my terminus—I mean that I am seeing myself on the very day on which, in due course, my face, passing from life to death, will undergo an accelerated cycle of transformations. Beads of sweat form on my brow. And it's real sweat; I can feel it by touching it…

Yes, it's my death-throes that I'm witnessing—death-throes whose spectacle is presented to me in the midst of life, in full health…

After surges of fear and a few moments of mad agitation in the studio—stupid ideas like calling someone, going to find a doctor, breaking the mirror in order not to see myself any longer, singing at the top of my voice in order to persuade myself that I'm not going to die—I calm down and become rational…

Evidently, I'm dying, but that happens to everyone, and, above all, I shall not really die until much later—if only I knew exactly how far I am in advance! And since it's given to me to witness my own death-throes, it's necessary not to miss such a spectacle; it's necessary to watch it calmly.

I've placed my desk, with paper and a pen, in front of the wardrobe mirror. I'm sitting comfortably, my face well-lit. I have only to raise my eyes to see myself in the mirror. I can't let myself down. I want to seize the moment in which I pass from life to death. A strange death-bed!

My waxen complexion is becoming greyer. Beneath my strangely jutting cheekbones, ashen patches are appearing, which enlarge like a charcoal shadow under the finger that blurs it. My mouth is slightly open and my lower jaw tends to drop as soon as I'm no longer holding it up. Was there ever a more lucid moribund?

From minute to minute, the swollen dullness of my eyes becomes ever blacker. The sides of the nose become pinched. The skin of my cheeks wrinkles like an elephant's trunk and takes on the same color. By contrast, my exceedingly blanched lips describe a kind of halo around my mouth, which opens like a flaccid buttonhole; I can't see the drool, but I divine it. According to these symptoms, what sort of death might I be undergoing? I wonder, and the spectacle is so distressing that I'm perspiring like a fountain. I can't see the drops of sweat, but I can hear them falling on to the paper, where, although they remain invisible to me, they nevertheless dissolve my ink here and there, which I see suddenly spreading out. What a struggle! Oh, dying isn't pretty.

No pity tempers the morbid curiosity with which my gaze fixes itself upon the spectacle that I am granting myself. On the contrary, I have to stop myself laughing. Will death—my death—be like that? No majesty; I find myself as vile as a piece of meat beginning to decompose. The swollen veins of the temples are a dark violet, one might take them for leeches. The greying eyebrows are agglutinated, like gross dirty paintbrushes that would like to be dipped in the hollow tumblers of the eyes. An occasional frisson passes over the skin of the forehead, so thin and tender that I almost expect to see it crack. It's still struggling, my old visage!

Five minutes have just gone by. Life is resistant.

A mute drama, a tragic pantomime of flesh at war with itself. I read on my face, as if on a musical score, the unfolding of a theme of which I can hear nothing—which is to say that I cannot sense within my flesh the pain which must be accompanying it. I see the grimaces and nothing more; it's necessary to interpret them. One might believe that a mosquito were tickling my skin here and there—but it's death's dart that's teasing me. I'm dying, and I'm making jokes!

The denouement must be getting close. Death takes too long, even speeded up. If I'm not dead in five minutes, I'll light a cigarette blindly, to kill time…

Are you giving up the ghost, you old beast?

No, I'm still defending myself. I don't want to spend the entire afternoon watching myself die though! Me, who has always had a horror of all the tedious ceremonial buffoonery that surrounds death! Fortunately, I'm spared the vision of the funereal apparatus. No candles, no priest, no final hand-holding on the bedclothes. Only my mug. A musical composition reduced to the essential, to a soloist.

What will I be thinking when I really have the face that I can see?

Will I recognize, as I feel them internally, the little spasmodic shivers that I can see being born near my temples, descending through the old skin of my jowls to the tucked-up lips which reveal glimpses of my gums and yellow stumps of teeth? Will I recognize myself at the final moment? Will I be able to say to myself: "It's the end" in spite of the assurances of "You're getting better" and "You'll be on your feet in a week" that people will not fail to lavish upon me? Here, at least, I'm dying calmly, without affectation, without commentary, in silence and perfect peace. I strip the spectacle of all its spiritual resonances, only providing myself with the sight of myself.

It can't go on much longer now. I grow impatient over the duration of my dying, as if it were a matter of an ordinary death. For two pins, I'd go back to painting while I wait for it to be over—but I don't want to miss my last breath.

Suddenly, a real anguish grips me. My hand trembles, to the point at which I can't carry on writing—what if, once I'm dead, *I can no longer see anything?* The dead are plunged into eternal darkness. In a moment, since I shall be dead, I might go blind. An atrocious prospect! Having reached the end of my tether, doubtless more rapidly for not having anticipated it, but having reached it all the same, I must, logically, enter into darkness. I'm arriving at the end of the film that was granted to me…

Autosuggestion? It seems to me that a shadow is already forming around me. In a moment, I shall be dead, these are my last glances, my last moments of light…

Look, quickly, look at the sky and the Sun, the light, transparent atmosphere…

No, it's necessary that my final gaze should be reserved for myself.

Oh, I can no longer contemplate myself with mocking detachment. The anguish that the mask shows in the glass, I feel as my own now, in every fiber of my being. It torments my mind. My sight is going to slip away, flee the time of people and things. My eyes, my poor eyes! Something vitreous appears in their orbs. Their fixity scares me. It's the end; I sense it. I see my own gaze become glaucous, seek itself, flee. I'd like to capture that light, the image of myself that is sinking behind the plane of the mirror. I plunge feverishly in pursuit of the gaze that is drawing further away, whose brightness is fading like a star at sunrise. Sun of death, halt! I want to catch hold of myself on the brink of the gulf. My gaze is sinking, like a plumb-line. Will my eyes plunge as rapidly as that fleeting ray which is becoming extinct? My eyelids are no longer fluttering. The pupil dilates, dilates, opening on abyssal depths. My taut features relax. As abrupt as a blade, a veil falls before my eyes. I'm dying…I'm dead…

O joy! I can still see!

I'm dead, but I can see! The mirror sends back my cadaverous face, my eyes fixed and vitreous, my complexion frightful, my features still marked by the struggles of the final agony. I see myself dead; never was a spectacle so dear to my heart, for if I can see myself, I can see, and I still have the light…

I weep invisible tears of joy.

My exuberance cannot be contained. I have to go out, to plunge into the midst of beings of light, the living to whom I still belong. I want to enjoy everything. After all, it isn't every day that one dies, and that day is a significant date.

Go out? With that face—what are you thinking, my friend? But others don't see me thus, can't see me…

Just to be sure, I've just taken a photograph. The print is very pale and old, but it reveals my usual face. I'm still their peer, in appearance. Champagne and women for me! If necessary, I'll close my eyes…

197

CHAPTER SIX

After my night of celebration, I went forth this morning, in broad daylight, through the avenues and the squares, to see what had become of the world. Oh well! Everything appeared to me in its customary degree of decrepitude: skeletons, cadavers, the carcasses of dogs and horses, vehicles worthy to be sold for scrap—in brief, everything to which I'm accustomed. I'm dead, and nothing has changed in the universe; may I say that it's a trifle disappointing?

Disappointment gradually turns to anxiety, obliging me to think rationally about my condition. It seems to me that yesterday's terror was not without foundation, and that my gaze should have been extinguished at the moment when I died. Nothing happened, fortunately—but why?

Ought I to suppose that humans can still see after their death? That spiritualist explanation offends my positivism.

Should I, on the hand, say to myself: my eyes, like the rest of me, are still incontestably alive. Nothing, therefore, is more natural than continuing to see. My optic nerves, still living, continue to offer the bacilli a culture medium in which they are quite naturally pursuing their march into the future. Little do they care that they have reached the date on which I shall pass away from life, which certainly holds no interest for them. So the process continues, I simply see things as they will continue to be after my death, without having any cause for astonishment in the fact that there has been no particular has change in the proffered spectacle.

All of that seems convincing. Here I am, though, dispossessed of my own time, if I might put it thus, of the pride of the thinking subject, who always has a tendency to believe that when he is gone, everything is finished. I have been reminded that I am of no importance with respect to the universe. I knew that, but still...

I make the further observation that, seeing things as they will be after my death, they are visible to me despite the fact that, in the normal course of affairs, *I would never have been able to see them.* I would never have been able to see my corpse, but I can see it! It is, in a way, the eye of purgatory that I direct at the world from now on. There are bound to be surprises in store for me…

Truly, I can no longer bear to look at my dead face, and I have just smeared my mirror with soap in order not to see myself any more. And when I write, I can't bear the sight of that fleshless hand, which is visibly decomposing. I had to go and buy a pair of gloves.

These gloves—new, as I have every reason to believe, and as my sense of touch confirms—offer me the indescribable appearance of moldy, stiff, cracked and split rags. Evidently, suede deteriorates sadly over time. How could I make a choice in such circumstances? I could have bought pigskin, which appeared to be more resilient, but the price put me off. The eye of purgatory can still count. It has to—my reserves are diminishing.

I wanted to know what my visual advance was, and I was lamenting the fact that I had no certain means of estimating it when chance came to my aid a little while ago in the Luxembourg. It's sufficient to look at the infants being taken for walks in prams. They can't be more than one or two years old, but I see them with the small serious heads of adolescents, like some kind of miniatures of boys of 13 or 14. In their turn, those individuals that I deduce to be schoolboys by the remains of satchels that they carry under their arms, have the faces of mature men. The entirety of humanity, marching in step, is progressing at an interval of about 15 years before my eyes, pushing at its head an avant-garde of skeletons in whose ranks are the dead of the next 15 years. Those corpses are playing croquet on the terrace of the Queens of France.

Armande's first visit since my death. She appears to me still alive, and will therefore live longer than me. I told her that, jokingly, like an old man flattering another—a tone that was much easier for me to adopt because she appeared to me wrinkled and grey-haired, at least 20 years older than she is. Was I mistaken in my estimation the other day? Perhaps I'm 20 years in advance.

There's no question of loving her as I see her now. My love for her is not the sort that lasts 20 years. It's necessary to make her understand that our relationship is sliding on to the plain of friendship. Is that a consequence of my coldness, or my death? Once a sweet and worthy girl, she is becoming bitter and acerbic. Our tiffs have become more frequent.

My ink is paling before my eyes to such an extent that I have to add Indian ink to it in order to continue to be able to write, and I can see the moment coming when I shall have to replace this yellowed paper with a piece of parchment, if I want to continue to keep my journal.

The idea that I can see what I should never have been able to see has revived my curiosity with respect to my own vision of the world. I have given up the photography that can show me nothing new—always the same trees, the same houses, the same women—in order to revert to the testimony of my eyes. I even record that testimony, with the result that my canvases are scarcely more than scenes featuring skeletons. People will think that I have a macabre imagination. I don't care. One must paint, first and foremost, that which one sees… and then again, these characters reduced to their bones are admirably suited to the yellowed, crusted and opaque shades that the brightest colors are for me, even as they come out of the tube. I see nothing on my palette but bitumen, greenish blacks and violets with winy glints, which are the very colors of decrepitude, in harmony with my new subjects, of the genre of *Fêtes galantes au cimetière*.[19]

---

[19] *Fêtes galantes* [roughly, "high jinks"—of an erotic nature] is the title of a famous collection of poems by Paul Verlaine.

Quite frankly, I no longer have much choice of genres. Could I dream of a career as a portrait-painter, hope to capture the delicate nuances of the psychological expression of a skull? Should I risk myself in dead nature, however appropriate it may seem? Dead nature, the three Cézannian aples, disappeared from my horizon some time ago. Nothing remains to me but the resource of paintings in which flesh, in the manner of Rubens, melts away, evidently treated after its passage to the grave; that is what I do, bringing the composition back to the format of Watteau, which is more economical.

Yes, I am letting myself be carried out to sea now. Attraction is not exerted by the world to which I belong, but by the one toward which I am going. And it seems to me that things are evolving with even greater rapidity than before. In the streets, entire houses and buildings are disappearing. The Eiffel Tower has been reduced to the condition of a shadow; the Opéra no longer appears to me in any form but that of a cloud of ash—is it fated to burn down again in the near future? On the other hand, the Obelisk lasts; the stone of the desert has seen other eras. Yesterday evening, while out walking, I saw something that struck me with amazement: miraculously suspended skeletons crossing the Seine in empty space. It took me a moment to realize that I was seeing the Academicians going home after the weekly meeting, using the walkway of the Pont des Arts, which is no more than a memory in the epoch attained by my gaze.

Remember that thou art but dust, and to dust thou wilt return.
No need for me to remember—I see it constantly. Nevertheless, one cannot help starting when, lowering one's gaze distractedly upon oneself, one encounters—as I have just done—through the dust veil that is a pair of trousers, one's own patellas and tibias exposed in broad daylight. Thus, in my turn, I have become a skeleton...

I have, however, only been dead for a little while. My cadaver will not last long, Does that mean that I shall die in a distant country, where my remains, exposed to the vultures, will be rapidly reduced to me bones? Or that, interred in the common grave with the poor, the quicklime will soon do its work upon my flesh?

I would have liked to keep my skin for longer.

I have cleaned the mirror in order to see myself full-length. I'm horrible. The gelatinous and transport muddy substance that my flesh will become only appears in places. In general, there are putrefied shreds with sticky gleams adhering to my bones. I was surprised to find myself wanting to tear them away, for the sake of propriety, instinctively clutching at the skin of my abdomen—which held firm, fortunately! Then I overcame my repulsion and began a "Portrait of the artist by himself" according to that vision, in the genre of the flayed man of Bar-le-Duc[20]—but I shan't raise my eyes toward heaven; it's too pretentious, and against my principles.

The forward march is accelerating; I have passed entirely into a skeletal state. I'm perfectly content with that. The last islets of decomposing flesh have disappeared, and neat bones appear from head to toe, with present no unpleasant malformation. Such as one is, etc. I contemplate myself in my definitive form. Pieces of clothing extend a very tenuous veil around my remains; it's discreet and decent—but the metallic buttons of the trousers, braces and suspenders set disparate patches of rust around my new silhouette. I've just got rid of these accessories. I want to be free and clear.

An odd way of attending to one's toilet and taking care of one's appearance!

---

[20] The Church of St. Etienne in the Lorraine commune of Bar-le-Duc contains a famous effigy of a partly-decayed corpse sculpted in white stone by Ligier Richier in the 16th century.

Having gone out this afternoon to visit my supplier of paints, I saw the first passer-by whose path I crossed start. An old maid of 30 or 40 uttered a squeal at the sight of me. A little group formed at a distance, whose members stated at me, sniggering.

A taxi-driver gave me the key to the enigma by shouting at me as he passed: "Are you getting some fresh air?" I had simply forgotten to put on the cloud of dust that comprises my trousers and had inadvertently come out in the nude! When one sees oneself in a skeletal state, the difference isn't so great.

I went back home rapidly, pursued by the cries of street-urchins, who shouted: "Madman!" Others proposed going to fetch a policeman. I almost gave myself away by shouting back: "Don't be so proud of your rotting carcasses!"

That won't help my reputation in the quarter.

A hilarious scene: a funeral procession on the road to Montparnasse cemetery. The horse drawing the hearse, the coachman, the widows and the orphans were all in a more-or-less skeletal condition. Only the dead man, enclosed in his massive oak coffin, remained impenetrable to the gaze and seemed fresh—I almost said alive. Comical, comical, those bones which had others in tow. They are not aware, since they do not see it, that everything ends up the same. I'm going to paint a little picture: *The Burial on the Boulevard*, which will outdo Père Courbet and his Ornans Maccabee.[21]

One cannot live in an environment of dust and dead men without suffering fits of depressive melancholy. I am like those prostitutes who, absorbed by their trade, know no more of humankind than a sad phallic vision. Oh, the voyage into causality is scarcely diverting, and the horizons of the landscape disappear beneath exceedingly grey mists. It is neces-

---

[21] Gustave Courbet's famous painting of a funeral ceremony in his native town of Ornans is on display in the Musée d'Orsay.

sary to learn to distinguish things by their contours alone, increasingly blurred, to cultivate the soul of a dung-beetle in order to be able to live in such putrefaction…

I have told myself over and over that I am the eye of purgatory, but it scarcely consoles me. I've just been wondering whether I might not do better to put on dark glasses, buy a white cane and simply declare myself to be blind. But I would excite pity! Anything but that. Then again, does one ever know…?

Why? Why this ordeal? I read. Books hold together much longer than humans.

An atrocious scene, sparked by God knows what: an Armande, older than I had ever seen her, burst into reproaches that I could more-or-less comprehend. Live with me was becoming impossible, it seems. I never did anything with her, never paid her the slightest attention. My monstrous egoism had finally killed all love, etc.

I looked at her coldly, as an old man looks at his aged companion, with no affectionate interest, with the detachment of a psychiatrist observing a hysterical crisis. Every woman is a hysteric when she wants to be. I watch various sorts of bizarre creases being born on her wrinkled cheeks.

"You could be 100 years old and not be more jaded!" she cried. "You're freezing my youth. Personally, I love life. Come on, how long is it since you kissed me? It's been so long, do you even know?"

My gaze does not leave her face. I know full well that I'm irritating her by looking at her in that fashion, but I watch her turning apple-green while her nostrils become pinched. An expression of distraction—or, rather, an absence of expression—congeals her facial features. One might think them a painted cardboard mask…

Abruptly, I realized that I was watching her die! Fate had brought her to my apartment on the day of her death!

Instinctively, so upsetting was the sight of her face, I murmured, as if I were kneeling by her death-bed: "My little Armande…"

"Your little Armande! You think that you can get out of it with words. I've had enough of your words that say nothing. It's too late now, too late."

"Too late?"

"Yes, it's over. I'm telling you that quite clearly, so that you'll understand: it's over."

And indeed, her eyes had taken on the glaucous appearance already observed in the mirror on the day of my death. In spite of everything, in spite of her furious tone, I was moved.

"We can't leave one another like this—you've always been so brave."

"That's it, yes—a brave girl, one that someone picks up and sets down like an umbrella. Have you ever thought about me—about what I might be thinking and feeling?"

That exhausted face of a dying woman hurling such reproaches at me—the conjunction was cruel.

"I'm only asking that we be polite…"

"Polite? Monsieur would like to be polite! It's enough to make one die laughing! You can keep your politeness—the time for it is past. I know now that you have nothing in your breast—stones have more heart than you have."

She was breathing hard. With the realism of an overly precise décor, the convulsions of her death-throes gave a semblance of verity to the imprecations emerging from her mouth. That was idiotic; I felt for her, because of the dolorous spectacle she offered to me—the compassion, or at least the pity, that one feels for a dying woman—but the violence of her language blocked all my good intentions. I would rather have surrendered to those lying promises that a death-bed calls forth.

"Calm down. It will get better."

I don't want it to get better; I don't want it to get anything at all. When one has felt as you have made me feel, that one is worthless, one goes away…I've been patient as long as

I can, Now I can't, any longer. I want to go somewhere else, where I count for something…"

Then, still because of that visage, I sighed: "Can one count for anything after death?"

"What I want is to sense a presence, an affection, someone who appreciates you… Anyway, if I talk to you like this, it's because I've found..."

"I rather doubt that."

"You're making fun of me! It's over!"

Indignation, or the approach of death—I couldn't tell which—made her move her head up and down nervously: little thrusts of the chin, which jutted out, abruptly stretching the creases of her old woman's neck. I ended up not knowing where we were. She made her preparations to depart, with a vague hint of comedy suggestive of a false exit. I felt an unhealthy desire to keep her with me in order to assure myself that she was really going to die. At the same time, the thought was haunting me that one does not throw a dying woman out into the street—that one ought to be kind, especially at such a moment. Oh, I knew well enough what the real remedy was: to furnish her proofs of my attachment.

I set my bony hand on hers, on which the veins were standing out in relief on a shiny crust, the tattoos of old age. To the touch, her skin was softness itself. She withdrew her hand.

"You mustn't hold a grudge against me," I said. "I'm sick—sicker than one can believe."

"Don't try to move me to pity!"

I smiled, conscious of the superiority of my role. "I'm not at all like other men."

"Yes, I know—your genius," she retorted, ironically.

"My genius, or something else—perhaps a keener way of seeing."

"And of feeling nothing."

"Of feeling, at least, that we're very stupid to argue when our days are so few."

I said all that because she was going to die, out of respect for tradition. She was stronger than me—but what good was that, since her 25 years gave her no suspicion?

I sensed her softening. At the same time, to avenge myself for having to be humble, for having allowed my secret to be penetrated, a horrible desire—a necrophiliac desire—was born in me. I wanted to deceive her with herself one more time, with that ruined flesh, so different from the one that I had loved—and to be completely honest, I wanted to soil the memory that I would have retained of her. It also seemed to me that by insulting death, I was affirming, with the rights of life, my entitlement to belong to a world from which I found myself unjustly expelled. She was only a dying woman, but when one is a skeleton oneself, has one the right to be choosy? From beyond the tomb, I could still return with the daughters of men. Like a fallen angel, I could escape my inferno…

Was it temptation, then, that she brought me? Were all her acid remarks, her reproaches, even her insults, nothing but darts to reawaken my ardor? In succumbing, if I decided in her favor, it was myself that I was condemning. Even that was tempting…

I no longer knew what I was thinking, but I took her in my arms and pressed my lips upon her firm, smooth face, flourishing with health and life…

When I opened my eyes, I perceived with a shiver of horror that I was no longer holding anything in my arms but a corpse, her sides ultra-Baudelairean[22] in their stickiness…

In the consequent disturbance of my recovery of consciousness, I thought I really had killed her. She remained inert on the divan. Her face spoke of the calmness of death, the release that follows the throes of agony. She was no longer breathing. Had I choked her in a crisis of dementia? I stood there mute with anguish.

---

[22] This citation acknowledges the manner in which this passage echoes Baudelaire's famous poem "Les Métamorphoses du vampire."

Finally, she breathed an "I'm dead…" that brought me back to life. Keeping her eyes closed, she repeated: "I'm dead."

And dead, she rose to her feet. Doubly dead for me, in fact. Her cadaver with the vitreous eyes was no more appealing than a scarecrow. I sensed, brutally, that I would never play out the comedies of the living again. She raised her arm in order to caress my hair with her hand. Before those fingers of death, which were approaching my face, I recoiled abruptly.

"One might think that I scared you."

One owes the dead the truth. Unblinkingly, I replied: "No, you horrify me."

With the staring eyes of a cadaver she shot me a glance—oh, what a glance! But I sustained the shock, as with a sword. Hated seemed to strike sparks in the silence. The dead treat one another harshly. Unceremoniously, I commanded: "Go away!"

She got up abruptly, as if stung by a whiplash. She didn't say a word; she left.

If she had demanded an explanation, my reply was ready: "I too want a living lover."

Is it really true that I want a living lover? Have I not passed the stage where one is free from all lust? When I look at myself full-length in the mirror, the disappearance of my sex has something symbolic about it.

I'm learning to understand the solitude of cemeteries. Dagerlöff, dead; Babar, dead; Armande and my concierge, dead; and me…

The circle of my acquaintances is evaporating around a center that has vanished itself. Life grows distant. Before my eyes, like a devouring canker, a nothingness expands that I sense to be infinite.

The skeletons to which my vision is getting accustomed are decomposing in their turn. See now how the rib-cages are losing their sides, permitting the sight of sad voids, like those of teeth. Elsewhere, it's a tibia that is missing, or clavicles. It's rare that I find a skull intact. One could believe that the whole human race were trepanned—trepanned by the future: the vengeance of time on those crazed brains…

Those missing bones permit me to identify my contemporaries more easily. Initially, when they enjoyed the integrity of their skeletons, I confused them all. Now, I'm more able to tell them apart. Babar, who must be buried in a damp and unhealthy place, has lost his arm-bones; nothing remain to him but the stump of a humerus. He doesn't understand why I call him the jovial one-armed man when I encounter him on the terrace.

For a few days now, I've also observed a femur-less cadaver that seems to follow me at a distance. One might think it the skeleton of a legless man, maintained at a good height above the ground by a phenomenon of levitation.

I'd like to invite a few comrades to the studio, to observe their reaction to my recent canvases before organizing an exhibition. I won't let on that I paint according to nature; they'll all be presented as imaginary compositions. If I'm thinking about an exhibition, it's not out of concern for fame, but in order to make a little money. My banknotes, already reduced to dust, are disappearing for good into the pockets of suppliers. The gas still has to be paid for…

I perceived the legless man, who seemed to be spying on me from the street-corner.

In the semi-darkness if the stairwell, as I climbed up with a bottle of varnish for my canvases, a voice that seemed vaguely familiar said: "Liar!"

Then I recognized the legless man, ensconced in a dark corner.

"What's that?"

"Liar—I know that you can see."

I shivered momentarily. Who, then, had succeeded in penetrating my secret? An abrupt intuition caused me to say: "Dagerlöff?"

The legless skeleton leaned forwards. I recognized the old madman's fashion of greeting someone.

"You didn't recognize my bones, eh? Vile liar, playing a role! Yes, I'm Dagerlöff—who is, moreover, your traveling companion. You tried to deceive me. In order to have a clear conscience, I tried the experiment on myself. Monsieur Poldonski, there are now two of us moving beyond the causal world, and you can no longer abuse me with false reports. I have the same eyes as you, with which to penetrate appearances. Oh, you may tremble in your carcass…"

Beneath his gaze, the power of which I knew from experience, I felt myself so suddenly naked, in fact, that I shivered and instinctively brought the flaps of my jacket back over my breast. He was talking loudly, though, risking attracting the attention of the neighbors. Better to continue the conversation and regulate our affairs in the studio.

To begin with, sitting face to face, we stared at one another—if one might put it thus—in silence. In bright light, we measured our reciprocal debris with severe but invisible eyes, like two women weighing up one another's costumes.

He had not only lost his femurs, but his rotting iliac bone was riddled with worms. A dull greenish mold was growing between the vertebrae of his spine and, the sutures of his skull having given way, he had the appearance of having taken for a head the carapace of an old crab, bristling with spines. Some kind of black corrosive slime was spreading over his sternum. His state of decomposition was much more advanced than mine.

"You should have had yourself cremated—that would be less sickening!" I said, to break the silence.

He made no reply, and I perceived that he was looking at the canvases that I had lined up at the foot of the wall with the intention of varnishing them. The interest that they appeared to inspire in him began to flatter my vanity.

Nodding his crustacean carapace, he said: "That's it—that's exactly it. Life itself, if I might put it thus, just as we see it…"

With that, my sentiments in his regard began to change. I forgot my grievances. The enthusiasm for solitude and the need to be on guard that a human interlocutor always reinforced within me were yielding in the present instance to a feeling of release. I couldn't see him, or so very nearly…he was dead, like me. We were the only two creatures in the world able to understand one another, to speak freely. In the final analysis, I found myself confronted by someone like myself.

He stood up in order to look more closely at the painting of the funeral, with the skeleton of the horse pulling the hearse in the foreground. Then he came back to the *Fêtes galantes*. Noticing that the femurs were crossed, retaining between them the distance of invisible flesh, he praised a modesty in those bones that the living did not have.

"It's because it has been preserved from impure contact that the skeleton is the most durable part of the individual," he said.

I would have preferred a more pictorial critique.

Running his eyes over the array of paintings once again he said: "You don't see the forms?"

"The forms? Do you mean the volumes?"

"No, no—the forms! I call them that for want of another name. Diaphanous forms, like immaterial tissues, which pass with immutable serenity through the crowd, through walls…" Seeing my incomprehension, he added: "It's true—perhaps you don't see them yet. Although I started second, I'm further advanced than you, having doubled the dose. All your visions"—his gesture embraced my canvases—"are of the residues, the last vestiges of a world that is receding before our eyes. The level of time is rising for us like a tidal sea, and we no longer see anything emerging but the high peaks, the most durable scaffolding—which, little by little, will turn to increasingly lacy filaments…but all in all, that still recovers the world to which we once belonged. By contrast, the dawn of a new world is bound to project its first gleams. The distant lineaments of the next position of equilibrium are bound to appear to us, who are suspended between two worlds. It is the glimmers, the harbingers of the new and unknown world, that I call 'the forms.' "

I was staring at his ancient jaw, which was trembling under his voice like the beating of the shutter of an abandoned house.

"The forms? Do you mean the angels?"

He laughed. "Where do you think I'm taking you?"

"I've begun thinking of it as a kind of purgatory..."

"The word is too precise, overburdened in a fantastic sense by a religious vocabulary operating without the support of actual experiences like ours. It risks diverting a voyage that, as you must be aware, no longer has anything predetermined about it, bathed as we are in a universal free will, far from any causal universe... In these conditions, the slightest influence might direct us along a false path. We must remain impartial, and wait to see around what residue the reconstruction will take place."

"But what about the forms?"

"I can't say anything more. You'll see them soon. What are they? Once again, I wouldn't want to influence you. Sometimes, I think about the dead, who have undertaken this same voyage before us. I've told you a little about the maladies caused by a hurricane of accelerated time. If there is one thing we have learned for certain from the experiment to which we have subjected ourselves, dead and alive at the same time, it is that the distinction between life and death is not as radical as vulgar minds believe. All hopes are permissible. The dead have gone before us; we are following in their footsteps. What if we catch them up?"

His skeleton shook feverishly, and an emotion came into his voice that I had never heard there before. He had forgotten to play his usual character.

"I will confess to you, Monsieur Poldonski, that there is nothing I desire more passionately than to find the dead. Finally, I would be able to see her again—her! I would be able to hear her voice again—my daughter! The drama of her disappearance is still as present in my mind as on that first evening. My child, my only passion, a unique being, a prodigy—she was prone to fevers—she left the shelter of my roof one evening, ran away...days followed one another. I only found out much later: she was dead—but she was haloed with the strangest of glories, dead but in possession of the secret that the living pursue in vain... My daughter Apolline—shall I admit it?—it's for her sake alone, fundamentally, that I've launched myself into this adventure, with the hope of rejoining her, of bringing her all at once the 20 years of affection that are waiting, accumulated in my heart, and finally to learn from her lips the ultimate meaning of the mystery of death..."

His voice broke with the emotion. I was strangely calm and cold, perhaps in a spirit of contradiction. He had stretched out his arm, and I felt, with a shiver of disgust, his warm and sweaty hand on the back of mine. If necessary, I could listen to him, but physical contact was too much. Any appeal to sympathy has always left me cold. He did not persist.

"Monsieur Poldonski," he said, heading for the door, "when you see the forms, tell me. We shall search together. Two of us will have more chance of finding her..."

I accompanied him on to the landing. Seeing his legless upper body, suspended in mid-air, effectuate a series of little aerial displacements, I understood that he was going down the stairs.

CHAPTER SEVEN

I looked for the forms all day yesterday, without success. It's fated that the old imbecile will trick me until the end.

The thought having occurred to me that the forms might be phantoms, I spent the night wandering around Montparnasse cemetery, peering through the gates into the pathways receding between the tombs. No phantoms, save for whores on the sidewalk unable to sell their virtue. One ends up being brought down to Earth when one goes in search of phantoms!

I brought three friends, collected from the terrace of a bistro, back to the studio, including the inevitable Babar, to show them my recent canvases.

From the corner to which I retired, in order not to influence them, I saw my visitors' bones passing back and forth in front of the painted bones. They said nothing, and obviously did not recognize themselves on the canvases. From a certain agitation of jaws, I understood that they were chuckling quietly—it's difficult to make out the laughter of a skull. It was, at any rate, inevitable that they would begin to talk nonsense.

"The idea's amusing, but a trifle monotonous."

"Probably not new."

"Unfortunately, one doesn't make paintings with ideas."

"I defended myself; I mentioned the Orcagna in the Campo-Santo.[23] They became more acerbic.

"There's no point seeking a literary effect in painting."

"Painting begins and ends with sex."

"You're forcing yourself into a blind alley."

The advice began to rain down:

---

[23] The Campo-Santo [Holy Field] is a cemetery in Pisa, which features a fresco by Andrea de Cione di Arcangelo (1308-1368), more familiarly known as Orcagna, on the theme of "The Triumph of Death."

"Stick to nature, then, and look at it like an animal."

"Paint anything at all, if you want, but paint what you see."

"It's the eye that counts, not the imagination."

Exasperated, I threw them out, and remained alone before my canvases—symbolically enough...

No! I shall not be one of those who persist and beg their contemporaries for a modicum of renown. Between them and me, the last bridges have been broken, and there will be a moat, an abysm of indifference. I shall remain on the side of my vision, my canvases, far from all the rest. It's not the bait, the externals of life that retain me, as they retain all those birdbrains. I paint the depths, and that's what they can't forgive me. I scare them with my truth. Well, if they're afraid, let them run away! As for me, all the bolder for being alone, I shall be able to plunge even deeper...

Rejected everywhere, what remains to me? My disease. That's enough! One is not oneself without one's faults.

The disease has made progress, by which I remain frightened.

Astonished only to encounter decrepit skeletons on the boulevard, almost missing the cadavers of yesterday, whose mummy-like skin was still slightly reminiscent of life, I wondered how far ahead I might be. I had recourse to my indicative clock, which is in the Luxembourg, along the wall of the Orangerie—the place where skeletal mothers exhibit the dear fruit of their loins in the sunlight. I interrogated 20 baby-carriages with my gaze, leaning over the youngest infants swaddled in their rags. Well, I found nothing but tiny skeletons!

Thus, even though it has just been born, a creature appears to me already dead. Now, it's inadmissible that all these children will die young. Some of them will reach maturity and grow old. If, even so, I see them all, without exception, in a skeletal form, the conclusion is unavoidable: my gaze is reaching at least a century in advance, an interval after which every-thing presently alive will be no more than bones.

"Smile at the Monsieur," said a mother flattered by the attention with which I was examining her progeny.

I don't know whether the monster hanging on to its bony rattle smiled, but I laughed, dully and sadly, for I knew that henceforth, I could not hope to see a living creature. I was alone in the middle of the 21st century.

No human gaze will ever again meet mine. For me, flesh has disappeared. I am living exclusively in a universe of death. It's a landmark, a definitive severance. Melancholy will not leave me alone this evening…

If I go to the Jardin des Plantes tomorrow, shall I see the elephant alive? Or perhaps the parrots…?

I was idling beside the large fountain in the Tuileries, to which my sadness had drawn me. Around me, skeletons of all sizes were following the ordinary routines of the living. Children were playing, rolling hoops of which I could only see the shadows, or maltreating some sort of boat, whose wake alone showed in the water of the basin. On the stone benches, adult skeletons with phalanges ornamented with ivory needles, were knitting empty space untiringly. Further away, under the rotten trees, whose foliage only existed in its rustling, other skeletons were pursuing the perennial amorous conversations two by two. I contemplated my universe of dust…

And abruptly, the forms appeared to me!

At a stroke, as if in superimposition on my grey reality, a host of white forms irrupted. They came from every direction, passing, running, stopping and starting again. Moving patches with human contours, which floated without regard for the ground, the sky or obstacles, gliding without any apparent effort through an impalpable ether…

I thought it was a hallucination, like those dancing spots that the Sun leaves on the retina; I rubbed my eyes, but the forms were still there.

Their comportment, quite different from that of humans, did not seem to be due to chance—like the fall of snowflakes, for example. Each of them gave the impression of going somewhere, but their activity did not cause the slightest disturbance in the progress of the real universe, that canvas background where the living continued to circulate without seeing anything of the incessant passage of white shapes. I stood there with my mouth open, and murmured: "The forms!"

They were extremely pale, almost transparent. As one of them came within range, very rapidly, I made out the features of a human face. The forms! I am not longer looking forward to them! I can see the forms! The chair on which I was sitting made the gravel grate beneath my trembling body. I rose to my feet, and tried to follow one, but it was gliding too rapidly.

Then, as suddenly as they had appeared to me, the forms disappeared.

"What are you doing, Riri?" cried the voice of a little girl nearby.

I rubbed my eyes again. Had I been dreaming? Had it been a hallucination, quite distinct for once? I was beginning to think so when, with the same suddenness as before, the forms reappeared. I blamed the hour, an effect of the Sun. I turned my back to the setting Sun. Everywhere, behind me as in front, the forms populated the gardens. A kind of fever gripped me. Like a child running after a rainbow, I set forth in pursuit of them. Taking advantage of a moment when one of them became motionless behind a couple, I threw myself forward abruptly. I encountered nothing but empty space—but people were looking at me; my attitude must have seemed strange. I made an effort to collect myself, and drew away at the pace of an innocent stroller. The forms had disappeared.

As I went home, though, they reappeared to me twice more on the Boulevard Raspail, firstly in front of the prison of the Cherche-Midi, and then further on, near the statue of Rodin, where they were moving through the cabs and buses cluttering up the crossroads. It was getting dark, but the artificial lighting did not change their appearance at all.

217

So I can now see the forms! A sort of delight grips me this evening in my studio as I write these lines. The sensation of a new and unknown power takes possession of me. Is my martyrdom not futile, then? I repeat, in a voice as soft as that of a child saying his prayers: "You have seen the forms, you have seen the forms..." And my head spins.

But why all that wasted time? Why haven't I seen them before?

The answer springs to mind instantly: the forms could not appear to me while there was still a living being in the universe accessible to my gaze. They could only reveal themselves in a world situated beyond all human life. Now, being more than a century in advance, but having conserved the faculty of sight, I am able to glimpse them in their movements without them suspecting it...

I'm sure now of not having been the victim of a hallucination. I really can see that which no gaze ought to see. I am plunging into the secrets of the afterlife through a crack in a mysterious doorway.

I've spent all day spying on the forms and studying them.

It is not enough to want it in order to make them appear. It's certainly necessary to think about them, but another unknown condition is also necessary. The superimposition appears abruptly, and the phenomenon can be manifest anywhere.

It's difficult to distinguish their features, so rapidly do they go past. They seem infinitely flat, while being obedient to the laws of perspective. They have human faces. One might think of them as photographs of some sort—or, more exactly, those engravings that preceded photography, in which shades are made of thin, tightly-packed parallel lines. They remind me of the illustrations in the *Magasin pittoresque*, or those photographs of celebrities that one finds in the historic pages of the *Larousse illustré*. They are undeniably very busy, but their occupations remain a mystery.

They do not talk among themselves.

What are they? I no longer think about anything but them at every moment of the day. Not only does their mystery excite my curiosity, but the appearance of life that they bring attracts me, restoring the familiar physiognomy of the world. They have faces, faces that I can barely make out, but which are nevertheless human. I am no longer alone in a décor of death. They are like sparks shining over ashes. In their company, however distant and mute it may be, something warms in my heart. In the evening, when mist falls, when gloom envelopes and lends substance to the skeletons and ruins of the real world, if the forms appear to me, I might almost believe that I am still witnessing the movements of living beings.

Whether it is the bizarrerie of their illumination, the transparency of their appearance, or some secret property of their nature, however, I feel incapable of painting them. A little while ago, when it was still light and they were racing through the crowds on the boulevard, I took a sly photograph while hiding from them. I've just developed it; they don't appear in the print, which only shows the ordinary passers-by in the grotesque costumes that I had forgotten.

The photographic lens does not see the forms. They must, therefore, be immaterial—and yet I can see them. Are they, then, the shades of the dead, as Dagerlöff appears to believe? But why should I see the dead revive because I see things 100 years in advance? I've only ever seen the present—or, more exactly, the fraction of the present that will endure for a long time.

Let's silence our imagination and appeal to the rationality that has never deceived me. What is it in the present that lasts the longest, and which is immaterial? Answer: ideas. After the bodies, the cadavers, the skeletons, it is the ideas of human beings that are most durable. I am therefore seeing the forms of ideas. Judging by the manner in which the majority of brains function, there's nothing astonishing in their being a trifle vague—but why do they have faces? An idea has no face.

Tried in vain to stare a little longer at a form yesterday evening, at the exit from the Opéra, when an authentic procession of phantoms came along the avenue of the same name. Their transparency renders observation uncertain. I need to go compare my viewpoint with Dagerlöff's.

They haven't yet appeared to me when I'm alone. Yesterday evening, at a moment when I was stretched out on the divan, dozing off, the sensation of a presence made me open my eyes. To my great astonishment, there was a form in front of me, as motionless as a large photograph on the wall. And it had Armande's face! Armande's face as I used to see it.

Strangely enough, though, the features that I recognized did not appear to me distinctly, by virtue of their plastic character. How can I explain clearly that which I saw confusedly? In the motionless face of the form that was considering me, I recognized Armande by the curious feature that something there must correspond to the fact that she always took the poorer of the two knives from the dresser. That was the striking detail, indicative of her physiognomy. One might have thought that the emotion formerly experienced in confrontation with that proof of delicacy had now become concrete in the face, permitting me to identify it, to give life an expression to the phantom's pale form.

I spoke to her—softly, in order not to frighten her—but she was unable to respond, for sure. As she moved around the room a little, I still saw in her face a tone that she had once adopted in order to sigh: "How difficult you are to love!"

At the clothing store's, where I discreetly interrogated the young page-boy, I learned that Armande was still on the staff, and that nothing untoward had happened to her. He volunteered to go fetch her. "Not on your life!" I replied.

It is sufficient for me to know that Dagerlöff's hypothesis is false. The forms are not dead people. I shall go tell him.

The house in the Rue Quincampoix was naught but ruins in the midst of an islet of rubble. The staircase whose steps had vanished gave me vertigo, but in the end, the old man was still in his hovel—which, for other eyes than mine, was still intact. He was still legless, obviously, but his skeleton had not deteriorated much since our last meeting.

I was making him party to my investigations, with an understandable volubility and excitement, when a whitish shadow became manifest behind him, and I saw his own form appear and then move distinctly around the room, resembling him so closely with its shaggy white hair that I began to follow it with my gaze as the conversation continued. The response, necessarily, came from the skeleton immobile in his armchair, to which I turned my head in order to bring me back to reality.

"Do you see it?" I asked the grimacing skull, then.

"See what?"

I turned back to the form. Signs corresponding to the visiting cards ordered at the fairground both, the reference to the génie—"military, no doubt"—appeared distinctly. I could even see the three bizarre holes, the murky hollows that had surprised me in the sketch I had tried to make of him—the sketch of his true face. And in its arms, the form was holding a doll, the doll in the green dress that I had once seen here. There could be no doubt about it.

"But, your…"

"Your what?" said the skull, in an irritated tone. "Go on."

Then something surprising happened. In the form with the living face, the skull appeared, the hideous, caved-in, flattened skull like a crab's carapace—and at the same time, I read there clearly that he was lying to me: that he had lied, and that the forms were invisible to him!

The discovery left me breathless. I had almost forgotten my grievances in his regard, the absence of scruples with which he had used me as a guinea-pig and my desire for vengeance—but learning that he was still lying to me was too much to bear, and brought out all my wrath.

Without suspecting anything, he said: "You can see the forms, good for you! I didn't wait for you. I've found Apolline by myself." Brusquely, he threw a large photograph at me and said: "Here she is!"

I looked at him in amazement. His deceit caused me some consternation. Not only did I know that the dead had no forms and that the forms could not be photographed, but how could he think me so ignorant as not to recognize on the photo the face of "The unknown woman of the Seine?"

"Yes, that's her—my daughter, Apolline. I never identified her, to allow her glory the prestige of mystery. Now I've seen her again, though, her very self, in the other world. Perhaps you expect to find me delirious with joy? The incredible, unthinkable thing that I desired above all else and against all else has finally been granted to me. The unrealizable has been realized. My daughter! It has been given to me to find her, to speak to her—but my heart has not burst with joy! I tell you that without any disturbance, almost coldly. Wait, listen."

He took the photo back and his skull leaned over it.

"Why does the interruption of a life end in that smile? One only has to look at that face, at that smile, which drives way back into the infamous kitchen of art and mystery the smiles of the Mona Lisa and that of Buddha, to comprehend that the being here present knows the secrets of the afterlife. The secret on which those lips seem to be forever sealed, in order to allow nothing to filter out but the upsetting testimony of a smile—that's what I went in search of, plunging into the abyss...and I've learned it from her very self...me, her father. And I'll tell you what it is…"

He paused for effect. I observed that his form took advantage of it to come and place itself behind him, and that it was cradling the green doll, the last relic of the dead Apolline.

"You resent me, Monsieur Poldonski. The stone resents the sling, the shell the cannon that fires it, the son the father who has launched him forth into the world. You won't resent me any more when you know the secret. Here it is:

"The world into which we have come is so utterly denuded of resistance that it gives us the frightening privilege of unlimited liberty. Made of our pure desires, the world is such that we can find anything there, exactly what we want to find there. Our desires, *and nothing more*.

"Nothing more!" His voice rose to a roar. "That is the consternating response, the nothingness in which all effort is swallowed up, the revelation that innocence alone can welcome with a smile, but which leaves us, those of damned to consciousness, nothing but the illimitable tedium inherent in Omnipotence…!"

I was hardly listening. I sensed in his speech a new perfidy, a desire to destroy the magic of the new horizons that had revealed themselves to me. My anger mounted—but my attention was attracted to the back of the room by a new fact: another form appeared next to his, a form with an unknown, antipathetic visage, surreptitiously marked with desire, with something cowardly and spineless in its expression: one of those vile and hateful faces of which one says that one wouldn't like to meet then in a dark alley…

Who was this prowler? The two forms appeared to know one another. Oh, he had nice friends, the old man who claimed to be searching for his Apolline!

Was this the obscure pimp who had been able to tip the body of the poor unknown woman into the river one night?

I did not have time to ask myself many questions. The two forms were now pursuing one another madly around the room. A presentiment of what was about to happen preceded the sight of it. I understood that the skull, the skull crushed into a crab's carapace, was about to be flattened, right there in front of me, by the pimp, who was raising a brutal menacing fist. By virtue of a reflexive movement, in order to protect myself, I turned around to seize the first thing that came to hand—a set of tongs placed on top of the stove. I heard a dull thud, followed by the sound of a collapsing body. The legless skeleton had quit its armchair and was lying on the floor. The two forms had disappeared. Everything in the empty room had become calm and silent. What did that settlement of a mysterious account signify?

I prodded the heap of bones on the floor with my foot. Nothing stirred; he had to be dead.

What would people think if I were found alone in company with a cadaver? Suspicion could not help falling on me. What explanation could I give the police? Sweat tricked down my back. The best thing to do was to disappear without alerting anyone. I set the tongs down noiselessly and went out, closing the door carefully—a door that locked by itself, fortunately.

Now I've returned to the studio. Was I followed? I don't know. How could I recognize the police, with my eyes? The whole scene unfolds gain and again in my imagination. The two worlds are overlapping. It's intolerable that the one I've left behind, that of the shameful living, is still pursuing me in the universe of forms that my gaze has finally attained…

Discreet enquiries made in a bistro in the Rue Quincampoix have just confirmed it. Dagerlöff really has been murdered. His concierge might have seen me, given my description. Judicial errors occur easily. Prudence commands me to move to a new neighborhood. I shall abandon the studio and cut myself off from my past and my habits. A suitcase will suffice for my personal effects. And by doing a moonlight flit, I shall save the last month's rent.

I'm taking my vision with me—that's the main thing.

CHAPTER EIGHT

I've found a little rooming-house far beyond the Nation. I told the landlady that I'm almost blind, in order to explain my groping in places that are unfamiliar to me. Such places are sordid, but one of the advantages of my condition is that I no longer see any difference between my lodgings and Claridge's.

My anxiety is easing. Little by little, I'm calming down, and I've already observed that the forms of the twentieth arrondissement lose nothing by comparison with those of Montparnasse.

I my organizing my new life—if I can still use that word—and plunging back into the world of forms. They appear to me now in an almost continuous fashion, so persistent that, far from seeming a superimposition upon reality, it's the real world that I have to strive to grasp behind the white veils that pass back and forth.

Since I've extracted myself from the familiar frame that gave it some cohesion, the old real universe glides even more rapidly through they greyness of its future ashes. What good is there in moving around and undertaking journeys? The landscape progresses of its own accord behind the window of my motionless apartment. I've adopted a kind of permanent observation post. Every day, I go to install myself on the terrace of the Tuileries, facing the Place de la Concorde, and I watch the world fall into ruins.

Cars, buses and passers-by, whose very contours tend to disappear, are no more to me than whirlwinds of dust beneath a vast sheet of immutable sky. If I close my eyes, life is there, close at hand, with its appeals, its cries, its ardors and its tumults, which press upon me from every direction; if I open them, I'm suddenly distanced by several centuries, and I see nothing more than a breath of wind stirring a desert of dust, a petty ripple running over the surface of a frozen planet.

That final agitation, whose manifestation is so vain and sterile, is the final adieu of the world of the living. It's a hand waving a handkerchief at a ship that has departed for eternity.

But is it true that I'm alone in the immensity of the ocean?

Suddenly, a host of sails surrounds me. The forms are there, very close, secretly bound to the evolution of the dust. These forms are the ideas exchanged during an instant of the world. The universe is losing its material face, and revealing its obverse of thoughts and sentiments. All the passions, ambitions, amours and smiles that are hiding in the whirlwinds of dust become visible to me. It is an abrupt emergence of stars in a sky overwhelmed by darkness. One might think it a change of lighting that makes the invisible light up, more durable and more eternal, while the perishable flesh blurs and recedes into the shadow of the tomb.

It's impossible to make out the skeleton of the chair-hirer in order to get away in time. Every time, I have to pay.

Why go out at all? Even in the depths of my miserable room, the forms come to visit me, and I can see them for longer, more distinctly. I've seen my mother—insanely—from whom I've heard nothing more since her last letter from Argentina. Does she still think about me, then, since her form has come? I've also seen Babar. He has recovered his trunk, which seems to be the symbol of the vulgarity that life demands of its faithful. I read more indulgence in his keen little yellow eyes than I had expected, and the kind of delicately narrow-minded intelligence that constitutes a solid and reliable tool for those bent on success. Form that he was, he must have been surprised that I didn't offer him anything to drink. I drink alone now. We looked at one another for a long time, but without our thoughts making a connection. How did I know that Armande had deceived me with him? On his elongated earlobes there was something like the marks of my former lover's fingernails—those pointed, red-varnished nails that I had always detested…

If I were a living man like others, that clairvoyance would be annoying...

My mother had not changed much, even though all the events of her adult life must have drowned all my retained memories of childhood in her features. I was able to see what a minimal role I had played in her life. On the nape of her neck, however, there were still the little blonde curls that caught the links of the gold chain from which her watch was suspended, so that it swung like a noose when she leaned over my bed when I was a child...

Experience now permits me to recognize the features and expressions that give each form a face that is the work of others' thoughts. The forms are supports of some kind, on which are inscribed and imprinted the thoughts and sentiments that they are able to inspire in others.

Oh, why have I not thought, felt and loved better? Now, instead of wandering among so many unknown faces, I find a thousand memories around me, a thousand opportunities for delight. Instead of being an anonymous crowd, the world of forms is a beloved crowd in which everyone speaks intimately to my heart. Why has my life been so poor?

I'm reduced to the reading of two or three meager faces. I'm paying the penalty for my solitary pride. Was it necessary for the error of my life to become visible to me for me to recognize it and repudiate it?

Of my father and Dagerlöff, no sign. It's certain that the dead no longer have forms.

I was trying blindly to work the gas stove on which the handful of pastries that constitute my dinner needed to be cooked, and my thoughts were lingering on the poverty into which I have sunk, when the sensation of a presence made me turn my head. A form was indeed there.

At first glance, its face told me nothing, although it inspired some repulsion in me. It should not be thought that all the forms are as lovely as angels; they are often hideous. This

227

one was not so much hideous as disagreeable in its choice of expression, which was suggestive of a pretentious mediocrity. It must be harsh and miserly, and even more sensual—I could see that in its nose. In the rather pronounced creases of the forehead there was something reminiscent of the lines of a hand that spoke of a spoiled future. To what forgotten acquaintance did it correspond? Was it the skeleton that addressed me intimately, but which I had never been able to identify?

I was asking myself that when it turned slightly, and I saw a little birthmark behind its left ear.[24] It was the form encountered in Dagerlöff's apartment—the form of the murderer! Shivering with fear, I adopted a defensive stance. What did it want from me? It circled around me. I never took my eyes off it. Had it come to kill me too? Or was it a warning that it was giving me? Confronted by my obvious hostility and resolution, it disappeared—but its visit upset me in the extreme.

Who is that form? It doesn't have a frank gaze. Every time I tried to meet its eyes, it looked away, like those madmen who mistrust an interlocutor. When I went to see my poor father in the asylum, the inmates turned their eyes away in the same way, in order not to see me, not to be distracted, to remain in confrontation with their sickness. The mystery intrigues me, and brings the Dagerlöff affair back to mind. Shall I be disturbed again by the police?

In the course of a period of insomnia, not long before dawn, Armande's form came quite casually through the window and stopped at the foot of my bed as if to study me. Was she moved to pity by my poverty? Personally, I felt no shame in her presence, and in a leisurely fashion, I examined the face in which intonations, nuances and meager memories mingled

---

[24] There is an untranslatable double meaning here; *envie*, which I have translated as "birthmark" because of the context, more commonly signifies "desire," and is used in that way a little further along in the narrative, by way of wordplay.

their features. "Oh! My beautiful hyacinth!" declared the cir-cumflex accent of her slightly taut upper lip, raising away from her white teeth. "Why are you always growling?" was the slightly ironic wrinkle that hollowed out a parenthesis on her left cheek when she smiled. Then, a more attentive study revealed—alas!—signs that I had not set upon the face myself, signs that originated in another, perhaps my successor: a sad projection of the cheekbones, a beauty-spot beneath the corner of the left eyelid, which clearly corresponded to thoughts of love emanating from a foreign source. A seed of posthumous jealousy crossed my mind, before yielding to a thought of re-nunciation that was instantly inscribed on her slightly over-sized mouth—which was open as if to speak, although she had not said anything. At the same time, I found an expression in her gaze so indulgent, so compassionate and fundamentally affectionate—a forgotten expression I had left centuries be-hind—that I wondered why I had not succeeded in loving her.

I was asking myself that gravely and regretfully, almost dolorously, when I saw Armande raise her eyes. I turned round. Horror! On the other side of the bed, the form with the birthmark was there, watching us both. What did it signify? What had it to do with our tête-à-tête? Armande seemed to be acquainted with it. Was it my successor? My surprise turned to consternation. How could Armande be interested in, and per-haps attach herself to, such an individual? Suddenly, all the love for me of which she had once given evidence seemed retrospectively soiled and vitiated. I wondered why I had been unable to love her? There was the answer, before my eyes: how could I love a woman capable of choosing such a lover? I, who, even in places of ill-repute, could not bear the sight of another man coming in to seek his pleasure…

I wanted to warn Armande, to put her on her guard, to tell her everything I knew. I cried out to her, under the spur of an irresistible impulse, without reflecting that the forms can neither hear nor speak. The neighbors banged on the walls angrily. The two forms disappeared—and I remain alone, racking my brains in the effort to understand.

How could Armande have met that specimen? What was it doing at Dagerlöff's apartment? Could she have sent him there to avenge herself for having been left by me? Had he killed the wrong man, thinking that he was killing me? My thoughts became lost in these enigmas. The world of forms scares me. It does not offer the security of the real world. Anyone can enter your place of residence at any moment. One is no longer in one's own home.

I have returned to the material. I was walking through the streets—which is to say, between two hedges of upright dust, representing that which will remain of the capital's stone in 1000 years—when I was suddenly dazzled. What were those marvelous flashes? I was in the Rue de la Paix, where the future lost gems of ancient Lutèce glitter in the jewelers' windows. A surge of enthusiasm lifted me up and dropped me again, quivering with lyricism. The last farewell of gold and platinum suns! Greetings, little rings of Saturn, bracelets worn on the arms of invisible elegant ladies! Perhaps the forms are no more than a mirage while you, your reality, truly defies the centuries, and the world is only turning to ashes in order to provide a better contrast, O sole truly precious objects in this casket of ruins!

Why should I not appropriate a platinum bracelet? Do archaeologists do anything different? My eyes tell me that I am in a desert, my thoughts tell me that there is no theft when one is all alone…be brave, then!

But there are the forms! Oh, I shall have spent my life not giving way to my desires!

Which way should I turn? Should I give in to the last temptation of matter? Should I, on the contrary, turn to the forms? There's still time to make a choice, if I don't want to fail in death as I've failed in life—but what lesson should I take from everything that has happened to me? One might think that I were being given a glimpse of the solution, that I am being urged on to the right path, but that, like an imbecile examinee, I don't understand anything, haven't discovered anything...

It's inexorably fated that I shall waste all my chances.

Going out on a sunny day, when all the forms are frolicking, is like walking along the sea-shore during a regatta, amid the ostentatious marquees, with the swarms of gulls, while the "white nations at play" wave scarves in the air from the balconies.

Seated in an arch of the Pont-Neuf all day, I never ceased watching the space traversed by those rapid courses, those faces, made more beautiful or uglier, but which never have the insignificant visages of reality. Each one makes of its neighbor either a caricature or an ideal painting, but at any rate, charges it with the meaning that it did not have in its natural state. And the whole of the invisibility that I am privileged to see extends like a vast deck of cards, playing God only knows what game!

It was warm, and I had automatically taken off my hat. When I went to pick it up from the stone bench, it was full of coins. I had been mistaken for a beggar! How pathetic I must look! At the end of the day, though, here is a kind of employment, for which I have been searching—one in which one is paid in true metal and not in invisible paper. The coins are encrusted, as if they had spent an eternity underground or in a numismatist's cabinet, but they are currency.

I shall go back to install myself there instead of the Tuileries. And since I'm good for nothing, why look for anything else?

If I were to date this journal with the millennialism of the world as my eyes see it, I would probably have to write 4000 or 5000. It's a long time since all the skeletons disappeared.

Everything around me is ashes, to the point at which, in the streets, I can only discern the passing cabs by the volume of their powdery mass. Machines and living things are combined in nothingness; only their movement still reveals them: "That's moving, beware!" is all that I can say.

What I have left to guide me is odors. Displays of food smell, like gusts of wind, and are my lighthouses—but one can't describe odors very well. Fundamentally, as soon as one can no longer see clearly, one has little to say. I sense things as the brain of a dog senses them, and like a dog, there are times when I am entirely accustomed to my poverty.

There are other times, however, when I groan: "Why have I been delivered to this fate? Why has my life been aborted?" I rebel; I clench my fists. Who can I blame? God? Destiny? Society? All of that is the same to me…

I go on and on! Even the forms are now changing their appearance. Their faces are blurring, seemingly less pronounced, less diversified. Individual visits are becoming rarer.

But why should ideas be eternal? They are a little more durable than material appearance, but in the end, time must reckon with them as with everything else. The forms' faces are paling because the thoughts, sentiments and remembrances of others that comprise their features are paling. Forgetfulness is doing its work; everything is subject to the mill of time.

Nothing remains of each form but a sort of vaguely-inexplicable supportive frame.

The only signs still distinguishable in the anonymity of forms are those corresponding to reputations capable of piercing the oblivion of centuries. Thus, on the Pont-Neuf today, I saw a famous inventor pass by, in the form in which he will be reproduced in the textbooks of the future, bearing by way of a caption an amulet saying: *The inventor of…God knows what!* I've also seen a great actress in Roman costume; a modern Ninon de l'Enclos (who could that be?); the shock-absorber king; and a saint who had, I swear, an authentic halo…

All ridicule and all glory makes a fine mixture in this elixir of renown. The spiritual universe is being distilled around me. I can only see what will remain of this sunny day in the eyes of the most distant future.

And what of me, the great painter, who thought himself a kind of genius? I have not seen myself pass by. That's the confirmation, the certainty, of my irremediable failure…

An odd destiny mine has become: the man dreaming on the Pont-Neuf. Today that brought me a little more than 20 francs.

"I don't feel well." Does that sentence still have any meaning when, for such a long time, one hasn't felt anything at all? My illness goes back to the day when the forms first appeared to me, or, even more distantly, to the day when, having decided to end my life, I began this voyage…

How can I define my illness? I'd like to know…why has my life been spoiled?

As Irma, my landlady, a former acrobat said to another of her lodgers about me: "Poor Jean isn't right in the head."

The odor of a cool wine-cellar exhaled in the torrid streets in the July sun caused me to go into an archway and plunge myself into its shade as if in cold water. Huddled up against a phantom pillar, I didn't take up much space. The place was calm and deserted, apart from the forms, of course, which were passing by as usual but are no bother when one is as used to them as I am.

A voice that called me "old chap" asked me what I was doing there. I didn't know myself. My interlocutor was nothing but a little swirl of dust that I could scarcely make out in the gloom. He reeked somewhat of snuff-tobacco, but his voice was more pleasing. We started chatting and, as one thing led to another, I told him a little about myself: "Personally, I've wanted to steal, I've wanted to kill, I've wanted to kill myself…"

"Did you think about the blackening of your soul?" he asked.

"Who still believes in souls?"

He started. I was talking to the curé of the church into which I had entered.

For some time, he talked to me in the fashion of the catechism, of the Hell that awaited me. I let him talk, in order to give him pleasure. I knew much more than he did about death and its consequences. Without making it too obvious that I was setting him a difficult question, however, I asked him what one could see when one made the great leap.

"The important thing is not so much what one can see as saving one's soul."

The priest still thought he could save his soul! Ironically, I said: "But what does one have to do in order to do that?"

"Love God and one's neighbor."

"As for God, I'll believe in Him when I understand why, having given me life, He has permitted everything I've attempted to fail lamentably. Things have happened to me that I can't tell you, but do you think that making me a tramp is pardonable?"

"My son, my son!" he sighed. He told me that he would pray for me, and gave me 40 *sous*. That was the least stupid thing he did.

To recommend me to love! Does he not know, then, that an intimate idea of oblivion paralyzes the very possibility of love?

Fundamentally, I've had it.

Reduced to the essential, to its four elements, my universe was holding firm against the millennial assaults, but now I have reached the point at which water, which had thus far continued to flow with the calmness of an eternal representation, has disappeared...

This morning, it did not run from the landing tap, although I could hear it glug-glugging. All day long, I didn't see a drop pass under the Pont-Neuf. The last bath in which the unknown woman of the Seine fished up her secret has run dry! And a little while ago, at the soup-kitchen in the Place Maubert, the jug seemed empty to me. The water was there, however, I could feel it. I was able to drink it—although I prefer wine—but I could no longer see it.

Thus, my gaze has reached a point in the fantastically distant future at which, in consequence of some cosmic catastrophe, some encounter with a comet, our planet's water has evaporated.

That I am *en route* for eternity, I can no longer doubt. I shall reach it at the moment of my death, my true death—that's certain. It will have been granted to me to see Time unravel all the way to the end of the reel, to witness the evolution of the world until its final moment, the end of millions of years. So shall it be, as my curé would say.

The Sun is so pale that I could see the stars in broad daylight today. It's going out, that much is certain.

To measure my advancement, to find a clock appropriate to the task, I need to direct my attention to the supposed objects of eternity; I got up tonight to watch the constellations. Well, two wheels of the Great Bear's chariot disappeared before my eyes! Constellations treated like vulgar taxis! Nothing escapes the Scythe of Time. The sphere of fixed stars is nothing but a soap-bubble, the immutable sky nothing but a sandcastle. Vanity of vanities!

When the Earth disappears, how shall I walk without suffering vertigo?

All day, in spite of cruel pains in my legs, I ran all over the city trying to find forms that still had faces, in order to catch the merest glimpse of life. Nothing—they're all as pale as blanched leaves, and they're shrinking. "This universe is disappearing like the other," I said to myself as I came back.

But just now, on going down to the office to fetch a quid of tobacco that I had forgotten on Madame Irma's mantelpiece, I saw the form with the birthmark appear in the mirror! Over that one too, the eraser of time has passed, but it has not lost its antipathetic expression, and I saw the birthmark clearly reflected in the mirror.

Just my luck that the only form conserving a distinctive mark should be the one that I can't stand! What good does it do to change the world, if the same ill-luck follows you everywhere? I went swiftly back to my apartment to escape the vision. It almost followed me upstairs. One might think that it knows that it irritates me, and that it's eager to impose its presence upon me.

It's becoming an obsession. I encounter it everywhere: whether I go to empty the dustbins in the Avenue Jean-Jaurès, queue for greasy water at the Belleville barracks or am at my post on the Pont-Neuf, that bitch of a shade torments me. It arrives, mingling with others, impersonally, without seeming to be doing anything, then stops on seeing me, makes as if to go away or come closer, turns so that I can see the birthmark...an entire atrocious routine. Who can it be, for God's sake?

In the middle of the Boulevard Voltaire, exasperated, I shouted names at it—the names of slight acquaintances of yesteryear, as if it might hear me and reply to me! A policeman told me to shut up. I was causing a scandal getting angry like that, with no reason.

The form is that of someone who is thinking about me. But who can still be thinking about me in this rotten world? And so disgusting an individual, to boot! I sometimes think that there was someone in my life who secretly wanted to do me harm. That would explain why everything I attempted has failed...and I shall die without knowing who...

The form with the birthmark has played a dirty trick on me; I jarred my hip as I was going down a stairway under the Pont-Neuf; yesterday evening a car knocked me down on the Boulevard Richard Lenoir. Something that must be after my blood has got its claws into me, and I don't know where it will end up. When one sees things from afar, one obviously sees things less well—but above all, no ambulances, no police. I got back to Irma's house as best I could.

I'm in my bed at present, but I'll have to get up to go out in search of something to eat. Whatever it is, it will make amends, the bitch. Needless to say, it's holding up better than the others; instead of shrinking, it's retaining its dimensions and even an appearance of physiognomy. Taking advantage of the quietness of the room, I look it straight in the face whenever it's motionless. It's a head that respires mediocrity, with a receding forehead and the fearful expression of a hunted beast: the head of a degenerate, such as one sees in newspapers, without a collar. Might it be Death? No, Death is a myth, an allegory, and I know that the forms are real. Might it be a companion in poverty, a killer paid to murder me? But why? Everyone at the rooming-house knows perfectly well that Père Jean of the Pont-Neuf hasn't a *sou*. Vengeance? Armande, Dagerlöff—all of that's been obsolete for a long time…

It wishes me harm, however, and every time it's there, I feel ill. My heartbeat accelerates, I lose my breath. As a remedy after my accident, there are better ones.

It looks at me without looking at me—I mean that it doesn't catch my eye. I don't feel it in front of me. One would think that there is something between us, like a sheet of glass. Its gaze is directed toward me, but flees before my gaze as it attempts to catch it. It puts its hand behind its ear. Mimetically, I too put my hand behind my ear. What's that I can feel? A small bump…?

"Madame Irma! Madame Irma!" I called out, at the top of my voice.

Footsteps climbed the stairs slowly. They took a long time.

"What?" she said, as she came in. "Are you dying already?" She doesn't hide her thoughts, my landlady. Exactly the woman I need.

"Tell me something. Look here, behind my ear, above the nape of the neck. I fell over the other day…"

She looked; she touched.

237

"Nothing broken, that's for sure: a strawberry mark. In an old drunk like you, it's nothing extraordinary. You ought to wash a bit, especially your feet, before dying, so I don't have to do it for you…"

She said it jokingly, to reassure me.

It didn't matter what she said. I had understood.

Half way between my bed and the wall, the form is looking at me, as on the days of old when I looked at myself in a mirror. The memory is inscribed on its face. But we have exchanged places. I see, and I understand: the form with the birthmark is me, as others see me—worse, what they have made of me forever.

At the end of my purgatory, I finally have the answer to the question that has tormented me so much, and I can explain the perpetual failure of my life: the face that was looking at me was my own. The person that I thought I was: the "me" of my intimate affections, the "me" of genius being only an illusion. The "me" that others made was the only true and durable one…

I understand; I understand everything: I'm going to die, and that is my soul, awaiting me on the threshold of eternity.

And already, slowly forming on its degraded face, I can see the ineffable smile that lingered on the lips of the Unknown Woman…

SF & FANTASY

Guy d'Armen. *Doc Ardan: The City of Gold and Lepers*
G.-J. Arnaud. *The Ice Company*
Aloysius Bertrand. *Gaspard de la Nuit*
Félix Bodin. *The Novel of the Future*
André Caroff. *The Terror of Madame Atomos*
Didier de Chousy. *Ignis*
C. I. Defontenay. *Star (Psi Cassiopeia)*
Charles Derennes. *The People of the Pole*
Harry Dickson. *The Heir of Dracula*
Sâr Dubnotal *vs. Jack the Ripper*
Alexandre Dumas. *The Return of Lord Ruthven*
J.-C. Dunyach. *The Night Orchid. The Thieves of Silence*
Henri Duvernois. *The Man Who Found Himself*
Henri Falk. *The Age of Lead*
Paul Féval. *Anne of the Isles. Knightshade. Revenants. Vampire City. The Vampire Countess. The Wandering Jew's Daughter*
Paul Féval, *fils. Felifax, the Tiger-Man*
Arnould Galopin. *Doctor Omega*
Nathalie Henneberg. *The Green Gods*
V. Hugo, Foucher & Meurice. *The Hunchback of Notre-Dame*
Michel Jeury. *Chronolysis*
O. Joncquel & Theo Varlet. *The Martian Epic*
Jean de La Hire. *Enter the Nyctalope. The Nyctalope on Mars. The Nyctalope vs. Lucifer*
G. Le Faure & H. de Graffigny. *The Extraordinary Adventures of a Russian Scientist Across the Solar System* (2 vols.)
Gustave Le Rouge. *The Vampires of Mars*
Jules Lermina. *Mysteryville. Panic in Paris. To-Ho and the Gold Destroyers*
Jean-Marc & Randy Lofficier. *Edgar Allan Poe on Mars. The Katrina Protocol. Pacifica. Robonocchio. Tales of the Shadowmen* (anthos.; 6 vols.)
Xavier Mauméjean. *The League of Heroes*
John-Antoine Nau. *Enemy Force*

Marie Nizet. *Captain Vampire*
C. Nodier, Beraud & Toussaint-Merle. *Frankenstein*
Henri de Parville. *An Inhabitant of the Planet Mars*
Polidori, C. Nodier, E. Scribe. *Lord Ruthven the Vampire*
P.-A. Ponson du Terrail. *The Vampire and the Devil's Son*
Maurice Renard. *The Blue Peril. Doctor Lerne. The Doctored Man . A Man Among the Microbes. The Master of Light*
Albert Robida. *The Adventures of Saturnin Farandoul. The Clock of the Centuries.*
J.-H. Rosny Aîné. *Helgvor of the Blue River. The Givreuse Enigma. The Mysterious Force. The Navigators of Space. Vamireh. The World of the Variants. The Young Vampire*
Brian Stableford. *The New Faust at the Tragicomique. Frankenstein and the Vampire Countess. The Shadow of Frankenstein. Sherlock Holmes & The Vampires of Eternity. The Stones of Camelot. The Wayward Muse.* (anthologist) *The Germans on Venus. News from the Moon*
Jacques Spitz. *The Eye of Purgatory*
Kurt Steiner. *Ortog*
Villiers de l'Isle-Adam. *The Scaffold. The Vampire Soul*
Philippe Ward. *Artahe*
Philippe Ward & Sylvie Miller. *The Song of Montségur*

MYSTERIES & THRILLERS

M. Allain & P. Souvestre. *The Daughter of Fantômas*
Anicet-Bourgeois, Lucien Dabril. *Rocambole*
A. Bisson & G. Livet. *Nick Carter vs. Fantômas*
V. Darlay & H. de Gorsse. *Lupin vs. Holmes: The Stage Play*
Paul Féval. *Gentlemen of the Night. John Devil. The Black Coats: The Cadet Gang. The Companions of the Treasure. Heart of Steel. The Invisible Weapon. The Parisian Jungle. 'Salem Street*
Emile Gaboriau. *Monsieur Lecoq*
Steve Leadley. *Sherlock Holmes: The Circle of Blood*

Maurice Leblanc. *Arsène Lupin vs. Countess Cagliostro. Lupin vs. Holmes: The Blonde Phantom. The Hollow Needle.*
Gaston Leroux. *Chéri-Bibi. The Phantom of the Opera. Rouletabille & the Mystery of the Yellow Room*
William Patrick Maynard. *The Terror of Fu Manchu*
Frank J. Morlock. *Sherlock Holmes: The Grand Horizontals*
P. de Wattyne & Y. Walter. *Sherlock Holmes vs. Fantômas*
David White. *Fantômas in America*

SCREENPLAYS

Mike Baron. *The Iron Triangle*
Emma Bull & Will Shetterly. *Nightspeeder. War for the Oaks*
Gerry Conway & Roy Thomas. *Doc Dynamo*
Steve Englehart. *Majorca*
James Hudnall. *The Devastator*
Jean-Marc & Randy Lofficier. *Royal Flush*
J.-M. & R. Lofficier & Marc Agapit. *Despair*
Andrew Paquette. *Peripheral Vision*
R. Thomas, J. Hendler & L. Sprague de Camp. *Rivers of Time*

NON-FICTION

Stephen R. Bissette. *Blur 1-5. Green Mountain Cinema 1*
Win Scott Eckert. *Crossovers* (2 vols.)
Jean-Marc & Randy Lofficier. *Shadowmen* (2 vols.)
Randy Lofficier. *Over Here*

HEXAGON COMICS

Franco Frescura & Luciano Bernasconi. *Wampus 1*
Franco Frescura & Giorgio Trevisan. *CLASH*
 Luciano Bernasconi, Jean-Marc Lofficier & Juan Roncagliolo Berger. *Phenix 1*

Claude Legrand, Jean-Marc Lofficier & Luciano Bernasconi. *Kabur 1*
Franco Oneta. *Zembla 1*
Lina Buffolente, Jean-Marc Lofficier & Jean-Jacques Dzialowski. *Stangers 1: Homicron*
Danilo Grossi. *Strangers 2: Jaydee*
Claude Legrand & Luciano Bernasconi. *Strangers 3: Starlock*

ART BOOKS

Jean-Pierre Normand. *Science Fiction Illustrations*
Raven Okeefe. *Raven's L'il Critters*
Randy Lofficier & Raven OKeefe. *If Your Possum Go Daylight...*
Daniele Serra. *Illusions*

www.ingramcontent.com/pod-product-compliance
Lightning Source LLC
Chambersburg PA
CBHW060353030726
47497CB00003B/694